UNTAINTED

UNTAINTED

THE CRYSTAL ISLAND

LILIAN T. JAMES

Crystal Pages
~Publishing~

Crystal Pages Publishing is an imprint of Aleron Books, LLC

First printing edition 2023

Cover Design : A. T. Cover Designs
Editor : Allusion Publishing
Map Design : Chaim Holtjer
Chapter Heading Design : Eternal Geekery

Special Hardcover ISBN: 978-1-958763-04-9
Hardcover ISBN: 978-1-7378899-5-3
Paperback ISBN: 978-1-958763-00-1
eBook ISBN: 978-1-7378899-1-5

To every person who suffers from anxiety and self-doubt.
You do not have to accomplish a single one of your goals to matter.
You. Are. Amazing.

Author's Note

This novel contains content that may be triggering to some readers, including:

Abuse of power, consensual biting, child abuse (mentioned, not on-page), mild gore, misogyny, a morally gray love interest, profanity, sexually explicit scenes, torture (mentioned, not on-page), and violence.

Pronunciation Guide

Characters

Brex Jensen	Brex JEN-son
Dedryn Barilias	DEH-drin Bar-ILL-ee-us
Eithan Matheris	EE-thin MATH-er-is
Elric Lesta	EL-rick LESS-tuh
Jaeros Barilias	JAY-rows Bar-ILL-ee-us
Jaren Barilias	JAIR-en Bar-ILL-ee-us
Ryn Hayes	Rin HEY-s
Sulian Matheris	SUE-lee-en MATH-er-is
Trey Gibson	Tray GIB-son
Vaneara Arenaris	Van-EAR-uh Are-NAIR-is
Veralie Arenaris	VAIR-uh-lee Are-NAIR-is
Vesstan Arenaris	VESS-tin Are-NAIR-is
Wes Coleman	Wess COAL-man

Pronunciation Guide

Locations

Aleron	AL-er-on
Bhasura	BAH-sue-da
Cliffront	CLIFF-front
Eastshore	EAST-shore
Ebonbarrow	EB-on-BARE-oh
Kilmire	KILL-my-er
Matherin	MATH-er-in
Midpath	MID-path
Oskein	OH-skeen
Salthorn	SALT-horn
Southterres	South-TAIR-is
Sudron	SUE-dron
Westholde	WEST-hold

Other

Magyki	Mag-i-KAI
Thyabathi	Tie-yuh-BAW-tee

Prologue

Veralie

"**J**aren?"

"Shh…" he whispered. "You mustn't speak, Veralie. We must be quiet as the wind."

She glanced at him and dramatically rolled her eyes. She was fairly sure the wind wasn't quiet at all, but she knew better than to tell Jaren he sounded dumb. He liked to think of himself as an adult when he said things like that and tended to get grumpy when anyone disagreed.

He held one of her hands caged in his much larger one, so she made do with tugging on it as he peered around the corner. The corridor was dark, barely illuminated by the few torches on the walls. There was usually a constant hum of noise from servants carrying out orders, but tonight there wasn't another soul in sight.

Jaren had sneaked into her room and roughly shaken her awake, demanding she leave with him. She hadn't necessarily been surprised, just tired and cranky. He often slipped into her room when no one was looking to build fortresses and tell her stories about his training, or sometimes when he was lonely and wanted company.

Tonight had been different, though. The second she'd agreed to get up, he'd put a finger to his lips, laced his hand with hers, and dragged her toward the door. She was still in her nightdress, and it did nothing to protect her from the night's bitter chill.

"Jaren!" she whispered sternly. "We're not supposed to be out this late. Jaeros will catch us, and I—"

He whipped around and slapped his hand over her mouth. His green eyes bore into her, brighter than the emeralds in Queen Vaneara's crown. Veralie's hearing wasn't nearly as good as his, but concentrating, she realized she could hear something. Shuffling.

They weren't alone anymore.

Speaking their native tongue, a male's gravelly voice came, barely above a whisper, but still somehow echoing down the empty corridor. "I heard something, over there!"

The silence was punctured by the pounding of boots. Veralie felt her wrist pop as Jaren yanked on her hand and threw her behind him. Taking a deep, shaky breath, he withdrew two daggers. He rarely went anywhere without them, but it still sent a wave of unease through her to see him draw them from their sheaths.

He sandwiched her between his back and the wall, the cold,

rough stones grating against her skin through her clothing.

Two males rounded the corner, both dressed in all black, each grasping long swords in their meaty hands. They smiled cruelly when their eyes locked on to Jaren and her. Their bodies were massive, and the flames of the corridor's torches glinted almost blindingly off their white-blond hair and pale skin.

Veralie had enough sense to know she should be terrified, especially with how Jaren was acting. It was obvious these men, with their swords and mean smiles, wanted to hurt them. But even as her fear began to rise, she couldn't help but also notice that the males were identical. She had never seen anyone look so much alike before.

"What a surprise, already out of bed and everything. What do you think you're possibly going to do with those, boy?"

The male on the left laughed and held his sword up a few feet away from where Jaren stood in front of her. Movement on the blade caught her eye, and Veralie's heart started beating rapidly at the blood dripping off its tip.

Jaren's shaking vibrated against her body, down to the tip of her toes. He tried pushing her even harder against the wall, practically squeezing the air out of her lungs, as if he hoped to hide her amongst the stones.

"Don't come any closer," he said, raising his daggers.

Veralie dug her fingers into the back of his tunic, scared more for him than anything else. He was only five years older than her and had only begun training that year when he turned ten. He was no match for the giants before them.

"Get out of our way, boy, before I find this less amusing than

I do now."

Before the male could so much as huff another laugh, Jaren whipped his right arm back and released a dagger. He was still so close to her, the air kissed Veralie's face as his wrist flicked back above her head before flying forward.

She didn't know where he'd intended to throw the dagger, but when it only embedded into the male's arm, Jaren cursed.

The male hissed, eyes wide, as he looked down at the blade. "You will regret that." Sheathing his sword, he grimaced and pulled the dagger free, blood running down his arm.

Jaren reached back with his now-empty hand and laced his fingers with hers, whether to prepare to run or just offer comfort, she didn't know.

Before she could take another breath, the male whipped his arm forward and released the bloodied dagger back at them. Twisting with predatory speed, Jaren barreled into her, knocking them both to the side.

She heard the blade strike against the stone wall just as they fell. He rolled to the side to avoid landing on her, but that didn't protect her head from bouncing hard off the unforgiving ground.

He moved away from her, and the space he'd been occupying turned cold and empty. She heaved in air, fighting against the black dots invading her sight. She rolled to her side, blinking to clear her vision, and saw Jaren's dagger by her feet.

Groaning, she pushed up off the ground onto her knees. She tried to stand but couldn't get her legs to cooperate. Her head was pounding, and she felt sticky wetness on her fingers when she reached back to touch it. She slowly raised her head and felt an icy terror spear through her. The male stood a foot away, towering over her, but it was the scene behind him that made her feel sick.

The second male, who had thus far been silent, loomed over a moaning Jaren, with the point of a sword resting against his ribs, while the first male sneered down at her frozen form.

He dropped down into a squat and leaned forward. She reared back against the wall and clasped the dagger at her feet in both hands. She could smell the metallic tang of blood as it dripped down the pommel toward her hands. His expression turned malicious, and he glanced at the blade and back up as if daring her to use it.

He reached forward with his good arm, and Veralie instantly panicked, dropping the dagger. She threw her hands over her head in a futile, childish attempt to hide. Laughing, he continued reaching for her.

"I see you."

His breath landed hotly against her skin as he wrapped his thick, calloused fingers around her chin. With a bruising grip, he forced her face up out of the cage of her arms.

"Don't you touch her!" Jaren screeched.

She looked into his wide, green eyes. He looked so scared and helpless lying there. She held her hand out toward him, although she wasn't sure what for. All she knew was he needed her, and she needed him.

As her arm hovered in the air—a lifeline between them—they locked eyes, and something tensed and hummed in her chest. Someone spoke, but she couldn't hear the words over the buzzing in her ears. There was movement, and she was suddenly yanked up off the ground, forcing her eyes away from Jaren.

"I've got her. Get rid of him, and let's go."

Oh gods, they were going to take her away. No, they couldn't, she couldn't leave him. Screaming at the top of her lungs, Veralie started kicking and thrashing, tearing her fingernails into whatever pieces of skin she could reach.

Her foot connected with the male holding her. She must have hit something important because his grip loosened, and he spit a vulgar name at her. She fell to the ground, her shaky legs unable to catch her.

Something glinted in her peripheral, and she dove without hesitation, wrapping her tiny fingers around it just as the male angrily snatched at her again. He grabbed her by the ankles, and she cried out when his grip felt like it was crushing bones.

"*Veralie!*"

Jaren's voice cut through her pain, and she twisted her body, lashing out with the dagger and slicing into the wrist that held her. The male released her with a curse, only to backhand her across the face.

The hit vibrated through her skull, and for a moment she thought she might vomit. He leaned over her, trying to steal the dagger, but she clutched it with all her strength.

His mean sneers were nowhere to be seen, just pure hatred as he grabbed her wrist and squeezed. She felt a snap, and she screamed as she futilely tried to pull away.

Too late, Veralie realized she'd inadvertently yanked the blade back toward herself. The world seemed to move in slow motion as her fingers loosened around the handle, and the dagger dropped; fire exploding at her throat.

Angry shouts rang out above her, but her mind was no longer capable of focusing on the words. She wanted to turn and see Jaren, but her body wouldn't obey. A deafening roar split the air, stabbing into her ears, and she swore the ground beneath her shook.

Jaren.

Veralie's thoughts grew fuzzy. As the searing pain increased, she struggled to control her thoughts. She was so cold.

She needed to get to Jaren. She needed—

Chapter 1

Vera

FIFTEEN YEARS LATER

Holding a hand to her chest and gasping for breath, Vera lay sprawled across the ground in an undignified heap.

"Lie there any longer, and I'm going to assume you've fallen asleep."

Scowling, she looked up at the man leaning over her with a sword in his hand. "Stand there any longer, and you're going to join me."

He opened his mouth for a retort, but she didn't give him the satisfaction. Twisting her legs, she kicked out, knocking his right out from under him. She rolled to the side to avoid being crushed by the bulk of his body and heard the satisfying *humph* he made as his back collided with the ground. She glanced over and laughed at the expression on his face.

"I'm getting too old for this," he huffed as he tried to regain his breath.

"You're not old, Elric. I'm just better." Grinning, she attempted to jump to her feet, only to plop back down on her ass when the world spun slightly.

"I think you knocked my head loose with that last hit." She rubbed her temples, groaning, before pushing onto her feet again.

"You depend too much on your opponent fighting fairly. You must expect the unexpected hits too." He looked at her sternly. "Although, if it makes you feel better, I did feel like a heathen for landing a hit to your face."

Vera chuckled as she helped him up. Elric *was* getting old, but he still had the corded muscle and skill of many guards half his age. "Another round?" she asked, already knowing the answer.

"No, it's already later than I'd like. You need to get back inside and clean up."

He moved to rub his hand across his head. He'd recently cut his dark, coarse hair close to his scalp and sometimes still absentmindedly reached up as if to push phantom locks away from his weathered, brown face. He paused, glaring at the appendage as if its instinctual movement offended him. She fondly shook her head.

"I know, Elric. Never hurts to ask." She offered a small smile and, snatching up their swords, set off toward the armory that bordered one side of the yard.

The morning air was crisp and cool against her damp, clammy skin. The best part about working alone in a grimy shop was not worrying about what smells came from the equipment, and what came from her body.

She rubbed the back of her wrist against her throbbing cheek again. She couldn't do anything about the bruise that was sure to be there, but she could at least wash the grime from her face.

Closing the door of the armory behind her, Vera leaned back against the frame and sighed. She'd give anything to be allowed to stay out and train with the men, but it was a hopeless notion.

She walked past the racks of weapons waiting to be sent off, the smell of sweat and metal berating her senses. As she placed the dull-edged, sparring swords in their barrel, she was hit with a feeling she could only describe as claustrophobic. She closed her eyes and puffed out her cheeks with a rough exhale.

Ever since she could remember, this had been her sanctuary, but lately she'd started feeling more confined than safe, like the walls were closing in.

When she wasn't meandering around their cramped living quarters, she was in the workroom handling weapons. Elric typically only allowed her outside in the first few hours of the morning to train, and sometimes in the afternoons if he needed help with something. She was never, under any circumstance, allowed to leave the training yard unsupervised.

She used to take solace in the walls of weapons, but now the lack of freedom and limited sunshine just felt suffocating.

She should be happy. Life was easy here. Simple. Vera knew what was expected of her and what each day would bring. The less she left the armory, the less attention she attracted, and the less attention she attracted, the safer she remained.

She had limited memories of life before being Elric's ward. It had simply been too long ago, and she'd been too young. The few memories she did have usually bombarded her while she slept, blending until she couldn't tell what was real and what was imagined.

Some nights she dreamed of a beautiful woman, curled up in a chair, reading stories. She never could remember the stories themselves, but Vera often woke swearing she could hear an echo of the woman's laugh still ringing in her ears. Sometimes she dreamed of running through stone corridors, adrenaline pumping through her veins at the thrill of being caught.

But some nights, she'd have nightmares so real she could smell blood and feel the heat of a pair of bright green eyes staring at her before waking up with her heart lodged in her throat.

Elric believed it was a good thing she couldn't remember much because the more she remembered, the more she might have struggled to find contentment in her new life.

It didn't bother her. Not really. Part of her wished she could at least remember her family, but she also knew having little memory might be a gift. She didn't want to dwell upon what might have been. It was hard enough dealing with *what* she was.

Because she wasn't from the capital city of Matherin.

She wasn't from Aleron at all.

No, in the end, she wasn't overly sad about missing those memories. It would have only made life harder.

Vera knew she was lucky. She'd turned twenty that year, meaning it'd been about fifteen years since she became the ward of Elric Lesta, the Weapons' Master for Emperor Sulian Matheris.

Elric trained the Matherin city guards and inspected weapons before they were shipped to other parts of Aleron. He was a stern man and highly respected.

Fifteen years ago, a messenger had knocked on his door carrying a letter and a tiny Vera in tow. According to Elric, it was common for orphaned children to be given as wards throughout the city to provide free labor while also decreasing the orphanage population. But although common, Elric had never expected to be chosen for one.

It didn't take long for him to discover, not only was she not a Matherin orphan, she wasn't a human one either. To this day, she didn't know why he'd chosen to keep her, but she would never stop being grateful for everything he'd given her.

Vera couldn't recall her journey to the capital. Part of her wondered if she were even conscious for it. But Elric had told her the story enough times she felt like she could almost remember their first meeting.

He said she'd refused to talk for weeks, but would quietly listen and follow orders. She often flinched at sudden noises and cringed away from the blades to the point that he considered sending her away. Until one day, he swore she woke up with fire in her eyes and a silent, stubborn determination to help him around the workroom.

It was about three days later when she'd finally whispered, "I'm Veralie," while cleaning the worktable next to him.

He'd simply replied, "You look more like a Vera to me," and she'd gone by that ever since.

As a female ward, she'd only been expected to do basic servant duties, but when she'd expressed an interest in assisting with the weapons, he'd agreed to teach her. Elric had never admitted it, but Vera had a feeling he'd simply been eager to share his love of weapons with someone, regardless of her sex.

She'd been learning and working with swords for several years when she began sneaking out in the mornings to watch him go through his morning exercises. He'd been a sight to see. His movements had spoken to her in a way she couldn't explain. All she knew was that she wanted to learn it too.

He'd been furious the first time he caught her. "It is unseemly for a girl to witness anything related to battle," he'd said gruffly. He'd made her lay her hands flush against the table and smacked the flat of a sparring sword down on her fingers—his typical punishment for disobedience.

But she would not be deterred, and the next morning, she'd tiptoed out to watch him again. Of course, he'd caught her.

"This is not something I am allowed to teach you, girl. Stop dallying and get back inside."

Still, she persisted. She couldn't explain why, but her desire to learn how to wield a weapon was so strong, so deeply ingrained, she couldn't fight against it.

She refused to give up until finally, Elric didn't bother yelling. He'd simply looked at her for a long moment before turning around and saying, "Grab a sword."

It'd been over ten years, and she still loved it as much as she had that first day. But sparring with Elric each day, year after year, was no longer providing her with the same thrill or challenge.

What she would give to be allowed to train with the other

guards—young men with both strength and stamina. She wanted to spar with someone who would push her limits and allow her to truly test her skills.

But she had to accept reality. Women in the capital were not allowed to join the guard or wield a weapon. A fact that grated against her nerves every time she thought about it. Anyone should be allowed to learn self-defense, but even her working with the weapons was seen as taboo.

The guards were used to seeing her around, although Elric rarely allowed her out when they were present. Most chose to ignore her existence, but some sneered anytime they saw her handling the swords.

She hated it, but she couldn't judge them too harshly for it. They'd been raised to find such behavior improper, with her being the only evidence trying to prove otherwise.

Coming out of her thoughts, Vera turned and continued through the workroom. Attached to the far back of the armory were their living quarters—one small bedroom and a main room barely big enough for a basic kitchen, a bathing tub, and a table.

Elric had eventually given her the bedroom and set up a cot for himself squeezed in next to the simple hearth.

She eyed the tub in the corner longingly, wishing she had time for a real bath. Instead, she headed to the wash basin she kept next to her bed. Filling it with fresh water, she splashed her face, clenching her teeth to avoid gasping at the sharp bite of the cold. She patted her face dry and looked up into the scratched mirror hung on her wall.

No wonder she'd bested Elric today. Her appearance alone

probably terrified the poor man. She looked haggard. Some of her dark curls had even escaped and were sticking out all around her head like coiled serpents.

She grimaced at the sight. Sometimes she questioned whether she was even meant to be a woman. She *felt* like a woman, she just rarely looked like one—at least compared to the few Matherin women she'd seen. There wasn't a single thing dainty or soft about her. Reaching back to battle her curls into a tight plait, she scowled at her reflection.

Her eyes were a dull gray color, and her small nose was covered in freckles and somewhat crooked from one too many hits to the face. She had light brown skin, full lips that were often cracked or swollen, and her chin pointed out slightly, accentuating her heart-shaped face.

Vera finished her plait and tucked it down the back of her plain, gray tunic. She'd often considered cutting her hair since she constantly kept it tied back anyway, but she always talked herself out of it. It was the only feature she had that she thought was beautiful.

It also helped that the thick curls at least somewhat covered her ears. She glanced at them, running her fingers over the scars along the tops before pulling a few brown curls loose in front of them.

Sighing, she took one last look at herself before walking back out. She still had an entire day's worth of work to do, and she certainly wouldn't accomplish it by hiding away in her room. Elric would never let her hear the end of it if he walked in and caught her ogling herself in the mirror like a stuck-up noble.

She snorted at the thought. The day she started acting like a noble would be the day Elric finally decided to retire. Neither was ever going to happen.

Chapter 2

Vera

The remainder of the day went by quickly. Vera let herself fall into the rhythm and methodical motions of her work; the sounds and smells of steel and leather, their own form of comfort.

She was just finishing up her morning duties when a loud banging sounded against the outer door. She smiled, knowing the knock indicated Elric needed her, and she'd be allowed to step outside.

Making sure her plait was still tucked into the back of her tunic, she reached into her pocket for the length of fabric she always carried. She tied it around her throat, effectively covering and pinning her hair against the nape of her neck. Pulling the collar of her tunic up as much as she could, she secured a black mask over the bottom half of her face.

All Matherin guards and soldiers wore masks. The emperor believed they helped the men stay focused while looking intimidating. Not only did it force the men to fight without seeing their opponents' entire facial expressions, but it also hid their own and helped prevent them from forming attachments.

At least, that was the theory. But Vera had seen the way the guards spoke and laughed with each other and knew many were friends outside of training when the masks came off.

Personally, she hated wearing one. It fit just under her eyes and reached down over her jawline, effectively covering her nose and mouth before stretching back over her ears to latch behind her head. It made her face scratchy and sweaty.

She couldn't comprehend how the men wore them for hours at a time in the heat. It had to be miserable, and the thought of their potential tan lines underneath was humorous, to say the least.

Thankfully, Vera rarely had to wear one, so she tried not to complain, especially since wearing the mask was the only way Elric let her leave the armory during training hours.

Given that she was a *woman*, Elric worried—stupidly—that it would distract the men to see her walking among them while they were training. He wanted her to blend in. As it was, he'd only started allowing her outside during training hours in the past few years.

So far, as long as she wore a mask, no one gave her more than a passing glance or took any specific interest in her. For all they knew, she was just another faceless guard.

She cracked the door open and peeked out. The training yard was a large open area nestled between the palace walls and the Slumbering Peaks that watched over them. It was secluded and could almost pass for serene if you ignored the sporadic yells and grunts from the men.

Vera saw most of them sitting in the shade offered by the towering mountains behind them, drinking from flasks, while others were laughing among themselves, enjoying the short break.

She recognized most of them, even with half their faces covered. Their heights, body builds, eye and hair color, and overall mannerisms enabled her to tell them apart fairly easily.

Okay, not easily, but she'd observed them enough over the years to be able to at least recognize them while they were nearby. She also knew several of their names from the few times she'd witnessed Elric shouting at them. The few she couldn't yet name, she'd simply made up her own, which were probably better suited anyway.

Like Boulder Shoulders, a massive giant of a man whom she'd never heard speak and who usually kept to himself. He was either shy or hated everyone. Either way, he'd never been on Elric's bad side, so she'd yet to hear his name. She was pretty sure he could crush her head between his bare hands.

Then there were Snake and Serpent. Two sides of the same coin, from their bald heads to how they moved their bodies during bouts. They were fast and mean when they fought, and stuck together when they weren't, sneering and whispering like they believed themselves above the rest.

They also made a habit to stare at her anytime they happened to catch sight of her unmasked. It didn't occur often, especially not in recent years, but they never failed to give her the creeps.

When she confirmed no one's attention was directed at the armory, Vera slipped out and stood by the door beside Elric. She took a deep breath. The air was almost pungent with the smell of sweat, but she breathed it in happily, content to be outside.

Tilting her head toward him, she asked, "Miss me already?"

"If there was even a chance I did, it left the moment you opened your mouth."

"Don't be sore, Elric."

He gave her a loaded look, about to respond, but he cut himself off when he noticed all the men's attention directed to the far side of the yard.

They both turned and watched an unknown guard strut into the training area. From what Vera could make out, which wasn't much given the distance and his mask, she didn't think she recognized him.

Elric squinted and pulled himself up, looking like he was about to call out when the guard crossed his arms over his chest and spoke with force. "I find myself in need of a good spar."

He paused, apparently a fan of dramatic effect. "I will buy an evening of drinks for any man who can beat me." Uncurling his arms, he laid one hand on the pommel of his sword. "Don't be shy. Who would like to be first?"

Vera still didn't recognize him, and his voice didn't sound familiar at all. He had blond hair tied back at the nape of his neck, broad shoulders, and a tapered waist. He remained standing on the other side of the yard so she couldn't make out details, but he seemed relaxed.

Elric, however, was not. From the moment the guard opened his mouth, he'd tensed beside her, agitated and wary. It wasn't like him and instantly put her on high alert.

She was about to ask what was wrong, but he hissed under his breath, "Go back inside," and left her standing there alone.

Several guards had already stepped forward. The temptation of a free night of drinking was enough to entice most to try their hand at a spar. It was bound to be more entertaining than their usual training exercises anyway.

Vera frowned. She wanted to watch the newcomer spar, especially since Elric was apparently going to allow it without so much as a word. Her interest was piqued, and she'd always had a habit of making stupid choices when she was curious.

So instead, she remained where she was and pretended she didn't hear his order. If Elric noticed, she'd simply feign innocence and tell him to speak louder next time. No one was looking at her anyway, one of the perks of being invisible.

Vera grinned. It felt like forever since she'd last got to witness a good spar, and as she watched the guard rush at his first opponent, she had a feeling she wouldn't be disappointed.

Jaren

SWEAT POURED DOWN THE BACK OF HIS NECK AND GLISTENED across his brow, threatening to drip into his eyes. With no trees or structures around providing cover, the blazing sun was relentless.

He wondered if he'd ever get used to how vastly different the climate was on Aleron versus Bhasura.

He fought the temptation to wipe his arm across his forehead, knowing if he did, he'd likely just replace the sweat with a smear of blood.

Blood that wasn't his own.

Jaren gripped his dagger more firmly and stared down impassively at the trembling young man kneeling several feet before him. He couldn't have been more than eighteen. Jaren could smell his fear and was fairly certain he was about to piss himself.

Which may or may not have been because Jaren had already cut the man's right hand off and had just threatened to cut off the other. He tapped into his strength just enough to launch the severed extremity like a shooting star off the nearby cliff. The man's eyes practically bulged out of his head.

"I t-told you…it's just m-me here. I'm j-just…just a scout, a nobody!" Sweat flew off the man's head as he forcefully shook it back and forth. The pool of blood at his knees from his severed wrist was rapidly growing in size, and Jaren knew he didn't have long before the man passed out.

"Why is Sulian suddenly sending scouts to these shores? The closest civilization is at least a day's worth of travel from here on foot."

Jaren had traveled to Aleron more times than he wanted to count in the last few years. He always anchored his vessel on the eastern coast because, although all of Aleron was under the domain of Emperor Sulian Matheris, the eastern portion was largely inhabited by harmless farmers.

No one in Eastshore, the closest city to the coast, ever gave him a second glance as long as he kept to himself and his money was good. He was fairly certain some might have guessed where he came from, but no questions were ever asked.

He'd never run into a soldier this far out from the city before. He usually had to travel at least a day before he spilled blood. It didn't bode well for King Vesstan's plans if Sulian was now monitoring this area. Maybe it was nothing, but Jaren had stopped believing in coincidences a long time ago. Sulian was either plotting something or getting suspicious.

"I don't know! It's not m-my job to ask! I just w-walk my patrol and answer back. But I swear! I swear, I w-won't say I saw you!" The man was practically wailing.

Jaren's lip curled in disgust. *Tsiw*. Pathetic. What a waste of life. It made tactical sense for Sulian to send the newest recruits out east where the chance of conflict was minimal, but this man's youth and lack of experience were no excuse for his pitiful mewling.

"If I released you, I'm thinking your commanding officer might question where your hands disappeared to." He raised an eyebrow and watched fear enter the man's eyes at the intention behind his words. The fool tried to hide his remaining hand behind his back as if that might change the outcome.

Jaren cracked his neck and gave a cruel smile, revealing his sharp canines, and a rancid stench invaded his senses. The man had finally pissed himself.

"No man as weak-willed as you should be welcomed back into

any army, Matherin or not. And I have no sympathy for weakness." Jaren didn't give him a chance to beg again. He whipped his arm forward and watched his dagger fly straight to the man's chest.

The scout's mouth opened in a silent scream as the dagger flew true and buried itself to the hilt. His arms came forward, his remaining hand wrapping around the handle as if he needed the confirmation that it was indeed there.

He slumped forward, about to fall flat on his face, but Jaren stopped him with a booted foot to the shoulder. He reached down and yanked his dagger out with a grunt. Wiping the residual blood from both his blade and hands on the man's tunic, Jaren released him abruptly and let his body collapse to the ground.

Holding the dagger out before him, he looked it over as he ran his thumb along the handle. It was covered in the markings that told the story of his duty, his *aitanta*, and the soul bond that had been brutally ripped away from him before it could mature.

Jaren's fathers, Dedryn and Jaeros Barilias, had been so proud when his bond was revealed that they'd had two daggers specially crafted. They'd gifted them to him when he came of age to train. But after that night, the night he failed, only one dagger remained.

His second dagger had been used to—

Jaren shuddered and sheathed the blade. He could never seem to see it without remembering. But the second dagger was gone, as was she. He didn't know why it still got to him the way it did, why it still hurt so fucking bad.

He growled. Yes, he did. She had been his best friend, his mate, the other half of his soul. Even as children, he would have traded his life for hers in a heartbeat. But he'd failed. In his terror that night, he'd failed both her and their people.

His fists tightened, his fingernails digging crescent moons into his palms. He'd never forget the last look she gave him, like everything was going to be all right. He'd been *weak*. Thinking about it made Jaren want to stab someone all over again.

He took a deep breath and held it, shutting down all his emotions. They were of no use to him. He needed to focus.

About five years ago, King Vesstan and his advisers—which included Jaren's father, Dedryn—had begun to talk more seriously about waging war against the Matherin Empire to seize the eastern portion of Aleron for Bhasura's people, the Magyki.

Even before their land became tainted, the Magyki were overpopulating the island. The land simply wasn't large enough to house their steadily growing population. But now, well over a decade after the first signs of taint, it was more imperative than ever for them to consider leaving Bhasura.

There was no guarantee their people wouldn't suffer other consequences if they abandoned their homeland. Still, in the last year, King Vesstan had become more insistent that the positives would far outweigh the negatives. The rebellion had forced their hand, and they had to work with what fate had left them.

Jaren honestly didn't give a shit either way. The rebellion had taken everything from him, and no amount of land was going to change that. But he owed his allegiance to his king, a debt for failing him that could never be repaid. So, every year he came back to this wretched continent to scout and report back.

He looked down at the scout's crumpled form and again felt

a foreboding. Sulian was up to something. Maybe if he headed into the city, he might be able to pick up some information in a local tavern. Buy a few rounds of alcohol, and humans lost complete control of their tongues. Pathetic, but convenient.

Grabbing the corpse by the legs, he began hauling it toward the cliff edge overlooking the sea. He wasn't sure if, or when, another scout would come this way, but he wouldn't risk leaving evidence. Unceremoniously kicking the body off, he watched it fall and disappear under the waves. The weight of the sword alone should keep the body out of sight.

Finally daring to wipe his arm across his face, Jaren pushed stray strands of his dark hair out of his eyes and turned back inland. Gods, it was going to be a long day. He still needed to make it to Eastshore by nightfall and he'd lost precious daylight already.

Chapter 3

Vera

Well, it certainly hadn't disappointed. The new guard had quickly and efficiently beaten every opponent who'd stepped forward. Vera had been utterly shocked. Matherin guards weren't lazy, nor were they unskilled, so for him to best each one was honestly amazing.

She wanted to be impressed—okay, she was definitely impressed—but it was hard to respect him when he'd made a point to verbally bash every opponent afterward. Even the men he'd had to work hard to beat were not spared from his insults.

He didn't curse, spit, or slander their mothers, but instead critiqued and belittled their skill, which was almost worse. The entire training yard was tense as a bowstring, and none of the men looked remotely happy anymore.

Vera couldn't believe the nerve the newcomer had to disrespect the emperor's guard so publicly. A guard he, himself, was a member of. She was technically an outsider, and even she was growing increasingly irritated.

"This is the might of our empire? If the capital were to fall under attack from the north, *this* is what we'd have as our defense? Is our guard made up of nothing but boys and feeble men?" He pierced the guards around him with an icy glare.

"I must admit, if this is the best skill we have, we either need recruits brought in from the east or perhaps..." he raised his sword and pointed it toward Elric. "Maybe we just need a new Weapons' Master."

She couldn't make out his expression from under his mask, but she could hear the condescending tone behind his words, and she felt an overpowering rush of anger begin to build in her chest. How dare he. No one could replace Elric. It wasn't just his skill with a blade, but his knowledge, love, and care for each sword he held. He trained them hard and deserved some fucking respect.

The Weapons' Master in question didn't say a word in his defense. He just continued to stand straight, quiet and unperturbed. Vera's face heated, and her hands clenched so hard her arms shook.

"What? No more challengers?" he asked as he opened his arms wide and slowly turned in a circle, inspecting the men around him. "Well then, maybe I'll just have to challenge the great Elric Lesta?"

She saw the men shift and a blanket sense of unease settled into their postures as he spoke. He was tearing them down and spitting insults at each turn, stomping on their morale. These men worked diligently. They came here day after day and gave it their all, and this man, whom she'd mentally named Arrogant Ass, thought them beneath him. She couldn't understand why everyone was letting it get so far out of hand, and she was furious. Was no one going to say anything?

"How about it, Lesta—"

Before she knew what she was doing, she was double-checking her mask and grabbing a sparring sword. Within a few strides, she'd stepped forward into his line of sight and stopped him mid-sentence.

His eyes, which she could now tell were a pale blue, were all she could see above his mask as he took in her frame. Vera knew what he saw—a short, lanky man. He likely thought her no more than a lad. She smirked, knowing he couldn't see it. Let him think her young and foolish.

He laughed loudly. "I said I needed a challenge, not a toothpick." A few of the men surrounding them chuckled, eager to get on his good side, but the rest openly stared at her with furrowed brows, trying to place her. She didn't care, her rage overshadowing her caution.

Vera said nothing. Movement in her peripheral caught her eye, and she watched as Elric stepped to the front of their audience. His anger was so evident she figured she could see it steaming off his scalp if she looked hard enough. Refusing to acknowledge his presence further, she raised her blade and pointed it directly at the blue-eyed guard before dropping into her stance.

"You've got balls, I'll give you that." Lifting his sword, he shifted his weight and mirrored her stance. "Let's see how big they are."

Bring it, asshole.

Without waiting to see if she'd reply, the arrogant ass advanced. She knew he figured he'd take her by surprise, but she'd been closely watching each of his bouts. She expected his speed and was ready for him.

She caught the blade of his sword on hers and thrust it back toward his body with a strong block. His eyes widened just slightly, and he feigned pulling back before altering his tactic and lunging again.

Their swords hit over and over as they each altered defending and attacking. She wasn't sure how long they'd been at it, but her stamina had yet to dampen, and she'd never felt more alive. Her anger had burned away into a rush of excitement at the pure bliss of a fight.

Arrogant Ass was incredibly skilled. He assumed his strength would be enough to push her back as if her arms would fold on themselves with the force of his hits. He wasn't completely wrong; his strikes were powerful, and shockwaves shot up both her arms each time they met. When that hadn't worked, he began to focus more on speed. He truly was wicked fast.

But she was faster.

Vera grinned beneath her mask as she watched him lunge toward her again. She waited until the last possible second before deflecting his sword. Before he could regain his momentum, she launched forward at lightning speed.

She landed the flat of her sword hard against his arm before pivoting and kicking his legs out from under him. It was almost exactly what she'd done to Elric just that morning. As his back connected with the ground, she stood over him and pointed her weapon at his chest.

He lay there for a long moment, eyebrows raised and mouth hanging open. She waited for the snappy comment that was sure to come, a foul curse or some lame excuse for losing. But it never happened. She jumped slightly when he burst out laughing. It was a deep, baritone laugh that made her feel more than a little flustered.

"Lesta!" he hollered from the ground, "We're going to need a few more toothpicks!"

His laughter continued as he rubbed his arm and tried to sit up. Baffled by his reaction, Vera silently extended her arm. He accepted her proffered hand in a firm grip, the strength of his fingers obvious even through his glove.

She heaved him up, stumbling slightly with his weight. He steadied her with a hard clap to her shoulder, and she felt a sense of pride pulse through her body in tandem with the adrenaline of sparring. A second later, reality set in as she made eye contact with Elric. The horror on his face spoke more than words could, and she took an involuntary step away from Arrogant Ass.

Planning to make a hasty getaway before Elric could kill her where she stood, she twisted around only to come to an abrupt stop. Her jaw dropped beneath her mask, and her eyes bulged from her head as she took in the face of the man before her.

Arrogant Ass had removed his mask, and in its place was a well-formed mouth lifting into a stunning smile. It caused the corners of his eyes to crinkle and small dimples to appear in his pale cheeks. With his hair still tied back, she could see his closely shaven, squared jaw. He was beautiful. The kind of beautiful that could make anyone fall all over themselves for just a fleeting moment of his attention. The kind of beautiful that *did* make people do exactly that.

The kind of beautiful that was to be expected of the Crown Prince, Eithan Matheris.

Vera's entire body froze, all her adrenaline suddenly converting to acid in her stomach. She knew without a doubt, if she tried to speak, she'd vomit all over his boots. He chuckled at her obvious shock. Yep. One hundred percent chance of a spew fest. Gods, she was an idiot.

"Varian!" Elric shouted, making his way toward them, and using the pseudonym she went by anytime she wore the mask.

"Get back to the armory." He snapped his fingers before pointing angrily at the door. Mentally cursing her frozen feet, she forced them to start moving.

"I apologize and beg your forgiveness, Your Highness. Varian is young, and he is as mute as he is daft. He had no right to be out here and will be swiftly punished," Elric said from the deep bow he'd dropped into.

His words snapped her out of her blind terror, and Vera's legs came alive, carrying her as fast as possible toward the armory. Let the prince think her daft, just as long as he believed her to be a daft man. She heard him reply, but she couldn't make out the words over the pounding in her ears.

She didn't spare a single second as she arrived at the door. She flung it open and dashed in as if death were nipping at her heels. It might as well have been.

She'd struck the *Crown Prince*. And not just struck but pointed a weapon at his chest and humiliated him openly. Even if she'd been a man that would have been stupid, but as a woman? She ripped off her mask and rubbed a hand over her face. Holding her sweaty fingers over her lips, she tried to steady her erratic breathing, roiling stomach, and stupid freaking mind.

No wonder Elric had reacted the way he did. He'd known. Gods, of course he'd known, he'd trained the prince himself.

With her anger no longer controlling her, she realized just how badly she'd fucked up. Even if the prince didn't demand she return, any of the guards could now guess who she was and speak up.

It wouldn't take much for one of them to put two and two together that Elric had only ever had one ward. Her life would be forfeit, not to mention Elric's life.

Vera didn't move for several minutes, waiting and listening for someone to demand she return and face consequences. She nibbled on the inside of her lip, frantically trying to come up with an explanation that wouldn't incriminate Elric. He'd done so much and put up with her for so many years, and this was how she repaid him.

She suddenly felt like crying but refused to let the tears fall. Ignoring her burning eyes, she walked toward the back. Maybe if she were lucky, she'd be able to scrub some of her idiocy off along with her sweat.

Chapter
4
Vera

S he only allowed herself a quick wash before forcing her legs
to carry her back into the workroom. Having an already
angry Elric return and see she'd slacked off in her work
would end quite poorly for her. So instead of hiding in her bed
like she wanted to, she lost herself in her work.

The precise, repetitive actions of sharpening blades calmed
her mind and gave her a purpose. It was the best form of
meditation. She always knew what the outcome would be—could
rely on it. With a little love and attention, she could take
something worn down, something used and beaten, and make it
better than it was before.

It took focus, care, and patience, especially with a sword,
which she was currently working on. The difference between

sharpening a long sword and, say, a dagger, involved sharpening sections at a time rather than sweeping the entire blade across the whetstone.

By doing it in sections, there was the risk of the blade coming out slightly uneven, so Vera had to work slowly and meticulously. It usually ended up being a few hours' worth of effort per sword.

The trick was making sure she didn't over-work the blade. An overly sharpened blade sounded like it'd be deadly and vicious, but in reality, it often did less damage. Swords that were too sharp and thin tended to bounce off bone and chip rather than sever a limb completely. Thankfully, she'd long since perfected her technique.

Vera didn't often work on swords for Matherin city guards since they practiced with dull-edged blades in the training yard and rarely had to unsheathe their actual weapons while on duty. It was uncommon for an event to occur inside the capital that required more than brute strength to disband.

However, the emperor never stopped demanding more weapons be sent to the east and west territories of Aleron, which kept Vera busy.

Remembering all the history facts Elric had made her study as a child wasn't one of Vera's stronger skill sets. Still, she knew that generations ago, before the rise of the Matherin Empire, the different quadrants of Aleron were at a constant state of unrest.

According to Aleron history texts, it wasn't until the first Matheris, a Northerner, raised an army and went to war with The West that they all inevitably came under one banner. The East and South territories were vastly outnumbered once Matheris took The West so, to save lives, they surrendered without a fight. And thus, the Matherin Empire was born.

Since then, there hadn't been any real unrest or fighting, but that didn't deter the current ruler, Emperor Sulian Matheris. His paranoia only seemed to grow each year. Considering who—or more accurately *what*—was north across the Dividing Sea, most Aleronians didn't blame him; instead believing him some sort of great protector.

It helped that his paranoia kept work flowing for her. Vera knew she wasn't the only person working on blades that would be shipped out. She wasn't stupid, she knew one person couldn't possibly supply the entire army with swords no matter how diligently she worked. But she liked to pretend it was just her, a mere slip of a girl, helping to keep the soldiers armed and Aleron protected. She appreciated the ego boost, no matter what was true.

She'd just finished up for the day, enjoying the smell of worked metal and the twinge in her tired arms, when the door finally opened. Elric didn't say a word as he stepped in and pushed it shut behind him. She was instantly tense, her worries slamming to the forefront of her mind as if they'd never left.

Glancing at her briefly, his eyes moved over the finished swords next to her. He grunted in approval, and Vera's body relaxed slightly, a tiny weight lifting from her chest.

She had a dozen questions for him. Was the prince angry? Did he ask who she was? Did any of the guards figure it out? Should she run away and never return?

But instead, she asked the most important question, the one she was most scared of. "Will you be punished, Elric?" She bit the inside of her lip and couldn't help but shift side to side, waiting for his answer.

"No."

The breath she'd been holding whooshed out of her. She wasn't sure what she would've done if she'd gotten Elric in trouble. He was all she had. "Thank the gods. So…" She didn't finish her question. She didn't need to. It was apparent what she wanted to ask.

Elric folded his arms across his chest. "What on Aleron could you possibly have been thinking, Vera? Dammit, you knew better." He didn't raise his voice, though the disappointment coating his words was somehow worse.

"I know, I just got angry. I didn't really think it through… obviously," she added, at the look he gave her. "He insulted the men and blatantly disrespected you. I assumed he was just a guard, and I didn't—" she sighed. "I let my emotions dictate my actions instead of my intellect. I'm sorry, Elric."

Grumbling to himself, he uncrossed his arms and finally walked away from the door. "I can handle verbal spurs, Vera. I'm not a newborn babe. The fact you thought I needed to be defended wounds me more. And those men deserved his comments."

"I beg to differ. He was an asshole."

"For good reason. He came to inspect their abilities, and they failed. Those men had become complacent but will work twice as hard now. Wounded pride is a heavy motivator."

She fiddled with the tools on her worktable. "So, what happened after I left? Was he angry?"

He scoffed. "No. His Highness found it amusing more than anything else. He wanted you to come back, but I was able to persuade him to leave you to your duties as punishment for skirting your work." He looked at her sharply. "The work you should have been doing instead of sparring with the Crown Prince."

Vera wanted to curl up into herself. Maybe mold a nice shell out of her shame and crawl inside of it and never come out. At least the prince had accepted Elric's explanation and left her alone.

"But he expressed an interest in sparring with you again the next time he comes to inspect the guard, likely to recruit you."

She took a step back and raised her hands as if to ward herself against his words.

"But—"

"I wasn't exactly in a position to refuse, *Varian*," he said sharply. "However, the prince will spend the next several days preparing for a trip to Midpath to inspect the squadron stationed near there. The emperor has demanded His Highness become more involved in overseeing their forces, and Prince Eithan requested I join him."

He looked at her pointedly, "It will be several days before we leave, and several more before we return. So, you'll have a reprieve for a while, and if you're damned lucky, he'll have forgotten about you upon our return. If not, you'll have no one to blame but yourself."

Vera knew she should apologize again and let it drop, but as soon as "Midpath" left Elric's mouth, all his other words passed straight through her ears, suddenly unimportant. She'd never traveled outside the capital, at least not in the years she could remember, but she'd heard the guards tell stories about Midpath's pleasantries.

It was a stopping point about midway between the capital and the far eastern city of Eastshore—hence its name. Soldiers, travelers, and merchants alike all stopped there to rest and restock provisions. Midpath's popularity came not only from its convenient location, but from what it offered. Comfortable inns after days sleeping on the road, vendors, bars, brothels, entertainment, food—Midpath had it all.

Vera had wanted to go from the moment she'd heard of it, but Elric rarely left the capital, and she certainly wasn't allowed to leave alone.

"I know what you're going to ask, I can see the wheels turning behind your eyes. What are you going to do? Ride next to the Crown Prince and hope he doesn't notice you're not a man?"

He looked at her like she was the most idiotic person to ever stand before him. "Use logic, girl."

She chewed on her lip. There had to be a way for her to go. He was right, she wouldn't be able to blend in with the prince's personal guard. They were a selected few and would instantly notice her like a cuckoo in their nest.

"What if I go as Vera instead of Varian?" she blurted, watching Elric walk toward their quarters.

He didn't bother stopping. "Are you expecting me to answer that?"

"It's well known that I can be found in the armory. It may be highly frowned upon, but it's no secret you have a female ward."

She felt slightly flushed with a mixture of excitement and desperation. "Everyone knows you never leave here, you're practically a hermit. Which means it'll be no surprise for them to learn you've never left me before. Do you really want to leave me alone, knowing that all the men outside will *know* I'm alone? I'm just a defenseless woman, Elric. You wouldn't want to risk my safety." She batted her eyelashes. She was a genius.

"Don't be an idiot twice in one day," he threw out behind him. Not bothering to say anything else, he entered their main room, deliberately ending the conversation.

Knowing she'd have to walk past him to get to her room, Vera made sure to stomp the entire way and slammed the door behind her. She was acting like a child, but she didn't care. She had a good life, and she loved her work and looked up to Elric, but she wanted more.

This was the only home she'd ever known, but that didn't mean she wanted to stay there forever. Elric was content to stay because he'd already lived and traveled Aleron. She just wanted the same opportunity, the freedom to travel and see other cities and meet people. The thought of never seeing anything other than the armory walls for the rest of her life made her feel trapped.

She fell back onto her bed, dirty clothes and all. She was tired of being shut behind doors and told to keep quiet because she was born with the wrong equipment between her legs. It wasn't like men's fragile junk was anything to be proud of.

Vera's body could knock a prince on his ass *and* give birth to new life. No man on all of Aleron could claim the same. *That* was something to be proud of.

Men thought themselves so important, they put themselves on a pedestal, but it was the strength of the women who birthed, raised, and cared for them that kept their precious pedestal from crumbling.

Stretching out, she groaned when her stomach growled loudly. She hadn't had supper yet, but she was too cranky and exhausted to get up. Elric was grown and capable. If he were in a hurry to eat, he could make his own supper. She'd just close her eyes for a few minutes and apologize later.

VERA JERKED UP, still half asleep as she gripped the sides of her bed for support. She reached up to rub the sleep from her eyes when a knock against her door startled her. Realizing that was likely what woke her in the first place, she flung her feet off the bed. By the lack of light outside, she'd been out for a couple of hours. She smirked, Elric was probably starving.

Standing, she stretched her limbs before changing into a clean tunic and trudging into the main room. He hadn't knocked again, likely having heard her finally up and around. Sure enough, he was sitting at their small table, looking at her expectantly. Two mugs sat out, one still full and foaming.

Sitting in the empty chair across from him, she pulled her legs to her chest before grabbing the full drink and taking a deep pull. "Thank gods for whoever created ale," she said before resting her chin on her knees.

This was one of the things she loved most about her relationship with Elric. No matter how cross they got at each other, they were always able to come to the table and talk over drinks. When Vera was little, it had been over spiced tea instead of ale. She liked tea, but she loved ale.

He grunted, and she thought she caught a flicker of a smile before he covered it with his mug.

"You can go."

Freezing like an animal that'd just sighted a hunter, she felt her mouth pop open. She'd been mulling over her words trying to decide whether or not she would apologize, and now she was too terrified to think, let alone speak, in case he changed his mind.

Seeing her expression, Elric tipped his head back and released a hearty laugh. It wasn't often she was speechless, and the ass was enjoying every second of it. He took another large sip before setting his mug down and leaning over the table, his grin falling from his face.

"I am willing to try to bring you along, but if I feel uneasy about it for any reason, you will leave without argument."

Vera nodded, trying to rein in the squeal that fought to squeeze past her lips. She'd agree to tape her mouth shut and follow every rule he made if it convinced him to bring her along, although she certainly wasn't going to tell him that.

She wondered how he'd react if she jumped across the table and hugged him. Probably not her best idea. She'd likely give him a heart attack.

"This is not a guarantee, girl. Prince Eithan will presumably deny my request. Ward or not, it would be unconventional for a woman to accompany the prince out of the city, especially since he's leaving to inspect armed forces. You need to be prepared for him to say no."

He reclined and drained the rest of his ale. "But I will try because you're right, I don't like the thought of leaving you here. I trust these men to protect their emperor. I do not, however, trust them around you."

She dropped her legs back to the floor and pushed her mug away. Tapping her fingers against the table, she wondered if seeing her as Vera would make the prince suspicious of the Varian he'd met. She cautiously voiced her worry to Elric, scared he'd change his mind, but he just shook his head and asked if she planned on making supper.

Her stomach rumbled in response, and she jumped out of her chair. Patting him on the shoulder as she passed, she practically skipped toward their minimal kitchen. She wasn't the best cook by any means, but over the years, she'd grown to enjoy it. Throwing a few random things together to make a quick meal, she thought back over her question.

She hadn't needed to ask. No Matherin woman would risk being caught wearing a guard's mask, let alone know how to wield a blade. On Aleron, it wasn't just unbelievable, it was laughable. Prince Eithan would never question it because to do so would be admitting a woman had bested him in the heart of a city that claimed it impossible.

She doubted he'd so much as spare her a second glance, which was probably why Elric had agreed to let her go. She felt flutters in her middle as everything started to settle in. She might actually visit Midpath! Her face broke into a fierce smile.

What had seemed like the worst day was turning into one of the best. She'd gotten to spar an actual opponent, and now she might get to leave the capital.

Her excited thoughts were interrupted when Elric came up next to her and leaned against the counter. She glanced over, and the look on his face had her swallowing nervously. He looked like a feline cornering a rodent.

"You know, Vera, traveling with the Crown Prince means you'll have to dress appropriately." His eyes practically lit up. "You're gonna have to wear a dress."

For the love of all the gods.

Chapter 5

Vera

She fidgeted and yanked at her dress for the hundredth time that morning. How did anyone wear these? Since she'd had to lace it alone, combined with her inexperience, she probably looked as ridiculous as she felt. The bodice was significantly tighter than the tunics she was used to, and she hated how vulnerable she felt. It demanded she keep a stiffer posture than usual, which was sure to be extremely comfortable while riding a horse.

Elric had demanded years ago that she keep a dress on hand just in case, but she'd never actually worn it before. It was a dull, faded brown and snug since she'd obviously grown over the past few years. But although tight, the bodice reached her collar and covered the important parts. Even so, she was more than a little thankful for her travel cloak.

The skirt, however, was going to be a problem. It was too long, and the hem kept threatening to trip her anytime she wasn't actively holding it up. It probably didn't help that she'd chosen to wear a pair of roughened boots that kept catching the fabric as she paced back and forth.

She was almost tempted to change her mind and go back to the training yard. But if she stayed, she'd be stuck inside the armory from dawn to dusk, avoiding the guards who would still be using the area for practice. She'd already been miserable the past several days waiting for Elric to announce their departure. Staying was not an option.

How long did it take to ask a question? Elric should have been back by now. Vera swore under her breath. If she'd squeezed into this contraption for no reason, she might knock the prince unconscious this time.

Not to mention the pins she'd had to shove in her hair were biting into her scalp. She'd painstakingly styled her hair into two plaits wound around her head like a crown, accentuating her facial structure. She'd pulled loose a few small curls in front of both ears and made sure there was nothing about her that screamed *Varian*.

She was just about to risk venturing out to peek at the preparing party when Elric finally appeared. She studied his expression, but she couldn't tell whether he was about to deliver good news or bad news. Like the frustrating brute he could often be, he made her stew in silence for several agonizing moments before finally taking pity on her. He nodded to the side, toward the others, and turned without waiting to see if she'd follow.

Vera momentarily considered jumping up and down, but she was overtaken by a wave of nerves that halted her limbs. She was leaving the city, with the Crown Prince of all people. This was insane. She was insane. But she certainly wouldn't turn back now.

She followed the path Elric had taken to the stables, where the party was finishing up the last of their preparations. As she waited slightly off to the side, she was pleased to discover she'd be given her own horse.

She was about to thank Elric when he ruined the moment by reminding her to stay silent unless spoken to, and not draw any unnecessary attention to herself. His look was sharper than a freshly worked blade.

Rolling her eyes, she said, "I'm not pretending you know. I am an actual woman. I know how to act."

He laughed—literally laughed in her face—and said, "Sure."

She glared at him, silently promising pain, but he just continued to laugh as if her reaction only further proved his point.

She followed him to the back of the group, where a stable boy led two unclaimed horses. Both mares were brown, although the slightly larger one was a soft chestnut color, while the smaller had a sleeker, darker coat.

Circling the darker mare, she patted her and uttered sweet words. She hadn't ridden a horse in years, and even then, she'd only done it a handful of times to market with Elric. She certainly wasn't experienced, but she felt confident in her memory enough to not make a complete fool of herself.

Luckily for her, a woman of her background wouldn't be expected to be an excellent rider anyway. If she fell off, she doubted they'd be all that surprised.

Thankfully, her luck held out. She grabbed the saddle and successfully hoisted herself up onto the mare in one quick movement, even in the awful dress. She stood in the stirrups and bunched the annoying skirts around her before sitting and clutching the reins.

She gave the beast another soft pat and decided to call her Umber. Smiling to herself, she turned her head to find Elric and several guards staring at her.

Her smile slipped into a frown as she looked down at herself to see what had caught their attention. Double-checking the tight bodice hadn't ripped—or something equally appalling—she popped her head up and snapped, "What?"

Elric just shook his head, mumbling under his breath, and turned his chestnut mare away. One of the guards, a man with flawless, brown skin and closely shaved black hair, flicked his gaze at her legs and cleared his throat before saying, "It's just... uncommon to see a lady ride astride."

He made a small croaking sound, and she had the feeling he was trying to restrain a laugh. His mask may have obscured his face, but his brown eyes sparkled with obvious humor.

She probably should have apologized and feigned ignorance, but she found herself locking eyes with him instead. She wasn't ignorant, and she sure wouldn't pretend to be just because her spread legs flustered their delicate, masculine sensibilities. Elric was right, she had no idea how to act properly.

"Any man who expects a woman to ride side-saddle the entire trip to Midpath is a fool."

Vera looked him up and down with the iciest expression she could muster before facing straight ahead. She held her head high as she urged Umber forward, but not before catching a glimmer of surprise enter the guard's warm eyes.

THEY DISEMBARKED SOON after, not wanting to waste precious daylight. As long as they didn't encounter any hiccups along the way, they would reach the town of Kilmire by nightfall and, hopefully, have hot food and warm beds waiting at the inn.

She'd caught sight of Prince Eithan a few times throughout the morning, but he'd dressed as a city guard for safety precautions, so she had to actively search to find him.

She scolded herself every time she caught herself looking. Her fear was irrational and pointless. He wasn't going to recognize her. He hadn't even so much as acknowledged her presence.

Forcing herself to take a deep breath, she was painfully aware of Elric regularly glancing back at her. He rode slightly ahead, talking to a few of the guards. Prince Eithan had brought twelve in total. Three trailed behind Vera, and the rest rode ahead, either next to the prince or right behind him.

She let her head fall back and closed her eyes, enjoying the simple pleasure of being outside during the day. There wasn't much to see besides the beginning of the Lakewood Forest, but it was rare for her to experience the sun on her face, and she couldn't help but be inexplicably happy about it.

"It's a beautiful day for travel," a voice said from directly next to her. Startled, her eyes flew open, and she had to grip the reins tightly to keep herself steady. If she'd been riding side-saddle, she'd have fallen face first on the road.

She glanced over to see the guard from earlier looking at her. Readjusting her posture, she lifted her chin in a slight nod before facing forward again.

"Sorry, I didn't mean to scare you. Name's Trey Gibson."

He had a chipper voice with a mild accent common for southern citizens. If she had to guess, she'd say he hailed from Southterres. His eyes were warm and inviting, and he was tapping his fingers rhythmically on the pommel of his saddle.

She didn't recognize him, but she also didn't recognize any of the other men either. The prince clearly had a private training yard for his personal guards.

"It's fine. I was just lost in thought." She paused, unsure if she should introduce herself or not. Elric had forbidden her from talking unless spoken to, and Trey had approached her, so technically she wasn't breaking the rules. "I'm Vera."

His eyes crinkled, telling her he was smiling beneath his mask. Vera found herself wishing he could remove it so she could see his face. She had a feeling he was one of those people who had a contagious smile.

"So, you're Lesta's ward?"

She nodded. Hoping to steer the conversation away from herself, she asked, "How long have you been part of the prince's guard?"

"I moved to the capital and enlisted as soon as I was of age, but I've been a member of Prince Eithan's personal guard for about three years."

Raising her brows, she appraised him again. "How old are you?"

"I'm twenty-three, why? You interested?" He looked over, wiggling his eyebrows.

Before she could think twice about the consequences of insulting him, she scoffed. "Not even remotely."

She immediately regretted the words and sucked her bottom lip into her mouth, prepared for the verbal slap she was sure to receive. Most of the guards she'd watched train were quick to anger and chose violence for even the smallest transgressions against them.

Vera was not expecting the loud, bubbling laughter that burst out of his lean body. Several of the men riding in front of them turned their way, drawn to the noise. She made eye contact with a few and shrugged, unsure as to why he was laughing.

She looked at him hesitantly. Trey didn't seem like any other guard she'd observed so far, and she found herself liking him already.

"I don't think I've ever met a woman with a sense of humor before."

"What, you expected us to lack it just because we have breasts?" His eyes widened comically, and his eyebrows shot up toward his hairline. "Besides, who said I was joking?" she continued, looking down her nose at him.

Finally regaining a semblance of control over his expression, he shook his head and chuckled. Taking advantage of his companionable presence, she asked, "So who is everyone else?

Have you all worked together long?"

Although he appeared a little baffled at her interest, he pointed and named each guard, working his way toward Prince Eithan. "The two closest to his highness are his first-in-command, Wes Coleman, and his second, Ryn Hayes. Coleman is a quiet one, tends to keep to himself. Hayes on the other hand...well, to be blunt, he's a shady motherfucker."

She frowned. "Then why have him guarding the prince's back?"

Trey shrugged, "He's the best bowman the capital has seen. He's a loyal guard, but I wouldn't recommend telling him any of your jokes."

They spent the remainder of the morning and early afternoon riding together and talking on and off to pass the time. Besides their somewhat awkward start, she found herself enjoying his company.

Mostly she questioned him about his years of being a guard while dodging his inquiries about herself the best she could without raising suspicion. Anytime the questions got too personal, she'd steer the conversation back to something safer, like her assistance in the armory.

Trey didn't seem to notice, or if he did, he didn't care. He was lively and had an ornery sense of humor. He seemed too young and carefree to be a guard, but she knew he had to be highly skilled to be handpicked at such a young age.

Vera hadn't truly realized until then just how lonely her life was. Sure, she had Elric, and she respected him immensely, but this had been the longest conversation she'd ever had with someone close to her age.

As the sun began to set, Trey finally pushed forward to the front. They were less than an hour from Kilmire, and all the guards closed ranks to ride protectively around the prince. The town was completely loyal to Emperor Matheris, but it was always better to be safe than sorry.

Elric dropped back to ride next to her for the first time since they'd broken for lunch earlier in the day. He'd lectured her about talking so openly with Trey, but she'd only half listened. She knew she'd probably never see him again once they returned, but her heart refused to care, swelling as the possibility of friendship was dangled in front of her.

It was almost completely dark by the time they'd stabled their horses and entered the inn. She watched Prince Eithan speak to the innkeeper and realized he didn't plan on revealing who he was at all. He simply asked for one room for "the lady" and three rooms for the rest of their party.

She was stunned. He hadn't so much as said two words to her but had requested an entire room just for her. She looked around at the men, expecting hostile behavior, but none of them paid her any mind as they trudged up the stairs to their shared rooms.

Trey caught her eye as Elric held up the key to her room, "If you get cold, you know where I'll be." He aimed an exaggerated wink her way.

Speaking to Elric, she tilted her head in Trey's direction and said, "You hear that? Trey over there could use a cuddle buddy."

To her delight, Elric didn't so much as roll his eyes. Twisting so he faced him completely, he said, "I'll be up as soon as I'm done getting Vera settled. Try to snag us the bed by the door."

Trey's head reared back, and Vera feared his eyes might actually fall out of his head. He stuttered a reply they couldn't make out before practically sprinting up the stairs.

Unable to keep a straight face any longer, Vera burst out laughing so hard, she thought her chest might explode. Wiping her eyes, she glanced at Elric to catch a smile on his face. He turned, and she followed him up to her room, soft chuckles still escaping her lips.

The room was small and simple, much like her room at home. Standing near the doorway, she stared at the bed, trying to decide if she possessed the energy to wash before sprawling on the mattress in a very unladylike way.

"You need to be careful, girl."

She glanced at the bed again before looking at Elric with a raised brow. "Of the bed?"

He crossed his arms and looked knowingly at her. She sighed. She knew what he meant, but she didn't want to talk about it.

"I know. And it's really not what you think, Elric. It's just been nice to talk to someone." She couldn't keep the longing from her voice, and she cleared her throat before plopping down on the bed.

She busied herself with tugging off her boots. Her entire body hurt, and she knew she'd wake up even more sore and chafed.

"A girl your age deserves friendship, and I want that for you. But I also want to keep you safe." He gave her shoulder a light pat before leaving and quietly shutting her door.

Finally alone, she tried to busy herself by scrubbing a wet

cloth over her face and arms, but the quiet seemed to stretch on. After being surrounded by other people all day, it felt weird to suddenly have nothing but silence surrounding her. She curled up on the bed, both physically and emotionally exhausted.

Elric was right, she did need to be careful because she wasn't sure if she'd be able to go back to being locked up in the armory anymore. She wanted more.

Chapter 6

Vera

D
ay two went by similar to the first, although the scenery had improved. The forest to their right had thickened, and it was as vast as it was beautiful. Several times Vera caught glances of creatures running through the trees, and their freedom brought her a melancholy type of joy. She listened to the bird calls and allowed herself to imagine what it would be like if she could fly away and travel wherever she wanted.

Trey came up to ride beside her a few hours in, and she couldn't prevent the little leap her heart gave. He held a hand to his heart and gifted her with a dramatic retelling of how Elric hadn't shown up to keep him warm, swearing he'd nearly frozen to death. Vera laughed so hard she snorted.

"Something must be truly funny indeed, for a laugh like that."

She froze, almost choking on her laugh, and turned to her other side to find Prince Eithan looking at her. She gawked at him, completely at a loss for words. Her entire head emptied apart from the image of pointing a sword at his chest, and that memory wasn't the least bit helpful.

He chuckled, "Forgive me, I shouldn't tease you before even introducing myself. Eithan Matheris. It's a pleasure to make your acquaintance." He nodded and somehow made the motion look both relaxed and regal, even from atop a horse.

"The pleasure's mine, Your Highness." Vera wasn't sure if she was supposed to try to curtsy or bow while riding, and opted for the safe choice of lowering her head to stare at her hands. Her face warmed, and a blush crawled up her neck as she felt his continued attention.

She wondered if the well-formed lips she'd seen the other day were smiling under his mask, silently laughing at her uncertain, awkward behavior.

Daring to glance at him from under her lashes, her breath hitched as they locked gazes. The glimmer in his eyes alone told her he was, indeed, smiling, and she couldn't help but wish she could rip his mask off.

"I hope Gibson hasn't been giving you any trouble."

"No!" She cringed. "I mean, no, Your Highness. He's been the perfect gentleman."

He laughed, sending a wave of flutters through her chest. "Gibson's never been a gentleman a day of his life. How many inappropriate comments have you made to poor Vera today, Gibson?"

"Ten. Possibly fifteen, but definitely no more than twenty."

"A personal record, I'd wager." The prince winked at her, causing her blush to explode across her body until she was sure her skin would peel off from the heat. "Well, I do hope you have a pleasant day, Vera."

He nodded at Trey before urging his stallion forward to stop alongside Elric. Her mentor glanced back at her, and she fought the urge to hide her face, dreading what the prince was possibly saying.

Feeling a sharp poke in her shoulder, she twisted to find Trey's arm outstretched toward her.

"What was that for?"

"Your face is so red, I'm trying to figure out how you're not engulfed in flames."

She shot a death glare his way, "You shouldn't point that out to a lady, it's rude."

He cocked his head to the side and shrugged, "That's true, I suppose. However, I've never been one to follow basic manners, and you don't act much like a lady."

Against her will, Vera felt her lips quirk up on the sides, but she didn't reply. He wasn't wrong, and they both knew it.

She moved her gaze to the sky and frowned. She wondered what it would be like to truly be herself around other people.

Trey had already concluded she was raised differently, but would he still act friendly if he heard her curse like a drunkard or knew she could knock him out? Somehow, she highly doubted it, and the thought weighed heavily on her shoulders.

They rode in silence for a while before she was able to shake the weight off and dared to ask him about his home. His eyes glossed over, looking incredibly sad, before he blinked it away.

He told her about being born to a single mother a few months after his father and older sister had died from an aggressive sickness. Vera wanted to ask more, but he seemed disinclined to speak further about them.

She realized, like her, Trey may not have had the perfect family or happy start in life. Somehow it made her feel better. If Trey could make his way, regardless of how and where he was born, and find contentment, then maybe she could as well.

They continued chatting occasionally until late afternoon when he finally rode off to make plans with the guards up front. They'd traveled hard the previous day and had an early start on the second, so at their current pace, they were estimated to arrive in Midpath within an hour or two.

Vera was practically vibrating with excitement. She couldn't wait to walk among the vendors and wrap up the evening with a foaming mug of ale.

ONCE AGAIN, VERA was given a room to herself. But unlike at Kilmire, the inn was larger, and the men were able to separate between five rooms instead of three. However, with the sneaking glances she'd seen several of the men give to the women they'd passed, she wondered if a few would return for any sleep at all.

With the rumors she'd heard about the Crown Prince, she doubted he'd care. Apparently, he was quite popular with the women in the capital, both nobles and servants. Who knew, maybe he'd be off looking for company as well.

She stood awkwardly to the side as the men discussed their evening plans. It seemed like most were interested in visiting a local tavern, and she had to agree. After two days of travel rations, she'd kill for a warm plate and a large drink.

She made to follow them out, but Elric stopped her with a hand to her shoulder. "Go ahead up to your room, Vera. I've already paid the innkeeper for your supper, just tell him when you'd like it brought up."

She clasped her hands in front of her and glanced at the men walking through the door before looking back at him.

"Wait...what? No, I'd like to go with you. Please. I'll stay quiet, I promise. I'd like to walk around before the sun goes down."

He shook his head, narrowing his eyes. "A lady does not drink ale with the Crown Prince's guards and wander the streets at dusk. Go up to your room." He didn't wait for her to reply before turning and pushing through the door.

She stood alone in the center of the room. He expected her to stay inside the entire evening? What about tomorrow? If he thought she'd stay locked in her room while he accompanied the prince to the army stationed a few hours out, he had another thing coming.

But the longer Vera contemplated it, the more she realized that's exactly what he'd demand she do. She wasn't a guard. She wasn't even considered an apprentice.

Suddenly feeling like crying and stabbing something at the

same time, she spoke with the innkeeper about supper and trudged upstairs. A few minutes later, the lanky man returned with some bland, warm stew and bread.

She was just finishing up when a foolish, yet tempting, idea formed inside her mind. Elric had said a lady had no place wandering the streets, but as Trey had pointed out, she wasn't much of a lady to begin with.

Vera dug into her travel pack and pulled out the folded tunic, trousers, and cloak she'd stashed just in case. Grinning to herself, she began changing as quickly as possible. She didn't have a mask or the band she typically wrapped around her breasts, but with her hooded cloak on, she wasn't too worried about either.

Re-working her hair into a single plait that she tucked inside her tunic, she threw on her cloak, wishing she had a dagger or even a kitchen knife. She didn't expect to be attacked, but she also didn't like the idea of being unarmed in an unfamiliar place.

She finished lacing up her boots and cracked the door open to peek out. It definitely wouldn't end well if anyone believed they saw a strange man leaving her room. When she confirmed the coast was clear, Vera eased out and made her way downstairs as casually as she could.

Thankfully, the innkeeper was talking with another occupant and was facing away from the stairs, so she ran for the door and eagerly disappeared into the streets of Midpath.

It was somehow better than she'd imagined. It was more vibrant, more exciting, more overwhelming, more everything. Vera had occasionally visited a few of the markets in the capital with Elric throughout the years, but they were nothing like this.

The streets of Matherin were congested and stuffy, smelling like a combination of waste and an overpowering concoction of spices and perfumes. There was no magic or suspense, just normal people living normal lives.

Whereas here, everything was spread out so people could pass easily and see all there was to offer. The people were more animated and alive. Her senses had definitely picked up an eclectic mix of smells that she could practically taste, but it wasn't overwhelming.

Although, if Vera was honest with herself, her overall happiness about being out of the armory in general probably had something to do with her intense approval.

She walked at a leisurely pace. She had no coin to purchase anything, but she was content with strolling unhindered and unnoticed through the streets, enjoying the simplicity of visually shopping the different wares for sale. But what she enjoyed more than anything was the way she could unapologetically watch people.

At first, she thought seeing the brothel workers would make her uncomfortable. She'd never seen one before and had only the guards' descriptions to base her assumptions on. But she found herself drawn in by the women's soft words and seductive movements as they danced in the open windows.

Sex was not something she'd ever done, but she knew what it was and understood the mechanics of it. Elric had brought in a local healer to have "the talk" with her when she'd first bled, and she often overheard the guards make comments. It just wasn't something she'd ever had a chance to experience, apart from her own self-exploration.

The women were gorgeous, and it wasn't because of what they were wearing—or not wearing—but because of what they were projecting. They didn't look miserable or used like she had expected. They looked strong and confident. Instead of crying over the lot in life they had, they made the most out of it, and Vera found herself secretly wishing she had their conviction.

Forcing her legs to keep moving, she turned the corner and had to fight to control her saliva when the smell of freshly baked sweets smacked her straight in the face. She watched as two small children sprinted circles around their parents, squealing in joy as their mother handed them a warm, sticky bun to share.

She felt a pang in her middle at the sight and absentmindedly rubbed her chest. She wondered what it might have been like to grow up in a family, with forehead kisses and heartfelt smiles. She watched them a little longer before chastising herself.

Elric may not have ever been affectionate, but he'd shown her how to find her own strength and taught her to push her limits. He'd made her the woman she was, and she was grateful to him, even when he tried to lock her in an inn.

There was a slight chill in the air as the sun began its descent, so thankfully she didn't stand out in her cloak. No one even spared her a second glance. She was invisible and unimportant. But for the first time in her life, Vera didn't mind it.

The only thing that could have made the evening better was if she hadn't had to wander alone. She missed Trey's company. He'd been her almost constant companion for two days, and she missed his lighthearted banter.

She thought about heading to the tavern the guards had mentioned and sitting at the bar so she could listen to their conversation and pretend to be a part of it. Even considering it made her feel pathetic, but it didn't stop her from wanting to anyway.

She almost convinced herself to risk it, but the knowledge that Elric would likely still be there stopped her. Even hidden under a hood and cloak, he'd recognize her before her foot even crossed the threshold.

Vera was just beginning to head back toward the inn when she saw her travel party step onto the street and head in her direction, almost as if her thoughts had summoned them. One of the positives to the men wearing masks was they were easy to spot from afar. She immediately ducked in a doorway, hiding among the shadows. Thank gods, Elric didn't appear to be with them.

Several of the guards were talking animatedly. Although she couldn't make out their exact words, Vera had a feeling she knew exactly what they were discussing. The tone and inflection of their voices carried, and two of them used their hands to imitate what Vera was pretty positive was a sexual act. She rolled her eyes.

They seemed to be enjoying themselves and she realized, just like the other guards back in Matherin, they genuinely appeared to be friends. In the center of the loud group, she recognized the prince instantly. His head tipped back as he released a deep laugh, and she was surprised to see he seemed perfectly content and happy to meander down the street as a guard instead of a prince.

Against her better judgment, she was transfixed by him. He was nothing like what she'd expected. Taking full advantage of her hideaway and unobstructed view, she watched them walk across the far side of the street. She was still admiring the prince's relaxed nature when she noticed a slight shift in the shadows behind them.

To their credit, even in their cheer, the guards were attentive to their surroundings. Enough so that Vera shook off the apprehension creeping up her spine, telling herself it was just a trick of her eyes.

She was about to slouch back against the door and wait for them to leave her line of sight when she saw it again. Movement. So subtle, she had to lean forward and squint, honing her entire focus toward the shifting darkness.

There! Someone was definitely edging through the shadows behind them, so smooth and silent, none of the men had noticed. A cold tingle crawled up her spine.

She considered calling out to startle the stalker, but she was shamefully too afraid of drawing the group's attention to herself. She briefly thought about running to find Elric, but if he wasn't at the inn, she'd waste precious time, and something could happen.

In the end, she decided the best course of action would be to keep watch and alert the guards only if absolutely necessary. She was terrified of getting caught, but she'd never forgive herself if her action, or lack thereof, caused anything to happen to Prince Eithan.

She'd simply have to become the better stalker. She glanced down at herself and scowled, irritated all over again at being unarmed. But Elric had taught her to be lethal with or without a weapon. It may have been foolhardy, but she felt confident in her ability to overpower a man who had to resort to slinking in the shadows.

She grabbed the fabric she kept stashed in her pocket for her neck and wrapped it around her face as a makeshift mask. As long as he stayed ignorant of her, she should have the upper hand. She'd tail him until she discovered why he was following the Crown Prince of Matherin.

Chapter
7

Jaren

He hated it here. Hated the entire fucking continent. Everything about it set him on edge, but nothing as much as being forced to blend into the varying towns and cities. He'd been traveling for days, asking around to see if anyone had seen or heard anything about Sulian's men being camped somewhere close.

It wasn't like he could outright ask. No, he'd had to buy drinks, flash careful grins, and pretend he gave a shit about a land full of people who wouldn't hesitate to villainize him if they knew who he was. In the end, it'd been an epic waste of time.

Most people either had no idea what he was talking about or had instantly become suspicious of the hooded man asking questions and had refused to converse with him, no matter how many drinks he'd bought. It was maddening.

Finally, when he thought he'd have to threaten someone to get any real information, an ancient-looking man at the back of a run-down tavern pointed him toward the city of Midpath. The frail man appeared two breaths away from death, but he claimed to have spotted an entourage of Matherin soldiers traveling near Midpath.

Jaren should have guessed. The city was known for its convenient location and hospitalities. It was the perfect place to station a group of lonely men.

So, yet another day later, here he was. He hadn't seen any sign of soldiers so far, so either they'd already moved out, or they were stationed farther away from the city than he'd expected. It wouldn't surprise him. Sulian always had been a sneaky bastard.

He already wanted to leave. His entire trip to Aleron was supposed to be a quick one. He'd already been here more days than he'd ever stayed before, and he was antsy. His fathers would be pissed by the time Jaren finally returned home, especially Jaeros.

But he'd already come this far, farther inland than he'd ever traveled before, so he was going to at least scout the outer edges of the city before making the trek back to the coast.

There was a reason Sulian suddenly had scouts patrolling the east. Bhasura had expected him to launch an attack during their civil unrest, but fifteen years later, he still hadn't. This was the first sign Jaren had seen that Sulian was plotting *something*. He just needed to figure out what.

He was leaning against a building, trying to convince himself to go into yet another tavern to waste coin and ask questions when the door opened and none other than Matherin soldiers exited. No, not soldiers—city guards. Even with the fading sun, Jaren's sight could make out the capital insignia on their chests.

They were loud and laughing, clearly having enjoyed a few drinks. It was almost too good to be true, but then again, Jaren always had believed in fate.

He pulled his hood farther down over his face as he began to tail them. They were talking loud enough that he didn't have to risk getting close to make out most of their conversations. From what he could pick up, he'd been right about them being guards and not soldiers. They were apparently staying in the city for the night.

Jaren's interest was piqued. If the men were staying in inns rather than camping at the city's outskirts, they had to be high ranking. What the fuck were high-ranking guards doing so far out from their precious Matherin capital? From what he knew, the guards never left the capital unless they were protecting the royals or some other important noble. So, the real question was *who* were they traveling with?

Jaren didn't have to wait long to find out. The more he watched, the more he could make out that one guard, in particular, was always in the center. And while he did participate in the jovial mood, it was clear he held himself differently than the others.

Not once did he seem the least bit interested in the surrounding area, and his speech was clear and concise. While the other guards, although relaxed and loud, still regularly glanced around for threats and rested their hands on their weapons anytime someone passed too close to their group.

He'd been tailing them for a while and so far, none of their discussions had given away any information besides what kind of women they wished to bed. Until finally, just as they began to approach their inn, one of them slipped and uttered a phrase that made Jaren's entire body still.

Of course, Your Highness.

He'd expected some form of general, or maybe even a spoiled noble, but no. The Crown fucking Prince was in Midpath.

He smiled savagely as he watched him enter the building. He didn't believe in coincidence. Fate played out exactly as it was intended to, meaning there was a reason he'd been directed to Midpath. Threads had weaved and spiraled just right to bring him here at the same time the *chinbi srol's* party had arrived.

He slunk farther into the shadows and began to edge down the alley beside the inn to map all the exits. He'd either receive valuable information, or the princeling's head, before he left. He hadn't yet decided which he hoped for more.

He wondered how long it would take the royal brat to beg and plead when he started to slowly slice—

He felt the air shift behind him, but he'd been so caught up in his planning, he sensed it just a second too late. An arm whipped across his neck and grabbed his shoulder at the same time his attacker's other arm dug into his back, forcing his spine into an arch. Successfully pulling him to the ground, his attacker tightened his chokehold, cutting off the air to Jaren's lungs.

He wasn't stabbing or striking him in any way, so it wasn't some desperate pickpocket. This individual was smart enough to know he didn't stand a chance against Jaren face to face. His goal was just to knock him unconscious, and his form had been executed perfectly.

It was clear that one of the guards had somehow noticed Jaren and was hoping to capture and question him. He'd have laughed if he'd had the air to do so. Matherin guards were just as cocky as the soldiers he'd encountered in the past, and it would always lead to their downfall.

Sulian's biggest error was training his forces to fight *men*. He almost felt bad for his alley attacker. The man had no way of knowing his feeble human skills wouldn't be that impressive when it truly mattered.

The guard probably expected Jaren to go for his arms or face since that would usually be someone's first instinct. Instead, Jaren grabbed the man's leg and twisted his ankle up viciously in a direction it was not meant to go while simultaneously digging his elbow into his calf. The man yelped—actually yelped—and released his hold just enough for Jaren to duck his chin and shove him back.

Jaren spun and was on his feet within seconds, anticipating the guard to have drawn a weapon. The group he'd been tailing all carried swords.

The first thing he noticed was the man was not armed. The second thing was the man was not in a uniform. Instead, he was dressed almost casually, apart from the hooded cloak pulled far over his face. Jaren could barely make out the general shape of his jaw, but it was hidden under a mask of some sort.

Definitely a guard.

The third thing he noticed was the man's stature. He was

small, but as Jaren knew from experience, that didn't mean he was necessarily weak. He'd fought more than his fair share of opponents back home who were half his size and still kicked his ass. Jaren tilted his head, sizing him up. The man made no move to escape.

He found himself tempted to grin. This could be fun. Deciding to keep his dagger sheathed at his side, he rushed forward. He'd expected to catch the guard by surprise, causing him to upset his equilibrium and respond too slow, but it didn't happen.

The guard reacted instantly, dodging Jaren's advance and jabbing his elbow straight up into the side of his throat. Following the hit, the guard continued using the last of Jaren's momentum against him and attempted to spin his arm around behind him to dislocate his shoulder.

Tapping into his enhanced speed, Jaren was able to twist out at the last moment and distance himself several steps. The movement, however, caused his hood to fall back and he smirked when the guard immediately retreated a step. *That's right, little human, I'm not what you thought I was.*

But again, instead of running or attempting to arm himself, Jaren watched as the man simply widened his stance and reassessed his target. *Good luck.*

He found himself hoping the guard stood a chance against him. After the disappointing bout with the pathetic scout on the coast, he was itching for a good fight.

They both darted forward and met with a vicious flurry of motion. Jaren chose not to tap into his speed again, challenging himself to beat the guard on his own level. But as the man continued dodging most of Jaren's hits and landing almost the same amount, he grew increasingly irritated.

He'd never met a Matherin able to take him on for this length of time. He was actually breaking a sweat, and his excitement over a good fight swiftly turned sour.

Enhancing his speed just slightly, he started lashing out hits faster than the guard could block. Hit to the shoulder, kick to the thigh, blow to the arm, the side, and the head. One right after another. He could almost feel the man's mounting frustration, and it fed the beast inside him.

He landed yet another hit to the side of the man's head, but instead of stumbling back, the guard used the movement to his advantage and spun a kick into Jaren's side so hard, he was fairly certain he'd bruised his spleen.

The hit knocked Jaren to one knee, and he bared his teeth in a snarl. What the actual fuck? He couldn't even remember the last time someone had been able to land so many hits on him, and it pissed him off.

He instantly saw red and barely let the guard recover before he pushed up off the ground and, reaching for his dagger, barreled straight into him.

Vera

SNARLED. HE'D LITERALLY SNARLED AT HER LIKE SOME cornered animal, exposing slightly elongated canines. She was certain the sound would come back to haunt her in a nightmare later. She'd heard the guards tell stories of the "fanged people" of Bhasura, but she—apparently falsely—assumed they were nothing more than stories.

But it wasn't just the sounds and teeth that made him seem predatory. Everything about him, from the second his hood fell back, screamed *Magyki*.

He had high cheekbones, a straight nose, and a chiseled jaw clenched in anger. Every feature was well-defined and sharp. Several small scars marred his face and pulled slightly at his honey-colored skin, but they only seemed to enhance his appearance. His body towered almost a foot over her and was topped with a mess of black waves that fell and curled around his pointed ears.

But it was his eyes that had caused her to stumble. She had tried to regain her footing, but she'd grown tired and moved too slowly. And faster than she could react to, he'd lunged up and practically smashed his body into hers with incredible force.

Vera had barely registered his movement before the fight was over. It was so abrupt; she wasn't even sure she understood exactly how it happened. One minute she was landing a kick to what she hoped was an important organ, and the next she was being tackled by a rabid beast into a filthy, alley wall.

She raised her head but was unable to move her body when he slammed his forearm against her chest. She imagined the sensation was similar to how a battering ram might feel. As he pinned her to the wall, his other hand simultaneously held a dagger to her throat.

Energy nearly depleted and even more out of breath from his

hit, Vera tried to inhale, but was rewarded with a stinging sensation at her throat followed by the trickle of blood as she nicked herself on the blade.

She struggled to resist the temptation to release the breath back out, knowing with every movement she made, she'd only continue inviting the dagger to dig deeper into her flesh.

He growled, pushing his arm harder against her chest, every inch of him radiating fury and promising nothing but violence. "Who—"

Suddenly cutting himself off, she watched creases appear between his eyes as his brow furrowed. He cocked his head to the side in an almost animal-like way. He pulled his head back slightly, arm still pinned against her, and glanced down. To her horror, she realized his forearm was flush against her breasts—her *unbound* breasts.

His eyes flicked back to hers before dropping to her neck. Without removing his arm or his dagger, he lowered his head to the side of her exposed throat and inhaled deeply. The sensation caused gooseflesh to dance across her skin.

Was he...smelling her? Dear gods, she didn't want to know what she smelled like after a fight. At the same time, Vera became painfully aware of the tickling sensation of his dark, unruly hair against her cheek as an earthy smell entered her nose. Like freshly cut wood and summer rain.

Great. There he was, slicing her throat and grazing his nose along the column of her neck, and she was smelling him back like a lunatic.

He raised his head and sheathed his dagger with such

swiftness, it startled her. She finally released the nervous breath she'd been holding, only to practically choke on it as he gripped the front of her tunic and yanked.

She would have stumbled face first onto the ground, but he steadied her with one hand fisting her tunic and the other on her waist. The hand gripping her body was like a searing brand straight through her clothes and into her skin as he held her almost flush against him.

Just as quickly, he released her clothing and whipped his hand up to snatch her hood and fling it back. She could only stand there, limbs locked, blood pounding in her ears as he shoved her makeshift mask down, causing it to pool around her collar.

Rogue curls fell forward, having been loosened from her plait during their skirmish. Her heart beat a little faster when his vibrant green eyes widened, and he drew in a sharp breath.

"*Zhu.*"

It felt like another lifetime since she'd heard her native tongue, and it stunned her, sounding more foreign now than natural. Vera couldn't move, his penetrating stare making her feel bared and naked down to her soul. His eyes were like chips of emerald, hard and unforgiving, yet somehow still intimate.

She suddenly felt too hot in her own skin as a sense of familiarity overcame her, and she began to raise her hand with an acute urge to touch him. She came within a hairsbreadth of his jaw before the erratic impulse shot a spike of panic through her. Dropping her arm like it was on fire, she whipped her head to the side to break the strange connection.

Vera had no idea what to do. She knew without the element

of surprise she had no chance of overpowering him. She'd tried her best, and her best hadn't been good enough. The man's skill had no equal.

No, not man. *Male.*

She couldn't keep herself from wondering and fearing what he could be doing here. In her entire life in Matherin, she'd never even heard a whisper of a Magyki being on Aleron. Though, in truth, she rarely heard whispers of anything, so she wasn't exactly the most knowledgeable.

Wrapped up in her thoughts, she belatedly realized he hadn't moved so much as a single muscle. He stood with an eerie, preternatural stillness as he stared at the side of her head. Vera scowled, beginning to turn her face back to demand what he was staring at, when she felt the featherlight caress of fingers against the top of her ear.

Finally coming to her senses, she knocked his hand away and twisted her neck to glare at him with every ounce of anger she had. She was about to unleash the most vulgar curse she could think of, but it died before it could ever leave her throat when she saw the look of absolute horror on his face.

It was like being plunged into cold water, and she flinched. The heat that had been building between them evaporated as fear took its place instead, and she struggled to control her breathing.

Shit.

The hand on her waist contracted before vanishing abruptly as he pulled away. For the first time since Vera had seen him, his fury had all but disappeared, and he honestly looked lost. It was now or never.

Taking full advantage of his shock, she swallowed the battling emotions she felt from his gentle touch and piercing stare and rammed her skull straight up into his face. His head snapped back, and he roared as he gripped his gushing nose.

She didn't hesitate. Darting forward she snatched his dagger from his hip and slammed the pommel up, straight into his temple with as much strength as she could muster. He dropped like a sack of potatoes. A gorgeous sack of gloriously toned potatoes.

Dear gods, it was official. She'd completely lost her mind. Shaking her head to clear her ridiculous, unhelpful thoughts, Vera secured his blade at her waist. She'd bested him, so she felt no guilt at claiming his weapon.

If she were a guard, she'd be expected to alert their party to his presence, which had been her original plan anyway. Now that she knew he was Magyki, it only further supported that plan. And if she were smart and considered the ramifications for herself, she'd kill him. She knew Elric wouldn't hesitate to end his life in order to protect hers.

But the look of anguish the male had worn as he gazed at her kept replaying in her mind. So, against her better judgment, she threw one last glance down at him and limped away.

With the way her muscles were protesting, she'd be lucky if she made it up the stairs.

Chapter
8
Vera

Not wanting to risk waking anyone, she removed her boots as soon as she entered the inn. Walking on her tiptoes, she ascended the stairs and passed the other rooms, barely concealing her groans of pain.

She eased her door open as silently as she could, thanking the gods when it didn't so much as squeak. Stepping across the threshold, Vera's attention went first to the welcomed sight of her bed before venturing over to the figure sitting before the low-burning hearth.

She jumped back, barely restraining a scream, while her free hand clutched her chest to keep her heart from leaping out of its cage. For a moment, she feared the stranger had somehow beaten her to the room, but that wasn't who occupied the chair.

Her head tipped back with a groan. Dropping her boots by the door, she trudged past his rigid form. She desperately needed to wash.

"How did you know?"

"You forget, I raised you, girl."

"Helpful, thanks."

She felt Elric's stare burning holes into her back as she filled the basin with cold water, but he didn't say another word as she dunked a raggedy cloth and methodically washed the grime of the night from her face.

"Do I even want to ask what you've been doing?"

"I highly doubt it." She hissed when the coarse fabric rubbed against the cut on her neck.

Silence greeted her.

"I needed fresh air and then I...tripped." She knew she shouldn't be testing his patience, but she was so damn exhausted. She didn't want to talk about her failure tonight. All she wanted was to flop on her bed in peace.

Elric didn't take the hint, or—most likely—simply didn't care. "Were you...assaulted in any other way?"

Scrunching her nose in disgust, she cringed away. "Gods, no, Elric."

He closed his eyes and breathed out heavily. "Did you know him?"

She wasn't sure. "No."

Noticing her hesitation, he asked, "Did he know you?"

"No." She sighed, setting the dirty cloth on the counter and hanging her head for a moment. "At least, not exactly." She turned and looked him in the eye, refusing to be a coward when she told him.

"I've never seen him before." She remembered the sense of familiarity she'd felt when she looked into his eyes but shook it off.

"I spotted him tailing Prince Eithan's group, so I followed him back to the inn and tried to catch him off guard, but...well, it was obvious he wouldn't let me escape without a fight, so I defended myself. But then my hood fell back, and he saw—" She didn't need to elaborate. Elric knew what she insinuated.

Lacing his hands together in his lap, he looked toward the hearth and nodded. "He's dead." It wasn't a question.

She squeezed her eyes shut and said nothing before ducking her head and pretending to inspect her stubby fingernails. Noticing her awkward behavior, he looked at her again, fear creeping into his features.

"Vera."

"No," she said for what felt like the hundredth time. She swallowed and fisted her hands to calm her nerves. "I didn't kill him. I had the chance, and I should have but..." she paused before racing on.

"It doesn't even matter! I didn't kill him, and he's probably far away from here by now anyway. I don't know for sure." At the look on Elric's face, she stopped, rolling her lips in.

He stared at her for what felt like an eternity as he silently processed her words. Standing abruptly, he began to pace in front of the hearth, rubbing his hand across his head. "You knew better! Gods, Vera, you damn well knew better!"

Shame soured her insides, and the flush that spread to her cheeks angered her. Like always, when she was angry, words spewed from her mouth like vomit before she could think twice.

"Why does it matter? Yes, he realized I'm not exactly from around here, but so what? I'm apparently not the *only* one on this continent. He's in no position to blab." She threw her hand over her mouth, but it was too late.

"What did you just say?" Eyes wide, he grabbed at her wrist, fingers digging in almost painfully. "Was he from Bhasura? A Magyki?"

She didn't understand why he was freaking out. She knew the situation wasn't ideal, but his panic was different—precise and brittle—like he might hyperventilate at any moment.

She ripped her arm out of his grasp. "What aren't you telling me, Elric?"

"Dammit, girl, did it ever occur to you that you have been tucked away with nothing but me and iron for company for a reason? It would have been bad enough for someone around here to question your heritage, but a Magyki?" He closed his eyes, his stoic mask falling back in place. "Are you sure?"

Worried her legs might give out at any moment, Vera shuffled past him and sat on the edge of her bed. Her exhaustion was palpable.

"Positive. He called me *zhu*, the native term for a Magyki female. I think he could tell by the smell of my blood." She wrinkled her nose at the reminder. "And then he got the upper hand for a moment, and he touched my ear." She shifted and subconsciously reached for it.

"That's how I was able to get away. I took advantage of his distracted attention and knocked him out. After that, I just ran." She conveniently left out the fact it'd occurred right outside and how she'd stood there ogling him like a lunatic before leaving.

Elric came to sit next to her. He took a deep breath and held it for several seconds before releasing it loudly.

"The emperor will need to know this. Now—don't give me that look. The simple fact that a Magyki was this far inland is cause for concern enough, but also seeing you? I know that sounds extreme, Vera, but I just need you to trust me. I can't tell you more than that."

He patted her on the knee. "I would tell you if I could. Truly. But it's not my place. All I can say is that, depending on who that male was, and what all he realized, it could be a problem."

Vera stared at her hands trying to process that. The emperor? Magyki weren't welcome anywhere on Aleron. How could it possibly be safe to tell the emperor about her? And why would he care if another Magyki saw her?

None of it made sense. Elric knew something about her. He'd apparently always known something and had never told her. Something important enough to scare him.

She wanted to shake him and demand he tell her everything, but Vera had lived with him long enough to know he wouldn't utter another word.

Not his place. Okay, then whose place was it? She scowled and fisted her hands in her lap until she felt the bite of her nails against her palms.

Elric straightened his spine. "I will alert Prince Eithan that I encountered a Magyki tailing him tonight while out walking with you. Given your appearance, I'll have to admit he attacked you before he escaped." She bristled but otherwise remained quiet.

"That alone should be enough to convince His Highness to return. I do not feel it necessary to say anything else to him about your specific involvement. I suggest you keep any other details to yourself."

She looked down at her hands. "I'm tired, Elric. It's been a long night, and I had my ass handed to me pretty good, so I'd like to rest while I can."

He nodded, giving her knee one final pat before heaving himself up off the bed and heading for the door. Stopping with his hand on the doorknob, he turned to her.

"I'm glad you're safe, Vera. I should have said that from the beginning."

The second he stepped out of the room, she fell backward on the bed, pulling her knees to her chest. What on Aleron could he be hiding from her? Elric had quickly figured out her origin when she was a child, but he'd never admitted to knowing more than that.

Grunting in frustration, she rolled to her side, wanting nothing more than to curl into a ball. But a sharp edge dug into her waist. *Oh!*

She'd almost forgotten about the stolen dagger, and sleeping with an unsheathed blade would not have done her injured body any favors. She agonizingly sat back up and threw off her cloak. Removing the weapon from her waist, she jolted so hard she almost dropped it.

It wasn't possible. The coincidence was too great. But as she turned the blade in her hands and angled the handle toward the hearth for better light, she couldn't deny it. It was identical to a dagger she currently had hidden in a chest of clothes in her room back in Matherin.

The blade itself was rippled, designed as if to imitate waves, and it was deadly sharp. The cross-guard was curved in opposite directions on either side, giving it an 'S' shape. But it was the grip that held the true beauty.

It was crafted from bleached bone, and etched into the surface was the most elegant script Vera had ever seen. It circled the entire handle down to the pommel. She had no idea what it said, but it was beautiful, she knew that much.

She'd found the original dagger not long after Elric had begun training her. It'd been tucked away in the armory, dusty and forgotten with several other basic daggers. Matherin guards tended to only use long swords, so daggers often went unused.

There had been something about the blade that had drawn her to it. It was unique and enchanting. Even as a child she appreciated its raw beauty and had cleaned it up and hidden it in her room.

Vera let her body flop back on the mattress. It was a Bhasurian blade. Why would Elric have had it? It was just more evidence proving he knew something she didn't.

Did he also know what happened to her ears? Or maybe even how she got to Matherin in the first place? A nasty sensation coiled in the pit of her stomach that felt an awful lot like betrayal.

What did it matter where she came from? She was a nobody,

and she'd always be a nobody. Nothing was going to change that.

Reaching up to touch her ear again, she shuddered as she remembered how the stranger's touch had felt. He'd been nothing but searing hits and hard edges while they'd fought, but the glide of his fingertips over her ear had been hesitant and gentle.

She dropped her hand and shook the thoughts away as she tossed the dagger to the other side of the bed. Curling up on her side, she silently begged sleep to take her.

VERA JOLTED AWAKE to several loud knocks at her door. Heart beating rapidly in her chest, she'd never been more grateful to be awake. Her dreams had been full of horrors she couldn't escape, and a metallic tang lingered in her nose.

She rubbed her eyes, frustrated at the lack of restful sleep. Stress always brought forth nightmares, and she'd definitely fallen asleep ten-feet deep in worries.

Pushing hair out of her face, she looked toward the window. She was surprised to see it was still dark out. She hadn't expected Elric to fetch her so soon, knowing how her night had gone.

Another knock sounded, making her grumble. She sat up and grimaced, feeling like she'd been trampled by a fucking horse. She tried to push herself straight off the bed, but her muscles protested so much, she had to make do with pathetically rolling off. Part of her hoped they didn't leave today after all, because riding Umber was going to be pure torture.

She only made it halfway to the door before the knocking

came again. "I'm coming!"

She swore Elric lost more patience every year. It was irritating and certainly didn't help her current mood. She continued muttering to herself as she unlocked the door.

Swinging it open with force, she put on her best glower. "Gods be damned, Elric, I can barely—"

She stopped suddenly when she came face to face with a gorgeous pair of brown eyes. Wide, completely startled, brown eyes.

"Fuck. No! Oh gods, that's even worse. I'm so sorry, Trey, I thought you were Elric." She covered her mouth with her hands, her stomach plummeting to the floor.

She had no idea what to say or do. They'd been friendly so far on the trip, but she also hadn't spoken like a straight-up heathen before now. He was going to think her completely crazy.

Her thoughts came to an abrupt halt, and she felt all the blood drain from her body to puddle with her stomach at her feet when she realized he was no longer looking at her face, but at her body.

He wasn't laughing or joking or even cringing at her vulgar greeting. He was only staring at her in disbelief as if his brain hadn't quite caught up to his eyes. Even covered as it was, she could practically guarantee his mouth was hanging open.

She lowered her hands and glanced down at herself. She'd never changed clothes last night. She'd simply rolled over and pleaded for sleep. And as she stood in her doorway, battered and bruised, wearing a filthy tunic and trousers, in full view of one of the prince's guards, she had a sudden feeling she'd officially hit rock bottom.

"Are you hurt?"

Wait. "What?" His question pulled her from her thoughts, and she forced her gaze up in time to see him roving his eyes over her face, brows drawn in concern.

"You're bleeding." He took a step toward her but paused before crossing the threshold of her room. "Tell me, are you hurt?"

Damn, she'd forgotten about the splattering of blood on her tunic from the male's nose. "Oh no, the blood isn't mine, it's—" She froze. What in all Aleron was wrong with her? She'd been careful for fifteen years, and now all of a sudden she couldn't seem to stop making one blundering mistake after another.

Clearing her throat, she stood straight and desperately tried to recover what little propriety she apparently didn't actually have.

"I'm fine, Trey. Thank you for checking on me. Now, if you'll excuse me, I just woke up and need to get...changed. Is there something you needed?"

Speechless again, he continued staring at her, his mouth for sure hanging open beneath his mask. She might have laughed at his expression had the situation been literally anything else.

She'd almost closed the door when he finally stuttered, "We're leaving within the hour. There's been an urgent matter brought to His Highness's attention, and we must make haste back home."

So Elric had already talked to him then. She sighed. Everything was spinning out of control, and she highly doubted it was going to end well for her.

Summoning her remaining pride, Vera forced her lips to say, "Thank you, I'll be down in just a moment."

Not giving him a chance to respond, she shut the door and leaned against it. Shit, there was no way Trey would let this go, but speaking to him while dressed like this wouldn't help her case.

It wasn't like she could invite him into her room to speak anyway. She could only imagine Elric's reaction to that. She just needed to get changed and downstairs as soon as possible and speak to him before he said something to Prince Eithan.

What could go wrong?

Chapter
9

Vera

Stepping off the stairs to the main floor, Vera shifted again uncomfortably. She had tied her dress as loosely as possible without being considered improper, but it still hugged her black and blue torso more than she'd prefer.

When she'd finally removed her tunic, she'd been less than pleased to find her body riddled with slightly swollen, dark bruises. She certainly wasn't unaccustomed to them, but these were incredibly sensitive. The male had hit harder than Elric ever had.

By the luck of the gods, the largest marks were hidden beneath the fabrics of her dress, with just a few visible bruises on her arms and the thin cut on her throat.

Leaving her plait unpinned, she'd draped it over her shoulder to partially cover her neck, and then tucked her arms into her cloak. Thankfully, although she'd received several hits to the head, none had landed on her face.

She knew she needed to eat, but her stomach was already full of knots. Where was everyone? Maybe she should retreat upstairs to see if Elric was still in his room.

She'd just started turning back when she caught sight of a masked face standing by the front door. Trey. Noticing he'd caught her attention, he waved her over.

Taking a deep, soothing breath, she edged around the tables toward him. She could do this. It would be fine. Faster than she'd have liked, she reached him. There was the briefest flicker of uncertainty in his eyes before they crinkled in what she could only assume was a hidden smile.

"Right this way, Miss Vera. Everyone else is ready, but Lesta said to let you sleep as long as possible. He's out preparing your mount." He held the door open for her as if nothing abnormal had happened.

She hesitated a moment, a little flustered and a lot confused. Was he really not going to say anything? Deciding silence was better than humiliating herself further, she held her head high and stepped past him.

It was still fairly dark as she carefully made her way to the stables where the rest of the party was no doubt waiting. Before she could take more than a few steps, she felt a tug on her arm. She flinched as pain radiated through her sore limb. She looked over her shoulder to find Trey with a hand around the strap of her bag.

His eyes sparked with mischief as he took in her posture and silence. He had her on edge, and he knew it. Gone was the shock he'd shown that morning. She was at a complete loss on how to act.

"I'm just trying to take your bag. It wouldn't be very gentlemanly of me if I made a lady carry her belongings." Vera didn't even need to see his entire face to know he was mocking her and laughing at her expense.

Huffing an irritated breath, she let him slide her bag off her shoulder before she continued walking. It was obvious he found their morning confrontation funny, and it made her face heat with embarrassment. Mix that with the fact she'd barely made it down the road before tripping over her blasted dress, she lost her composure.

Hiking her garment up away from her boots, she all but stomped ahead. He didn't say a word, but she could hear his bubbly laughter trailing behind her and hoped it was a good sign.

Elric looked up as she approached and couldn't completely hide his reaction. She knew even in the dark, she looked rough, but it still sucked to have it confirmed. She opened her mouth to ask what the plan was but abruptly closed it when her eyes traveled over his shoulder and met Prince Eithan's.

Upon meeting her eye, he made his way toward her, and she felt her heart rate pick up.

"Miss Vera," he paused and held out his arm. Hesitantly, she placed her hand in his outstretched one. He planted a quick kiss on her knuckles that she felt down to her toes. She knew her face was on fire and clasped her hands together as soon as he released her.

"I must formally apologize for what you have experienced. I cannot imagine the fear you must have endured. I have already expressed to Lesta my gratitude that he was able to protect you." He placed a hand on his chest, and his concern appeared genuine. She didn't really understand why he cared.

"It's fine," she said. "No apology needed, Your Highness." She vaguely wondered how close Elric was to having a heart attack next to her.

"I must respectfully disagree. When Lesta approached me and requested to bring you, I admittedly had my reservations. However, I agreed when he explained his reasoning. I trust our guards as a whole, but men will be men."

Vera bristled at the crude sentiment but said nothing as he continued.

"I truly felt you would be safer here, under the protection of myself and my guards. You have my sincere apology that I was wrong." He turned, and she saw Elric nod at her before accompanying the prince back to his mount.

She stayed where she was, watching them leave. She was trying to understand just how surreal her life had become. It hadn't been that long ago she'd knocked the prince on his ass, and less than a day since she'd failed to apprehend an enemy, and yet *he* was apologizing to *her*.

"I can't help but wonder something."

She jumped, not noticing Trey had come to stand next to her. She raised her eyebrow in answer.

"I can't help but wonder, since Lesta protected you and all, how you managed to get both blood and bruises. Makes one a tad curious."

She turned sharply in his direction in time to catch his departing wink before he followed after the others.

THEY'D BEEN RIDING for hours, and Trey still hadn't come to travel next to her. She was nervous at first, both at the prospect of what he might say and also at the chance she'd lost the only friendly face she'd ever known.

But twice now she'd caught him glancing back at her, and she would bet three rounds of ale he was purposefully trying to force her to approach him.

She tried, gods did she try, to fight the desire. But as the sun hit its highest peak in the sky, she found herself urging Umber forward, cursing Trey the entire way.

"Afternoon, Miss Vera, fancy seeing you up here. Are you enjoying today's trip so far?"

His eyes practically glittered, and she saw his fingers tapping away on his saddle. She'd questioned him about the habit the other day, curious if he was playing out any particular tune. But he'd shook his head and confessed the movement helped him focus when trying to juggle his thoughts.

She chose to focus on that memory as she looked over at him, trying to remind herself why she liked him.

"Yes, I have quite enjoyed the solitude the back of the party provides."

"I'm sure the solitude is quite welcome when you're cursing up a storm over the discomfort of riding a horse in your condition. You know, from your harrowing night as a damsel."

The bastard. "Gods, I get it. You can save your passive comments. You saw me covered in grime and bruises—"

"And trousers. Don't forget trousers."

"I said I get it," she snapped. "Nothing I say will change what you saw. So, spare me the lecture and taunts, and just tell me what happens now."

She heaved out a breath and looked away. She still didn't know him well enough to predict his reaction, but she was already so knee-deep in shit, there was no point in mincing words anymore.

"Hey," he said, softer now, "Nothing is going to happen. You don't even have to talk to me about it. You just…well, you just bring the mischievous ass out of me I suppose." He reached over to nudge her shoulder, but glancing around their party, thought better of it.

Vera contemplated his words, watching him for a minute before riding silently for a while. He truly didn't appear to care that—according to Matheris—she was doing things no lady had a right to do.

Then again, Vera didn't exactly have experience with people to base her assumptions on. But, with what Elric had said about the emperor looming over her, she decided to take a risk. A different type of risk.

"I avoided most of your questions the other day. The ones about myself," she said.

"Yeah, I noticed," he said, chuckling.

She felt her lips tip up. "I didn't answer because I didn't want to have to lie to you. I don't live the most appropriate life for a Matherin woman, and it's not something I'm usually safe to admit."

"You're the ward to the Weapons' Master. I don't think anyone expects you to be a noble lady."

She pursed her lips and nodded. True. "It's more than that." She paused, debating what all she was comfortable telling him. She wouldn't risk Elric, so admitting she could fight was still a no for now.

"I hate dresses. I agree they can be beautiful, but they're completely impractical. This is literally the first time I've ever worn one."

Trey's eyes flicked down to her body before training back on her face. His hands, she'd noticed, were no longer tapping. "So, what I saw you wearing this morning?"

"That's what I always wear, yes. Can you imagine helping out in the armory wearing this?" She gestured to her dress. "And I hate that it's seen as a big deal for me to dislike the typical female ware. Because it's not. It's just self-important Matherin men who make it one." She shrugged.

"You're not wrong," he said, "but in all honesty, it wasn't your choice of clothing that bothered me." His demeanor became more serious. "It was what you looked like. I wasn't expecting you to open the door looking like someone had just beat the shit out of you."

She turned away, schooling her expression. He wasn't angry

or disgusted. He cared about her, and the knowledge did something to her middle. A pleasant warmth spread through her, and she suddenly wished she were sitting with a giant mug of alcohol rather than miserably riding atop a horse.

"There's more to it than my clothing preference, but I won't explain it. I can't. What I can guarantee is it's not what you think. It looked worse than it was." Kind of.

He was quiet for a moment before glancing to Elric, who rode ahead of them with Prince Eithan. Something like understanding flickered across his eyes, and he nodded. "Fair enough."

She couldn't contain the sigh of relief that burst out of her, and he snickered. "So, what *will* you tell me about yourself, Vera? Something you wouldn't have told me yesterday but will now because you owe me." He wiggled his eyebrows.

Keeping a straight face, she said, "I can out-drink Elric."

He laughed so abruptly, he choked and was thrown into a coughing fit. It was several minutes before he could speak again.

"You know, Trey, I think I like you better like this. With your tongue controlled, you almost seem like a well-behaved—"

"No," he interrupted, "Somehow I think you'd like me even better if my tongue weren't controlled at all." He grinned suggestively at her, and she snorted. She knew they were drawing attention and tried to smooth out her expression, but every time she glanced over at him, she'd lose it all over again.

"You know, Vera, you just might be my new favorite person."

She could only smile as her heart swelled and her throat seemed to close. Maybe this trip hadn't been such a disaster after all.

Jaren

HE LURCHED AWAKE, INSTANTLY FOCUSING ON HIS surroundings. He enhanced his hearing, but there were no sounds within yards of him except for the scurrying of creatures. He couldn't even make out anyone walking down the street. He was alone. Looking at the sky, he could make out the beginnings of dawn and cursed.

He'd been lying unconscious and fucking defenseless for hours. Anything could have happened, and for all he knew, anyone could have seen him while he'd been a pathetic lump of uselessness sprawled out in filth. His lip curled in disgust, and the sticky layer of blood that had dried on his face pulled at his skin.

Oh, he was pissed. He inhaled deeply to try to settle his rage but faltered. Over the stale smell of blood clogging his nostrils, he was suddenly overwhelmed with the lingering scent of *her*.

It swirled all around, threatening to suffocate him. It was so strong; Jaren almost couldn't believe he'd missed it when she'd first attacked him. He'd been so focused on meeting her strike for strike, he'd smelled nothing but the mild tang of sweat. Nothing to hint at what lay beneath her clothing.

Fuck.

She'd been *zhu*. One-hundred percent, utterly female. He couldn't say he felt any shame in his inability to notice. Her loose clothing had hidden the feminine figure he'd later felt, and her scent had been well masked.

Up until he'd cut into her neck, she hadn't given him any

reason to look closer. Not to mention he'd never even heard of a woman on Aleron possessing fighting skills. Women here weren't respected the way the *zhu* on Bhasura were. He wouldn't make the mistake of underestimating her again.

Gods, he'd almost killed her. Thinking her just some guard for the puny princeling, it had unnerved him more than he'd liked to admit imagining Matherin men fighting with such speed and skill. And after her last kick to his side, he'd been so lost to hatred, he'd been seconds away from opening her throat and watching her choke on her own blood.

His thoughts had come crashing to a halt when he'd realized his arm was pressed against breasts. Obvious, full breasts. When he'd leaned in and caught the rich smell of her blood, he'd had to practically throw his head back to avoid inhaling deeper.

Her scent had been intoxicating. Smelling like wind, flames, and iron all rolled together, he imagined it was probably what the stars themselves smelled like. He growled as it infuriated him all over again.

Like a runt fresh out of training, he'd let her damn smell distract him, and he'd lowered his defenses. Because she hadn't just been some Aleronian woman. The potency of her blood had told him she was a fucking pure-blooded Magyki.

Jaren's shock had been so strong, he was surprised it hadn't knocked him off his feet. But in hindsight, he should have known by her speed and strength alone.

Even though she'd obviously yet to unlock her full power reserve, she'd still naturally excel at fighting compared to any human. No person on Aleron fought with that kind of grace. At least, none whom Jaren had ever encountered.

If all that wasn't already enough, she'd been fucking breathtaking. Determined gray eyes under long lashes, dark brown curls framing her face and sticking to her sweat-coated brow. Her full lips had been parted in surprise as if she were just as transfixed as him. He could scent her shifting emotions and her cheeks had reddened under his gaze.

She'd raised her hand, and he'd thought for sure she would touch him. He'd wanted to ask her name. He'd needed to know it. But his voice refused to cooperate when she'd turned, and he caught sight of her ear.

Her fucking scarred ear.

He'd never seen a Magyki's ears clipped before, but he could tell it hadn't been some backroom hack job. Whoever had altered them knew what they were doing. Jaren doubted any human would ever second-guess her heritage.

Against his better judgment, as if his hand had a mind of its own, he'd been compelled to touch the pale scar. But the second his skin grazed hers, her entire body had stiffened, and she'd reacted like he'd struck her.

Her scent had shifted, her fear shooting through him like a hit to the gut, forcing him to instinctively step back. He'd still been trying to simply breathe around the potency when she'd glared at him with hatred a split second before breaking his nose.

Coming out of his thoughts, Jaren probed his fingers around the bridge of his nose. He'd lost count of how many times he'd had it broken during his younger years, but this had been the first time in a while. Just another reason to hate his time on this damn continent.

Taking several deep breaths, he settled himself before reaching up to straighten it. The pain was intense but over quickly, making his eyes water and fresh blood seep out. He grimaced as he focused some of his power to heal enough to prevent any bruising and used his cloak to wipe his face.

Jaren couldn't blame her for taking advantage of his momentary lapse. She'd instantly taken note of his shock and made the most of it. He was honestly impressed with how quick her response had been, but dammit if he didn't hate having his fucking nose broken.

Deciding he'd better head out before the streets filled, he stood and brushed the dirt off his trousers the best he could before freezing abruptly. Slowly, as if he could deny the truth by refusing to visually acknowledge it, he looked down at the sheath at his waist.

The empty sheath.

She'd moved so fast; his brain had somehow irritatingly failed to notice she'd used his own dagger to strike him unconscious.

His eyes darted around the alley in the futile hope she'd thrown it before running off. He clenched his fists when his search came up empty, and bit back the roar building within his chest.

He'd thought her smart until now. If she thought she could steal from him—steal *that* from him—and live, she was going to be painfully disappointed. She should've killed him when she had the chance.

Fuck. She *could* have easily killed him while he'd laid there like a helpless lump. He tucked the information away. It spoke volumes about both her character and general lack of self-preservation. Jaren highly doubted she'd ever had to take someone's life. He'd use her innocence to his advantage.

Her scent still lingering in his nose, he set off out of the alley. He'd track her down, and this time he'd know what to expect. He sure as shit wouldn't be caught off guard again, and she'd regret ever daring to approach him.

That dagger was the only remnant he had left of his *aitanta*, his soul bond. He'd get it back. What he did with it once he caught her, he hadn't yet decided.

He couldn't keep the cruel grin from his face as he pulled his hood over his head. She'd started this game, but he didn't think she'd like how he played it.

Chapter
10

Vera

It was only a few hours past noon when they approached the outskirts of Matherin. Their dreadful early starts and long nights having worked in their favor.

Vera was used to being up before the sun to train, but between her aching body and lack of decent sleep, she felt halfway dead in the ground. She was so ready to be off the damn horse. As she thought it, she swore Umber snorted in agreement.

She'd spent the first day riding next to Trey, and she couldn't remember ever having laughed so much that she swore her diaphragm hurt. Actually, she knew she hadn't. Elric wasn't exactly known for his humor.

But this morning when she sensed someone ride up next to her, she'd been disappointed to see it was Elric. He hadn't said much to her since that night at the inn, and she was fairly certain it was because he was trying to prevent himself from throttling her.

He hadn't been talkative, just a comment here or there about things they were passing. He'd asked how she was feeling, and she'd answered honestly, *everything hurts and I'm dying*, but he'd only nodded like it was exactly what she deserved.

She'd tried to urge Umber forward to move away from him, but he'd only matched her stride. Narrowing her eyes, she tried to figure out his scheme. It wasn't until she'd finally spotted Trey, looking back at them and shrugging, that she'd put two and two together that Elric was purposefully preventing her from spending another day with Trey.

After an hour or so of trying—and failing—to leave him behind or get a rise out of him, she succumbed to defeat. He cared for her in his own frustrating way, and she knew he was just trying to keep her from emotionally hurting herself more than necessary.

She accepted the fact she wouldn't see Trey again after today, accepted that the tentative friendship they'd created wasn't long term, but she'd still foolishly hoped to have one last day of pretending.

So, she'd spent the remainder of their trip in quiet submission, replying when Elric spoke to her and eating when prompted. She understood where he was coming from, but she couldn't help but feel slightly resentful for it.

It wasn't until the capital began to take shape in the distance that all thoughts of Trey and Elric vanished. Her body went rigid, and she suddenly felt like turning and bolting in the other direction. Somehow she knew, without a doubt, once they entered

Matherin, her life would never be the same. *She* might never be the same.

They'd just finished stabling their mounts when Prince Eithan approached them. He acknowledged her with a polite nod before speaking to Elric.

"I sent a messenger to His Majesty upon our arrival. As long as he isn't tied up with his advisors, he should be expecting us. I trust Vera can handle your belongings?"

She felt her knees go weak, and she had the sudden, impulsive urge to hug him. She wouldn't have to join them. Thank the gods, she was going to take the longest bath in the history of baths.

"Your Highness, I would like Vera to accompany us to the palace."

She whipped her head around, eyes wide and mouth hanging open. Why was Elric suddenly so intent on throwing her to the wolves?

Prince Eithan's eyebrows raised slightly. "Lesta, I understood your desire to bring her on this trip, as pointless of a trip as it turned out to be, but this is to be a conversation about matters of security. It would hardly be appropriate for her to be present."

He darted a glance at her and winced at the blatant insinuation that she was unfit for such conversations.

"I apologize, Your Highness, but I must insist. His majesty will want to speak with her." The prince opened his mouth, but Elric continued, "I'd wager my position on it."

The prince took her in again, his gaze contemplative, before looking back to Elric.

"Let's hope your intuition is right Weapons' Master."

THEY MADE IT to the palace gates in record time. Vera practically jogging to keep up with their long strides. It was amazing to witness the kind of daily life the prince lived. People bowed and gates groaned open. Even his cloak was taken without him so much as raising a finger.

She tried to control her head when they entered, but she'd never seen so many servants or been so close to such finery. Her head swiveled like an owl, taking everything in and logging it away to remember forever.

If this was going to be the last thing she saw before the emperor inevitably imprisoned her for life, at least it was shiny and impressive.

They turned a corner and headed down a hallway, empty apart from two guards blocking a set of double doors at the end and the flickering light from the sconces. A faint memory tickled at the back of her mind of another hallway, one she sometimes dreamed about.

Maybe she'd been here before when she first arrived in Matherin? She tried to remember, but the more she focused on it, the more the memory slipped away.

As they approached the end, Prince Eithan glanced at Elric. "Someone will retrieve you when His Majesty is ready." He motioned toward the statue-like men, and they wordlessly opened the doors, allowing him to slip inside.

Vera wanted to have a panic attack. Like, she *really* wanted to. Elric seemed so calm next to her, and it only further confused her poor, chaotic emotions.

"I can't do this. Oh gods...I'm about to meet the emperor. I don't even know the correct way to meet an emperor!" She yanked on her plaited hair, biting her lip and pacing back and forth. The two men guarding the door gave no reaction, perfectly ignoring her minor meltdown.

"It will be fine. Just stay quiet unless addressed and answer every question honestly." Elric looked at her sympathetically, which did nothing to soothe her frazzled nerves.

Several more agonizing minutes passed before a knock came at the door, startling her out of her pacing. The two statue men appeared to know what it meant and instantly responded, reaching their arms toward the doors.

"Vera?"

"Hmm?" She decided it was probably best she didn't open her mouth, worried about what word vomit might explode in front of an audience.

Elric looked down at her with a small smile, "You're a lady. Make sure you curtsy, not bow." Glaring in his direction, she shook her head in mock anger, but he only laughed.

As the guards finished pushing the doors open, she took a steady breath and tried to clear her thoughts the same way she did before a sparring match. She could do this. If Elric wasn't worried, she shouldn't be either, right?

Keeping her head high, she walked in next to him. The butterflies in her stomach threatened to overwhelm her, but she made it across the threshold without tripping or fainting, which she considered a riveting success.

The room—if that's what you could call it—was massive. If she yelled, her voice would likely echo back to her just as loud. She certainly hoped they didn't execute people in a room with those kinds of acoustics.

Pillars adorned the entirety of both sides with varying banners hung on the walls between them. The colors and emblems appeared to represent the highest noble families.

The floor was a polished gray stone with a single, midnight blue carpet running from the doorway to the bottom of a raised platform. On both sides of the runner sat long tables that were, to her relief, empty. She definitely would have bolted if the entire noble court had been present.

Behind the platform were three floor-to-ceiling windows, with tapestries showing the royal crest between them, and settled right in the center of the dais, was a large throne. It had nothing adorning it, no details or gems, no banners or etchings. Just solid, smooth stone. Its simplicity somehow making it that much more intimidating.

It projected the confidence of the man sitting upon it. She supposed you didn't need an intricate throne when you held power over an entire continent.

On either side of the dais were smaller thrones of the same design, apart from their indigo upholstered backs. Prince Eithan stood before one, while the other sat empty. The emperor's consort had died during childbirth and he'd never remarried.

Finally reaching the center of the room, she stopped just a second after Elric and curtsied deeply as he lowered into a bow. When they rose, she caught a glimpse of confusion on the prince's face before he again controlled his expression into something akin to boredom. She looked away, only to be ensnared by a set of similar, pale blue eyes that did not belong to the prince.

With his eyes and shoulder-length blond hair, Vera was taken aback by just how much the prince resembled his father. Even with the emperor's full beard, their likeness was uncanny.

He continued to stare at her with an almost expectant look on his face, although she wasn't quite sure what he was waiting for. He lounged lazily against his hardbacked throne and laced his fingers together. She exhaled a shaky breath when he finally released her from the weight of his gaze to look at Elric. When he spoke, he didn't bother trading pleasantries, and his voice was as rough and terrifying as she'd expected.

"Weapons' Master, Prince Eithan has informed me you believe to have encountered a male from Bhasura while at Midpath. From what I understand, you and your…ward," the corner of his lip quirked up, "witnessed the male specifically tailing my son, but failed to kill or apprehend him. Is this accurate?"

Vera fought the urge to hunch her shoulders as she again felt his stare on her.

Elric took a small step forward, "Yes, Your Majesty. But to describe the events in full, there are other details I would need to discuss with you regarding what occurred that night."

Out of the corner of her eye, Vera saw him glance deliberately her way before shooting a glance toward Prince Eithan, who now wore a blatant look of confusion.

The emperor's posture changed in an instant. He sat forward, and his eyes hardened as he continued to stare at her. *Did he ever blink?* He seemed to be contemplating something. Looking over at his son for a moment, he rubbed a hand over his beard before nodding to himself.

"You may speak freely on the subject."

Elric glanced at the prince one last time before taking a deep breath and widening his stance. "The Magyki in question had been tailing His Highness, and we were, indeed, unable to discern his exact motives or what he might have sought to attempt."

He swallowed, "The male chose to abandon his intent on His Highness when he unintentionally discovered Veralie. He was able to corner her before eventually making his escape."

Vera fought the urge to turn and gape at him. Elric hadn't used her full name since she was a child. It sounded foreign to her, like it belonged to someone else. Someone she no longer was.

She breathed a little easier when she realized he wasn't going to willingly admit she'd been the one doing the ambushing, not the other way around.

She glanced at Prince Eithan again in time to see his eyes narrow slightly. "He ambushed your ward? You never mentioned that." He closed his mouth, his brow furrowed. He was clearly displeased at not being told the entire story, but he controlled himself and settled for just crossing his arms.

The emperor, however, showed zero surprise. He knew exactly what she was. If there had been any doubt in her mind that he knew, it was long gone now. He pushed himself up off his throne with such force, it startled her, and she took a hesitant step back.

"What happened then?" he demanded.

"Well, Your Majesty, he—" Elric began, but the emperor silenced him with nothing more than a raised hand.

"I'm asking *her*." He looked straight into Vera's eyes as he took a single step forward. "What happened when the male cornered you? What exactly did he say?"

Every nerve in her body was begging her to look away, but she forced herself to maintain eye contact. This man could order her death with a snap of his fingers.

"He—he did not speak at all, Your Majesty." Her voice stuttered and came out as barely more than a hoarse whisper.

"Not at all? You're telling me that a Magyki male was able to infiltrate, unnoticed, this deep onto my land and spy on the sole heir to my throne, only to abandon it all when he found you. Yet he said nothing?"

More like he abandoned it when she knocked him unconscious, but she obviously shouldn't say that. She cleared her throat, "Yes, Your Majesty. He honestly seemed too shocked to say anything. He didn't—"

"Did he know what you are?" he interrupted.

She paused, and in her peripheral, she saw the prince look up at his father, "Y-yes, Your Majesty."

Silence. She felt like she might pass out. Silence had never been so gods damn loud before.

"Tell me, Veralie," he drew out the syllables of her name and trailed his eyes down her body with a smirk, "do *you* know what you are?" He hadn't moved from the top of the dais, but he might as well have been standing before her with a sword at her throat.

"Yes."

"Which is?"

Her hands began to shake, and she turned to Elric, but he wouldn't meet her eyes. Refusing to look at the prince again, and too scared to meet the emperor's stare, she lowered her head and nodded. "Magyki."

She didn't even need to see the prince to sense his powerful reaction. She felt her cheeks burn under their scrutiny. It was clear the emperor hadn't shared his knowledge of her with his son. She wasn't sure if that made her feel better or worse.

Why would the emperor keep her around, knowing what she was? Was he the one who sent her to Elric? If so, why? Thoughts thundered through her head so fast, it made her dizzy.

She waited for his judgment, his disgust, maybe even anger or suspicion. But it never came. Finally daring to raise her head, she could only stand in another round of thick silence as the emperor continued staring at her with that same smirk.

"You look tired. Let's continue this conversation tonight after you've rested. You will join Prince Eithan and myself for dinner." He looked her over once more. "Try to wear something a little more appropriate, yes?"

He seemed to catch the way her eyes widened in alarm and added, "I suppose that might be difficult, given your living arrangements. I'll send someone to help you ready."

Dumbfounded, she lowered into a clumsy curtsy before noticing he'd already turned away, dismissing her. "Yes, Your Majesty."

Sparing a nervous look toward the prince, she locked eyes with him. He no longer looked shocked. In fact, she thought he looked almost excited. It only served to strengthen her growing apprehension. If the Crown Prince was excited about her revelation, she highly doubted it meant anything good for her.

As soon as they exited the large double doors and stepped far enough from the guards to not be overheard, she grabbed his arm and forced him to turn to her.

She'd never before been so demanding or ill-tempered with him. She was his ward, and she'd always treated him with respect, but at that moment, she was bombarded by so many emotions, she was barely holding it together and just didn't give a shit.

"What on all Aleron was that?"

"Calm yourself, Vera."

"Nope. Not a chance. The emperor. We're having dinner with the emperor." Gods, knowing her luck, she'd wind up *as* the dinner. She'd never felt so threatened as she had when he'd forced her to utter 'Magyki' to his face.

"What does he want with us?"

Elric's gaze softened at the tremor in her voice. "Not us, Vera. You. He invited only you to dinner. I will, of course, escort you if you desire, but I cannot stay."

"WHAT?!"

She was going to hyperventilate. She forced down the instinct to run from the palace, the capital, maybe even the entire continent. Her life was crumbling down around her all because she'd been stupid enough to confront a stranger. If she'd never approached him or never told Elric, none of this would be happening.

She needed air and maybe a stiff drink.

"It will be all right. Emperor Matheris has always known about you. I don't know the specifics, but I do know he's had fifteen years to imprison or harm you, and he's chosen to do neither."

They began walking again, leaving the grounds in tense silence. As they finally crossed the training yard toward the armory, Elric patted her shoulder.

"I have a matter I must see to, but I will return in time to escort you back to the palace. I suggest you use this time to clean up and settle your nerves best you can." With that, he spun on his heel and strode away.

Closing the door behind her, she took several deep breaths and tried to slow her racing thoughts. Elric was right. The emperor had possessed every opportunity to call her out and hadn't.

There was a reason she was here and as terrified as she was to return, her curiosity demanded answers. She plopped her traveling pack on the closest surface, freezing when she heard the loud thud it made against the table.

The dagger!

Drowning in anxiety the last few days, she'd completely forgotten about it. Snatching her pack back up, she sprinted through the workroom she hadn't seen in days, eager to get to her room.

Chapter 11

Jaren

He'd been following her unique scent ever since leaving that alley. Tracking her had been easier than he'd anticipated, but he wasn't sure if that fact pleased him or not. It was like once her star-fire essence had entered his senses, Jaren was both physically and mentally incapable of flushing it out.

He'd instantly picked up on it with the smallest breeze and followed it. There were scarcely any people meandering the streets at the cusp of dawn, so it had practically been child's play to locate. The scent hadn't diminished until he reached the main stables on the west side of the city.

Though faint, it was still there, but intermixed with a fuck ton of *pizlath* ones. He tensed at the idea of her being with a large group of human men. The stable was empty, confirming what he'd already suspected. She'd departed Midpath.

It didn't take him as long as he'd feared to find another stable. Quickly knocking out the stable hand, he prepared a horse and set out on the main western road. If the little star-burning *zhu* was indeed traveling in a group, they would move much slower than he'd be capable of. Jaren had no doubts he'd catch up with her.

Sure enough, within a few hours, he sighted a decent-sized party making their way toward Kilmire which, if memory served him, was halfway toward the capital of Matherin. Before the start of the forest, the flat expanse of land between Midpath and Kilmire made it easy to pick them out. He'd never traveled so far inland before, but he'd thankfully memorized a map of the land years ago.

Even miles ahead of him, he was positive it was the same group. An instinctual pull in his core told him that although he couldn't see her, she was there.

Jaren's initial assumption upon meeting her hadn't been wrong after all. She may not have been a guard, but she was associated with the royal *chinbi srol,* which only further angered him. He cursed, wanting nothing more than to shake her violently and demand answers. A Magyki mingling with a Matheris was an insult to their entire people.

Quelling his deep-seated need to strangle her, he allowed his horse to slow to a walk. He'd traveled hard so far, and the poor beast wasn't accustomed to it.

He wasn't too worried about keeping them directly in sight. Being too close would put him at an unnecessary risk of discovery, and he knew where they were heading.

What grated against Jaren's nerves the most wasn't that she worked for the prince, but of how in-tune his senses seemed to be to her. Even with the strength of her scent reduced due to distance, he swore he still knew exactly where she was. There was this incessant *tug* he couldn't ignore. It was as if his body was a compass and she, north.

It was fucking ridiculous.

Was he that lonely for companionship, or was it some bullshit primal instinct that demanded he find and protect her? Granted, it had been several moons now since he'd felt a female's skin against his own, but that wasn't unusual due to how often Jaren left Bhasura. None of his previous *dunduwaw* had ever been serious. They were just casual encounters whenever he felt the need to scratch the itch.

He didn't crave closeness. Most of the time, he didn't even know their names, or knew but forgot them soon after. He wasn't interested in anything more. He'd had his chance for more once, and had lost it.

Then, this *zhu* shows up out of nowhere, and gods damn him, but he wanted to know her story. He wanted to know why the fuck she was traveling with Sulian's brat, just as much as he wanted to throttle her for daring to confront and steal from him.

He needed to control his thoughts and stick to the truths he knew. She was a thief and nothing more. If she was in danger, it was her own fault for putting herself there. His only business was getting his dagger.

He was traveling to the capital, the heart of Aleron, and he needed to focus. His father, Dedryn, would skin him alive if he knew the risk he was taking for that dagger, and Jaren couldn't blame him.

He was endangering more than just himself by foolishly heading so deep into Sulian's territory, but he couldn't turn back. Something seemed to be pulling at him, whispering in his ear and urging him on.

Requiring more effort than he liked to admit, he closed off his emotions and fell into the calm he knew so well. The calm that centered him and allowed him to revel in one of his favorite activities...plotting.

His lips pulled up slightly in the corner. If nothing else, this was bound to get interesting.

DISMOUNTING ABOUT A mile outside the edge of the sprawling capital, Jaren offered an apple to his exhausted mare before smacking her hide and sending her off. This close to civilization, someone was bound to find her soon and give her the care she deserved.

A horse would've only brought him more attention than necessary. He could stick to the shadows and travel much faster on foot. He pulled his cloak farther over his face as he entered the city itself, concealing his unique features.

Most of the people he passed glanced uneasily at him and naturally moved out of his way, but none seemed unnecessarily suspicious. They were too busy trying to survive their own business to bother nosing into his.

Jaren couldn't pick out her scent among the sea of people around him, but praying to the gods he hadn't lost his mind, he continued to follow that annoying tug in his chest, letting it guide him deeper into the city. Unsurprisingly, it led him directly to the palace.

Growling, he rubbed a hand over his brow, fighting the impulse to hit something. It would obviously be really fucking stupid to try to follow her there, but that didn't mean he couldn't make good use of his time.

If he played his cards right, his presence in Matherin could end up proving beneficial in more ways than one. He'd come all the way here, so he might as well make use of his time. Assessing the area for weaknesses would at least bring him one step closer to getting back into his fathers' good graces.

Jaren took his time stalking the perimeter, scouting where each guard was posted. He was looking for the best way in when her scent suddenly hit him like a solid, stone wall.

Fuck. She was close.

To his right, almost hidden behind the palace, appeared to be some kind of training area, and it was definitely where her scent was coming from. Interest piqued, he edged closer until he could hear the low murmurings of a conversation.

Moving farther around the structure, he knew, as sure as he knew his name, she was directly on the other side. Just as he was about to risk glancing around the corner, he heard a door shut and the conversation died. Heavy steps, definitely not belonging to her, started his way. He quickly retreated, creeping, instead, around the back.

Strangely enough, there were only two windows for such a large building. He peered into the first to see a poor excuse for a living area with a tub and cot tucked into the corners. No sign of any occupants.

Moving to the second window, he could make out a sparse bed chamber. It didn't contain much besides a few pieces of simple furniture and a wash basin. The only thing of interest was the female form leaning back against the closed door.

She was slightly flushed and wearing a dress rather than the clothes he'd previously seen her in. Plain and ugly as it was, it accentuated her curves in a way that was irritatingly mesmerizing.

Grinding his teeth, he watched with rapt attention as she sprinted across the room, stumbling slightly, before dropping in front of a worn-looking chest. She was alone, distracted, and clearly distressed by something.

Roving his eyes along the frame of the window, Jaren realized almost gleefully that it wasn't latched. Reaching out, he couldn't stop his wicked grin when it opened silently.

Time to play, little star.

Vera

PRACTICALLY SLAMMING THE DOOR IN HER HASTE, VERA rushed across her room, tripping over her dress, and dropped to her knees before an old chest.

It had seen better days and creaked loudly when she opened it. Reaching in with trembling fingers, she removed the sheathed dagger tucked inside among her spare clothing.

Her breathing was labored, and her heart beat rapidly as she sat back on her heels and carefully removed the blade from its covering. It was still just as beautiful as the first time she'd seen it.

Pulling the stolen dagger from her belt, she laid them side by side in the crammed chest. They were identical in every way, from the tip of the rippled blades to the etchings on the handles.

Vera paused, scrunching her forehead, and leaning her face closer. With a start, she realized the etchings were not the same at all. They both used the same script, but each looked to say something different.

Although she'd already begun to suspect the blade's origin, seeing the identical weapons side by side confirmed it. She was fascinated and wished she had the time to sit and study them, but she'd have plenty of time later.

Sighing, she closed the lid. She was running out of time to wash up and prepare. She needed to use every minute wisely and decide on the best course of action for the night.

Lost in her thoughts, the sudden sensation of being snatched from behind had her screaming out. She was so caught off guard she could do nothing as she was slammed into a wall of her room.

Stars burst behind her eyes, and she felt the strong grip of fingers clasp around her throat. Struggling to clear her vision, she choked out a strangled breath and clawed at the hand.

Hot breath tickled her face, and a deep, menacing growl vibrated against her body. "*Kültha kpiybo, b'u mod.*"

Hello again, little star.

His voice was somehow both gravelly and smooth, making

the words sound almost sensual. She blinked a few more times, clearing the dots clinging to her sight and focused on the individual attached to the hand at her throat. He showed no visible signs of their skirmish, and his jaw was now lined with scruff, but it was definitely the stranger.

He'd found her.

"*Mbi mi tra thou.*"

She blinked rapidly, trying to mentally translate, but he spoke too fast, and it'd been too long since she'd heard or used Thyabathi. She was more than a little rusty. "I don't—I don't understand." She pushed the words out, struggling to speak past the pressure on her throat.

His eyes narrowed slightly, but to her relief, he switched to the common tongue. "You took something of mine. Shall I take something of yours in return? Your air, maybe?"

He squeezed, causing her eyes to bulge and her lungs to burn. She thrashed in panic, scraping her fingernails down his arm to no avail. Oh gods, he was going to kill her. She'd been so stupid.

What did she think would happen? That'd he spare her life just because she'd spared his? She tried to think, to form even one coherent thought. She'd beaten him before; she could do it again.

Who was she kidding? No, she couldn't. As black spots again began to fill her vision, she realized she had no chance at all. If Vera was honest with herself, she'd had no chance the first time, just dumb luck. She was unarmed and completely at his mercy.

"I quite like this game. Shall we continue playing?"

She couldn't speak even if she wanted to, and he knew it. She felt a single tear trail down her cheek. She'd never in her life felt so completely helpless.

His fingers abruptly relaxed, and air violently rushed back into her lungs as she took huge, heaving breaths. His face leaned in close, and his rugged, earthy smell caressed her senses.

"I will have my dagger back. If you try to fight, you will lose, and I will make you beg me not to bury it in your heart."

Gods, she didn't want to beg him for anything, but she sure as hell didn't want to die here in this room. She shook her head back and forth—as much as she could with his hand still in place—trying to clear her panicked thoughts.

"*Pha?*" He practically flung the word at her, and she realized he had misinterpreted her action as a refusal. "You value your life so little? I would step over your corpse and retrieve it. Your denial is stupid, not courageous," he spit.

She took a shaky breath as her heart continued hammering against her ribcage. She would be brave. She could do this. Elric's lessons echoed in the back of her head like a mantra.

Fear is a flame. It cannot be extinguished by will alone. You can let it burn you alive, or you can do something with it. Alter it, bend it to your will, forge it into a weapon.

She looked directly into his eyes. "I could have killed you, yet I only disarmed you and let you live. You owe me a life debt." Her breathing was still ragged, and her voice came out raspy and hoarse.

She saw surprise and something akin to admiration flicker across his face, but it was so fleeting she was certain she'd imagined it.

"I don't owe you a thing, *duwabi*. Whether I allow you to live or not is still undecided, but I will take back what is mine either way."

Vera nodded. She might have been drawn to the beautiful blade, but she wasn't stupid enough to value it over her life. A life that, quite literally, rested in his hand. Still drawing from the tiny reserve of bravado she had, she tapped his arm, indicating he needed to release her.

He smirked. Lifting his fingers one digit at a time, he slowly removed his grip from her throat. He took a small, calculated step back, but those green eyes never left hers. She wasn't naïve enough to run. His posture and arrogant expression screamed it's what he expected, and he was more than prepared to give chase.

Vera eyed him warily before finally daring to look away. She crossed the few steps it took to reach the chest and tried not to completely put her back to him while she leaned down.

She grabbed the edge of the lid but froze when she sensed the heat from his body directly behind her. She hadn't even heard him move. Trying—and failing—to ignore his presence, she continued. The silence was so heavy, she swore it was practically its own entity.

The creak of the lid echoed out painfully as she raised it. She paused again, eyeing the spot where the blades were hidden beneath her clothes. She knew which one was hers, of course, as it was safely in its sheath, but a question bubbled up the back of her burning throat.

"Are all Bhasurian blades designed this way?"

She sensed him stiffen behind her, but he didn't immediately answer. It'd been worth a shot.

"*Pha*. Mine was crafted specifically for me."

He spoke possessively, like the dagger was an extension of himself rather than a weapon. She wasn't sure what was more surprising, that he'd answered, or that he'd lied.

Or perhaps it was that someone *else* had lied to *him*. Vera's curiosity overpowered her common sense, so like always when that happened, she did something stupid.

"Interesting." She slipped her fingers under the clothing and unsheathed her dagger. Grabbing the other, she stood and gradually turned to face him, holding both out on her palms as unthreateningly as possible.

"Sorry, but I'm not sure I remember which one was yours."

Yep. Curiosity made her really stupid. She figured he'd be shocked, that she'd be able to catch him off guard again, and maybe he'd divulge something about the blades. But she did not, in any way, anticipate the violence with which he responded.

Moving faster than her eyes could process, he knocked both daggers to the ground. She vaguely heard the sound of them sliding across the floor before his body was upon her. His weight crashed into her, and within seconds of her finishing her idiotic sentence, she was on the floor.

His body loomed over her with one knee between her legs while one hand held her wrists above her head and the other was, again, at her throat.

Vera shuddered as the chill of the floor soaked through her clothing and clashed with the heat of his body as he pressed down into her. Her dress had hitched slightly up from her fall, the open air kissing her naked legs.

"*Ngil egyoch chow mbi thoots?!*" She flinched as he half yelled, half snarled in her face. He'd seemed angry before, but now there was a good chance he might actually hurt her.

Gripping her more firmly and shaking her by the throat, he repeated in the common tongue, "Where. Did you. Get that?" His voice had dropped back down to a calmer tone, which only terrified her more.

"I've…" She swallowed and tried again, "I've had it for as long as I can remember. I found it here among dozens of other daggers."

"Here?" he asked, glancing disbelievingly around her room.

"I mean, in the armory." She flicked her eyes to the door. "I was drawn to it, and I've had it ever since." She didn't know why she'd admitted that last part, but it was true.

He stared into her eyes, and she could practically see her words circling in his head as he tried to decide whether or not he believed her.

Vera lowered her gaze and noted, a little late, that she was pinned to the ground by a strong, attractive body. His tunic was a deep, forest green that only further enhanced his eyes, and his tan trousers were snug in all the right places.

With powerful-looking thighs, a taut torso, and well-defined arm muscles, he was definitely *not* a sack of potatoes. Even the fingers wrapped around her neck and wrists were attractive. Wedged between her legs, his knee was pressed against her center, and she was suddenly acutely aware of his proximity.

Vera's next words came out as nothing more than a whisper as she desperately tried to change her thoughts back to their conversation. "I don't know whose it was before me."

"Mine."

Her eyes instantly locked back with his. The emotion hiding behind them was intense and devastating, and she felt her body shudder in response. His nostrils flared, and she swore he glanced at her lips before pushing back to his feet above her.

"Those two daggers were given to me when I became old enough to train." He opened and closed his mouth as if he'd almost added something else.

"Training for what? How did one of them get here then?" The questions burst out from her before she could stop them, and she mentally cursed herself for letting her nosiness get the best of her. Again.

His expression hardened. "It was stolen from me. Highly convenient for me to find it, well over a decade later, in the hands of the same *duwabi* who recently stole the other." His fists curled, and she belatedly remembered she was still prostrate at his feet.

"I knew Matherins were barbarians and thieves, but I certainly never would have guessed one of my own would also steal from me." His stare was damning.

She sat up, and when he made no move to stop her, she slowly climbed to her feet. Feeling somewhat more confident since he seemed less inclined to kill her now, she crossed her arms and glared back at him. If he were going to kill her, he'd have done it by now.

Right?

"I'm not one of you."

Looking her up and down, his lip curled as if he found her severely lacking. "Guess I don't need to bother asking where your loyalties lie," he sneered.

Vera felt herself growing angrier by the second. Throwing her arms up in the air, she asked, "Okay, Green Eyes, enlighten me. Why should I feel any loyalty to Bhasura?"

She should probably have been concerned by her sudden lack of fear, especially considering the look he was giving her. Not to mention there were still two weapons somewhere on the floor. But the longer he stood there, the more she believed he didn't plan on harming her.

Green Eyes took a quick step forward at her question, causing her to reactively step back. He said nothing at first, but she saw his eyes flicker to the sides of her head.

"Your blatant disrespect toward your own kind is appalling." He looked down his nose at her before switching gears and asking, "Why does Matherin welcome you, a *zhu*, to work for Sulian's spawn?"

Vera supposed she didn't need to ask how the Magyki felt about the emperor. The complete dismissal of his title spoke volumes by itself. She couldn't help the small spark of pride that he thought her capable of working for the prince. Lie, she told herself. Lie your ass off.

But she didn't.

"I'm not welcome here. I was kind of forced to blend in. It's not like I was exactly given a choice." She bitterly gestured at her ears. "And I don't work for Prince Eithan," she added. "I'm just a ward in the armory."

Uncertainty crossed his features, and his posture relaxed ever so slightly. "How long have you been kept here? Do you even know what you are?"

"Why does everyone care so much about what I am?" she snapped. She was angry, exhausted, and suddenly felt on the verge of tears. Swallowing hard, she tried to force them back. Tears were the last thing she needed right now.

He didn't respond to her outburst besides raising an eyebrow and looking at her like she was an emotionally unstable child. She certainly felt like one.

"Sorry, it's just—" Why in Aleron was she apologizing? He'd tried choking her to death just a few minutes ago. It was further proof that her mind and her mouth were not on the same page.

"Yes, I know," she said instead. "But I've been here since I was a child. Young enough that I have no memory of being anywhere else." She looked down and exhaled roughly, letting her arms fall limply at her sides. She didn't want to talk anymore. She didn't even know why she'd started.

At his silence, Vera looked back up only to be completely and utterly captivated by his eyes. They had widened, and he was looking at her in a way that made her heart flutter.

"Exactly how long has that been?"

"Fifteen years, give or take."

Taking a step toward her, he whispered, "Untainted." But he said it so quietly, she wasn't sure she'd heard him correctly.

"What?"

Suddenly his head whipped toward the door, and he tensed,

hand snapping to the empty sheath at his waist. His jaw ticced, and he stood with that eerie, preternatural stillness of his. She was about to say something again when knocking disrupted the silence. She turned toward the noise just as Elric's voice came through.

"Unless you want me to treat you like a woman, stop acting like one by hiding in your room. We have a few things I'd like to discuss before your dinner."

She spun back around to gauge the stranger's reaction, but he was gone. She looked around wildly, but he'd left through her window just as silently as he'd appeared. She looked down at the floor to see he'd left both daggers where they lay.

The sight of them brought only unease. Green Eyes had followed her for days to retrieve what she took. There was no way he was going to forget about them, which meant he'd eventually be back.

She carefully placed both into the chest, knowing they'd likely be gone by the time she returned, but still hoping they wouldn't be, all the same.

Chapter 12

Vera

She didn't tell Elric about what happened. If she did, he'd only demand she inform the emperor, and for some insane, illogical reason, that just didn't feel right. Green Eyes had two separate opportunities to kill her, yet he hadn't.

Plus, there was that weird thing he'd said. *Untainted.* She had no idea what he meant, but he'd looked at her like she was precious. Like she was a lost treasure he hadn't expected to find.

As stupid as it was, she wanted to see him again. She had so many questions, and against the voice of reason, she trusted he'd answer. He was dangerous and violent, but he just didn't seem like the kind of male who would outright lie. She couldn't say the same for the Matherin men she knew.

She groaned loudly, startling the poor girl who was styling

her hair. Not long after Vera had spoken with Elric, the girl had appeared with an entire palace worth of torture devices. She was short, pale, and incredibly thin, but had turned out to be rather vicious with deceptively strong hands.

Vera had been poked and prodded, plucked and yanked, then squeezed so tightly into a deathtrap of a dress, she'd mentally written a nice eulogy to her already bruised ribcage.

As the girl finished attempting to wrangle her unruly curls, Vera knew without a doubt, she never wanted to go through such a torturous process again. No wonder noble women were said to be nothing but vipers, who could blame them? She hadn't even left for dinner yet, and she already wanted to punch someone in the throat.

She'd tried to strike up a conversation, but Lady Strong Hands never replied. Anytime she asked her a question, the girl would just shake her head and continue working as if she wouldn't—or couldn't—answer.

Maybe the emperor was afraid Vera would start spouting out secrets about herself if someone happened to be friendly with her. She wouldn't put it past him. He certainly hadn't seemed overly impressed with her.

When Vera finally stood, Lady Strong Hands gathered up the supplies in record time and rushed out without so much as a nod. She heard the door to the armory open and close, then nothing but silence. Steeling herself for what she was about to see, she walked over to her small mirror.

Even though her mirror had a slightly cloudy film, she could see enough that it stopped her in her tracks. The red stain on her lips brought her focus to the now prominent shape of her mouth, and the soft kohl smeared across her eyelids made their normally dull gray color appear almost bright.

Her hair was pulled into some kind of extravagant up-do she couldn't fully see, and perfectly placed curls hung loosely around her face. She dragged her eyes away from her reflection to look down at herself. The bodice of her dress was a creamy white that cut deeply between her breasts, showing off the jagged scar just above her collarbone, and more cleavage than she even knew she had.

Although it technically had sleeves, they were skintight and see-through and ended with tiny loops that wrapped around her middle fingers to keep them in place. There were no embellishments anywhere on the gown, but it didn't need them.

The skirt was slightly shimmery, looking either white or lilac depending on how she twisted. It weighed less than she'd imagined when she saw it, and it swooshed around her ankles when she moved.

The person staring back at her was beautiful, she could admit it. And the dress truly was exquisite. But it just wasn't *her*.

She was disrupted from her assessment when she heard Elric's boots coming toward her doorway. Looking up in time to see him appear, she felt self-conscious and unsure. She instinctively went to chew on her lip, but the bitter taste of the stain had her releasing it with a grimace.

Instead, she stood bouncing on her heels, clasping and unclasping her hands. He only stared, eyes wide, but he didn't speak.

Her face flushed, and she busied herself with picking up the shoes sitting on her bed—flats, thank the gods—and said, "I'm guessing it's time to go."

Elric nodded. His lips twitched as he decided what to say. "I know you're angry with me, Vera, but no matter what you believe, just know that I'm sorry you're having to go alone tonight." He stepped to the side to let her pass. "Just remember what we talked about earlier, and you'll be fine."

After Green Eyes disappeared, Elric had shoved her in a chair and instructed her on everything she shouldn't do at a royal dinner. He'd even somehow gotten his hands on dinnerware and taught her what pieces to use and when to use them. It was incredibly confusing, and she wasn't sure she actually remembered any of it.

"I'm sure it'll be fine," she said, her tone coming out flatter than she'd intended.

Gently grabbing her wrist, he asked, "Are you all right, girl?" The wrinkles decorating his forehead had deepened and his eyes were glossy. He looked worried in a way only a father could, like he could sense the storm of emotions wreaking havoc in her mind.

Yes, she wanted to say. She'd be fine. She always found a way to be fine.

"No, Elric, I'm not. I mean, look at me. I don't look like myself, and I don't feel like myself. You threw me to the wolves, and now I have nothing but hairpins and bare skin to protect myself with." She pulled her arm out of his grasp, carefully edging past the worktables so as not to smudge or tear her gown.

"I'm going to be perfectly ladylike, don't worry. I'll nod and

134

smile and act like I have no thoughts of my own while I silently hope the gods bless me with a painless death." She opened the outside door and let the evening air whip across her face and soothe her raging soul.

"Holy shit."

She barely managed to avoid shattering her nose on the door when she realized someone was standing just on the other side speaking to her. Elric was at her side instantly and didn't relax when he saw who it was.

"What are you doing here, Trey?" Her smile felt like it was stretching her entire face. She didn't think she'd get to see him again, especially so soon.

"Did you think I'd miss a chance to see you all dressed up?" He winked as he closed the distance and offered up an arm. "Prince Eithan insisted that one of us escort you to dinner. I volunteered. Can't say I regret it in the least." She reached over and smacked his arm, eliciting a laugh.

"You're the worst."

"And you're delectable."

She flushed all the way down to her toes and fought the urge to cover the exposed swells of her breasts. "I find it unfair that you keep seeing me in all manner of dress, yet I've yet to even see your face," she joked.

"I tell you what, Vera, show me yourself in a manner of *undress*, and I'll show you my face." Taking her arm, he hooked it through his, wiggling his eyebrows suggestively.

She could not have blushed harder if she tried, but she covered it by pinching the underside of his arm. He gave a satisfying yelp but didn't let go. She found herself leaning into him, already more relaxed.

Turning to look at a glowering Elric, she gave a small wave. "I don't know when I'll be back."

He crossed his arms and grunted, staring daggers at Trey. "I'll be up."

Trey had the good sense to look a little worried as they started walking toward the palace. "Why do I get the feeling Lesta doesn't think too highly of me?"

"Don't take it personally, I doubt he'd trust anyone showing interest in me." He looked at her curiously, but she just shrugged. "It'd probably help if you kept your ornery comments to a minimum when he's around." He chuckled in agreement but made no promises.

They walked in companionable silence the rest of the way, Trey somehow knowing she needed the time to organize her thoughts. It wasn't until they'd entered the palace that he broke the peace.

"This way. We'll be heading to the west wing. They like to use it when they entertain guests and dinner parties." As they neared their destination, Trey released her arm and took a step back to walk just behind her. She immediately missed the comfort of his proximity.

They stopped outside a set of large doors settled between two stoic guards. The doors were a deep navy with smooth iron knobs embellished with vines and thorns. Engraved into the panels themselves was the royal crest, and the sight of it froze her feet to the floor.

She had no idea what to expect. Emperor Matheris hadn't seemed remotely unsettled about her obvious origins; in fact, he seemed thrilled. But given he didn't know the exact details of her involvement with Green Eyes, she couldn't quite understand his interest. He wanted something from her, she could safely assume that much. What he wanted, however, was an entirely different matter.

"Since when is feisty Vera nervous around a few *self-important* Matherin men?" Trey gently chided from behind her.

She didn't know much about him. If she were honest, she didn't know him well at all. But there was something about him that she trusted. Maybe it was because, besides Elric, he'd been the only person who seemed to like her exactly how she was. Granted, he might not know everything, but she didn't think he'd care if he did.

"I don't know what he wants with me." She crossed her arms over her body, desperate for any form of protection against the impending dinner. "Did Prince Eithan tell you anything about me?"

She turned, looking him in the eyes, terrified all over again. He flinched at whatever he saw in her gaze and cupped his hands around her elbows.

"I'm sorry, Vera, but I couldn't tell you even if he did."

She nodded. "Yeah, I understand."

She took a shaky breath, straightened her shoulders, and dropped her arms. She wasn't used to this constant sense of fear, and it was starting to drain every bit of energy she had.

Fear is a flame. Bend it to your will and forge it into a weapon.

She repeated it until she was able to re-take control of her emotions.

"I'm ready."

As soon as the words left her mouth, the two guards framing the doors moved to open them. She picked up her skirts just enough to allow her to take steady, concise steps, and willingly entered the wolves' den.

THE TWO MEN were seated at a large, rectangular table set for ten. She wasn't sure if the table was perpetually set for guests, or if it was done purposefully to make her second guess who all would make an appearance.

According to Elric, royals and nobles were fond of mind games, and he warned her to expect them. In hindsight, the advice probably wasn't going to do her any favors, considering her current mental state. She was likely going to see games and traps everywhere, even where there weren't any.

They instantly stopped their quiet conversation and stood when they saw her. It took her a little by surprise. The two most important men on the entire continent just showed her respect. Was *that* a mind game?

Dammit, Elric.

She allowed herself a quick peek at the prince, and it took her a moment to understand what it was about him that had snagged her attention. Then it hit her. He was wearing a simple white tunic and dark gray trousers tucked into plain, black boots. He had no crown, no weapons, no vest or adornment of any kind.

Stealing a glance at the emperor, she noticed him dressed nearly the same, except his tunic was navy. He was also sans crown.

In her gods-forsaken gown, Vera stood out like a sore thumb. The emperor had demanded she be primped and dolled up while they dressed down as if this were just a basic nightly dinner for them. If the intention was to unsettle her, it was working. Whether it was the emperor or both of them, she had a feeling they were trying to make her uncomfortable.

She felt a tingle of anger crawl under her skin. Whether intentional or not, they'd already put her in her place without saying a single word.

It didn't help that as she came within a few feet of the table, she realized she had no idea where she was supposed to sit. They were both standing on opposite ends, and there were several chairs between them on either side. She looked at the open chairs and decided the middle seemed like the safest bet.

But to her relief, Prince Eithan came around the table and pulled out a chair for her. She mentally applauded herself when it was the middle chair. Focusing far too much on keeping her skirts out of the way, she suddenly lurched forward when he pushed the chair in, almost knocking over a wine glass.

"My apologies, I didn't mean to startle you." He flashed her a devastating smile before reclaiming his seat. Vera's face turned a vibrant shade of molten red, and it had only partly to do with embarrassment.

He'd barely finished sitting when servants scurried about,

placing plates of mouthwatering food before them. She had to actively work to contain the saliva accumulating at the sight of the fresh meat before her. She and Elric weren't starving by any means, but they certainly couldn't afford meals like this.

Following their lead, she desperately tried to remember all of Elric's tips regarding appropriate dinner etiquette as she chose a utensil and took a small, ladylike bite. Oh gods, she'd have to allot a few minutes tonight to moan about this later.

"You look beautiful this evening, Veralie."

She swallowed her half-chewed bite, uttering a quick, "Thank you, Your Highness," before taking a generous gulp of wine. The prince's smile never faltered; his eyes riveted to her as if she were a puzzle he desperately wanted to solve.

"My son spoke true; you do look quite lovely." *This time*, he didn't need to add. The emperor sat back against his chair and cocked his head, appraising her. She took another sip of wine, hoping to mask her nerves with a slight buzz.

"I must confess, Veralie, I'm not one for idle chitchat. I find it rather tedious. So, I will do us both a favor and get right to the topic at hand."

She nodded, pleased. Small talk wasn't a skill she possessed either.

He drummed his fingers lightly on his armrests. "What all do you know about Bhasura and its people?"

"Not much, Your Majesty. I know the island resides over the resting place of the gods. And I think somewhere I heard, or maybe read, that the gods blessed the Magyki with superior physical abilities. That they're faster and stronger."

"Yes and no." His lips quirked and he looked down his nose at her as if he found her to be an adorably naïve child. "You're correct that the island does sit above where the gods slumber. However, the gods did not bless the Magyki. The Magyki have such abilities because they stole the power."

Vera's eyes widened, and she moved to lean forward before thinking better of it when the prince's eyes darted below her neck. "How did they steal power from the gods? And why?"

"Come now, Veralie, what motive would one have for such a thing?" He tsked. "Greed."

"But...how?"

"According to history, the gods left a remnant of their power on the island—a relic of some kind. The how and why has never been clear. The Magyki, who were, of course, natives of the island, swore an oath to protect it. But they lied." He took a slow, measured sip from his wine.

"They began to experiment and discovered they could drain its essence and imbue their bodies with a power they were never meant to have. It gave them strength, speed, heightened senses, and longevity. The average lifespan for a Magyki is around two-hundred years."

Vera tipped her head back; food forgotten. Her mind went immediately to her green-eyed stalker. He'd appeared not much older than she, but if his lifespan were at least double a human man's, who knew how old he was. She stiffened at the next thought that entered, unbidden, into her mind.

"Veralie?" Prince Eithan was looking at her, concern etched into his face.

"I just realized, if my life span is longer than what I thought it was, I might be completely wrong about my age." She chewed on her bottom lip, ignoring the bitter taste.

"Elric believed I was around five years old when I was sent to him. But what if I just looked younger than I really was?" She stared down at her lap, twisting her hands into her skirt. Verbally acknowledging how little she knew about herself left a hollow feeling in her stomach.

"You will physically age slower than a Matherin, but your age is correct."

She raised her head abruptly. "How do you know that?" Belatedly, she realized she'd just demanded an answer from him without addressing him respectfully. He narrowed his eyes, but after a slight pause, he answered.

"Because the Magyki who smuggled you here told me." He smirked; his tone annoyingly arrogant. He was trickling out information, dangling it by a hook and reveling in the sight of her trying to grasp at it.

Her eyes burned with unshed tears that desperately wanted to fall. He was taking advantage of her ignorance and teasing her with knowledge. And the worst part was she had no way of knowing if he was even telling the truth.

She swallowed hard, looking away toward the windows. There was a pregnant pause as she internally wrestled for control.

Risking the chance she was digging an even bigger hole, Vera asked, "Your Majesty, may I speak freely for a moment?" She didn't look away from the view outside.

He didn't instantly reply, and she had the distinct feeling he was sizing her up. "I'll allow it."

She forced herself to turn and make eye contact with him. His eyes were lit with amusement, clearly wondering what silly little question she might have for him.

"You told me you prefer to get right to the point rather than make idle chitchat, but I don't feel like you're getting to the point at all. Allow me to just tell you now, I have no memory of my life before becoming Elric's ward. I don't remember how I got here. I don't even remember my family. So, if your hope was to get me to admit to knowing something, I have to say, Your Majesty, I will only disappoint you."

His response was to smile openly at her, and it was almost as beautiful as his son's. It caught her off guard, and she found herself glancing at Prince Eithan to gauge his reaction, but he was smiling at her too. What the fuck in all of Aleron was happening?

"You know, Veralie, for someone with absolutely no experience in court, you're rather good at this." The prince winked at her, "I suspect we can thank your family line for your natural talent."

She felt the blood drain from her face. Did he mean—

"You know who my family is?" Her voice came out higher pitched than she would have liked, but he didn't answer. Instead, choosing to lean back and look toward his father.

She followed his gaze and felt the world fall out from under her when the emperor said, "I know everything."

Chapter
13

Jaren

For the third time since encountering that damn *zhu*, Jaren had found himself shocked to his core. He'd barely been able to force his legs to move and launch himself back out of the window before whoever was at the door came in.

He stood, plastered against the outer wall next to her window, and listened as a man droned on about wasting time and something to do with forks. There was a moment of silence before he heard the shuffling of feet followed by the click of a door closing.

Not trusting her to stay quiet, he took off before she and the unknown man had the chance to come around looking for him. But he didn't go far. He physically couldn't. His instincts demanded he protect her, and like the fool he was, he couldn't resist.

She wasn't *just* a Magyki female. Gods, she may not have even set foot on Bhasura her entire life and was clearly still locked. She could be completely unaffected. Possibly the only one left. Her blood could be the key to figuring out the taint and helping their people. There was no guarantee, of course, but Jaren couldn't take the risk of losing her.

Everything that had occurred since he landed on this barbaric chunk of land had pushed him to her. The scout, the nudge to Midpath, happening upon the prince only to be attacked by *her*. It was all too perfect to be taken as anything other than fate. Especially considering his lost dagger. There was no way that was a coincidence.

She was either an exceptional liar, or she'd been telling the truth about finding the dagger in the armory. Given how easily flustered she was, Jaren's gut told him it was the latter. It was as if fate had dropped the dagger at her feet so that years later, she would be tempted to steal a matching one, ensuring he'd follow her and lead them to this exact moment.

That exasperating tug he couldn't rid himself of? It meant something. She had to be important.

So, bracing himself for the fight he knew she'd give, he forced himself back into the miserable bustle of the city streets to buy a larger pack and supplies. He'd need food for two, an extra flask, and probably some extra materials for her monthly bleeding, just in case.

On his own, he didn't usually carry much. Sleeping on the ground didn't bother him, and it was easy to catch food along the way. But he wouldn't be traveling alone this time, and once he had her with him, he couldn't risk any delays, hunting included.

He didn't know her role within the Matherin borders, but given her recent travels with the *chinbi srol* and his group of merry guards, she wasn't just some nobody to them. He had no idea how long it would be before someone noticed her missing and raised an alarm.

It had taken a couple of hours to get everything done. Besides purchasing basic supplies and food, he'd last-minute decided to buy a few extra pairs of clothes. It'd taken the majority of his coin. He'd barely have enough left to stock up one last time in Eastshore.

After Jaren had everything he needed, he made sure to pinpoint a convenient stable with a mount capable of bearing two riders, and planned the best way back out of the city. There were guards at every gate, so no path was going to be without its challenges, and it put him on edge. There were so many ways this could go wrong.

Although, the quickest route would be to knock her unconscious, restrain her, and throw her ass over the horse, he obviously couldn't ride through the city that way. No matter who she was, someone was bound to notice and report such a sight.

He was somehow going to have to persuade her to go with him willingly, and he honestly had no idea how to go about convincing her. She had no reason to trust him, and although he begrudgingly respected that—he did threaten to bury a blade in her heart, after all—it was going to prove rather inconvenient.

She couldn't have been more than a few years younger than

him, which meant she'd basically been raised by humans. She, at least, knew she wasn't one of them, but she'd also made it clear she didn't know much else. Gods, she didn't even speak their native tongue. He had to hold out hope he could feed her information to pique her interest enough to leave.

Jaren needed to tempt her to the point she'd risk trusting him enough to leave. The idea had his entire body tight with tension. He wasn't known for his ability to connect with people. Quite the opposite. Jaeros had tried to instill communication skills into his repertoire, but he'd just never cared. Until now.

IT WAS LATE into the evening when he finally made his way back to the training area and peeked into her window. The room was empty. He stole a glance into the other to find it empty as well.

Fuck.

He took several deep breaths to refocus. It'd be fine. She'd return eventually, and even if she didn't, he knew without a shadow of a doubt he'd be able to track her again. Her scent was practically engrained in his senses.

He slipped back through the unlatched window—a stupidity he'd make sure to throw in her face later—and slunk over to the chest he'd seen her pull his daggers from before.

It was obvious she'd set them inside with care, and his chest hummed with approval. His blades were his most priceless possessions, and it pleased him immensely to know someone else saw them for the treasures they were.

147

His hands shook, and his heart felt like it was in his throat when he picked up the one tucked safely in a simple, leather sheath. Jaren hadn't seen it since the night he'd lost it.

Touching it was like reliving his worst nightmare, and he swore he could still taste the thick fear that had choked him that night. He'd been just a boy, but his failure had triggered a domino effect of events no one had known how to fix. The taint, the growing unease, the death, all of it stemmed from his inability to save his best friend's life.

Attaching the sheath to his belt, he couldn't bring himself to pull it out just yet. He knew he wouldn't be able to trust his emotions if he did, and he needed to keep a clear head. He grabbed his other, the one that had served him well over the years, and placed it at his other side. Feeling the weight of them at his sides was surreal.

He left her room and circled the building. If—no, when she returned—he'd need to confront her outside. Jaren truly hoped he'd be able to reason with her, but just in case he couldn't, he needed the freedom to restrain her since she'd be sure to put up one hell of a fight.

But even if her blood was useless, the little star deserved to be with her people. She deserved to learn about what she came from and not have to hide her identity.

She might not see it yet, but he'd make her understand, even if he had to whisk her away against her will to do so.

Vera

"ALMOST TWO DECADES AGO, BHASURA WAS HIT WITH massive civil unrest. The citizens were unhappy with how King Vesstan and Queen Vaneara were ruling, and a rebellion formed. They tried to usurp those in power, and it ended with major bloodshed on both sides.

"You see, the rebels didn't just want the king and queen out of power, but also every noble who had supported them. The queen was killed in cold blood, and entire families were wiped from existence. Men, women, and children. They showed no mercy."

Vera sat transfixed. Once they'd finished dinner, they'd shown her through a doorway to the right that led to a sitting area before the largest hearth she'd ever seen. She'd never been more thankful for anything as she was that fire because after the emperor had dropped his I-know-who-your-family-is revelation, she'd felt cold as ice.

He was lounged across from her, an ankle crossed over a knee, completely at ease with his story. Prince Eithan sat to her left, leaned forward, elbows on his knees with his chin resting on his clasped hands, watching her as she listened. His unwavering attention made her uncomfortable at first, but she quickly became so invested in what the emperor was saying, she almost forgot the prince was even present.

"Your parents were born to two of the highest born noble families and were, therefore, targeted by the rebellion. It was they who sent you here. They paid a group of loyalists to smuggle you off the island with the hope you'd survive. You were born Veralie Palacia."

She couldn't stop the tears this time. They trickled out, leaving hot trails down her cheeks. Palacia. She hadn't been abandoned or discarded. She had a name, a family. One that loved her enough to do anything to save her.

She'd told herself so many times over the years that it didn't matter. That her past didn't matter. But she'd just been lying to herself. It *did* matter, and a wound she'd never wanted to acknowledge started to heal.

A hand curled around her own and she jumped, ripped out of her thoughts. Her eyes tracked the arm back to its owner to find Prince Eithan. He didn't speak, he just smiled softly and laced their fingers.

In a moment of weakness, she decided not to worry about how improper it was or what his motives might be. She just curled her fingers around his and enjoyed the simple comfort from the gesture.

"So…" her voice cracked, and she had to swallow and try again. "So, I was smuggled off the island. But since you knew about it, I can only assume that we were caught."

The emperor's attention was on their joined hands. "I have always had scouts, but I doubled them during the rebellion. I didn't know if their war would come to my shores. So yes, my men discovered the vessel carrying you. The Magyki on board were willing to forfeit their lives in exchange for a single meeting with me." He smirked.

"They informed me of who you were and why they'd brought you. They begged me to give you sanctuary. In return for valuable information about Bhasura, I agreed. I had my personal healer alter your appearance, and sent you off as a ward where no one would expect to find you."

Realizing she was gripping the prince's hand, Vera forcibly relaxed her fingers. Her head was starting to pound. The *emperor* had saved her?

"Why?" It was a stupid thing to ask, but she had to know. "I mean, I understand that you bartered for knowledge, but you could've tossed me anywhere after. Why place me with Elric? Why not an orphanage?"

Because that's what he had done. He hadn't just accepted her on his land, he'd made sure she was hidden from discovery and raised close to the palace.

"I am not altruistic, Veralie, I always have a motive for my actions. I wanted you somewhere no one would think to look, and I wanted you guarded. My Weapons' Master was one of the few people I trusted enough."

She tensed before releasing the prince's fingers and tucking both her hands underneath her legs. She felt jittery, like a swarm of insects had taken over her body. This was it, the moment she found out why she was here.

"You're a highborn Magyki, Veralie. Your family had strong ties to King Vesstan, and he still lives. Not long after you arrived, King Vesstan and his supporters extinguished the rebellion. From what I know, they've had peace ever since. Except with us."

She nodded. Everyone knew Aleron and Bhasura had

stopped trade decades ago and rarely communicated. They were self-made enemies. But she still didn't understand what that had anything to do with her. Did he hope to send her back to speak on his behalf? She highly doubted it.

"I should probably add that your father was a cousin of King Vesstan, which makes you an incredibly valuable female to them."

She choked. "I'm related to their king?"

The emperor abruptly stood and approached the hearth, his back to her. Completely switching topics, he said, "We gain much from our trade alliance with Sudron, but we lost much when trade with Bhasura ended. My predecessors believed the Magyki were growing too greedy, too demanding. They resented that they had stolen power from the gods and acted like they were so above our own people." He crossed his arms behind his back, staring into the flames.

"But I do not share their sentiments. The current populace of Bhasura is not to blame for their ancestors' choices. They did not ask for it." Finally turning, he looked straight at her.

"I want peace, Veralie. I want fair trade and communication. And I believe King Vesstan wants it too. Their island is becoming overpopulated, and they need more land. Land I currently rule over. I believe with the right steps; we could form an alliance with them and both benefit."

His eyes bore into her, and she shifted uneasily under the scrutiny, unsure what role he expected her naïve ass to play.

It was Prince Eithan who said, "The strongest alliance we could make with Bhasura would be an alliance through marriage."

She nodded. That made sense. It would bond the two lands

together permanently, maybe even allowing them to someday live peacefully together. She was still bobbing her head when the prince reached over and pulled her hand out from where she'd hid it under her legs.

"King Vesstan has no living children and never remarried. That leaves you, Veralie. You are the only living relative he has left. With you, we can forge a bridge between our two peoples. A marriage between us could change everything."

Chapter 14

Vera

She didn't move. She wasn't sure she remembered how to blink as she stared at Prince Eithan, his words running on repeat in her mind.

When he gently squeezed her hand, she started shaking her head, soft, broken chuckles leaving her mouth. She must have lost her mind. That was the only explanation. She was just crazy.

"Veralie, imagine what we could accomplish, what we could create." He smiled at her, that beautiful smile that would usually have her blushing, but now just worsened the coiling of nausea building in her stomach.

"You knew about this? The entire time we traveled, you knew?" Her voice came out hoarse and accusing. Had everyone she'd ever met known about her and lied?

He pulled back, looking affronted. "I knew my father's

intention for me to take a Magyki bride, yes. I've known my entire life that would be my future, and I'm honored. But no, until today, I did not know that it would be *you*."

She could feel panic clawing its way up. "I don't understand. If that was your goal, why not just keep me here in the palace and tell me?"

"Because the nobles here are not trustworthy," Prince Eithan said at the same time the emperor replied, "In case I changed my mind."

He sent a glare at his father, and Vera felt his thumb brush the top of her wrist. This couldn't be her real life. She'd only just learned who she was, and now they expected her to be okay with the knowledge that she'd been tucked away with the purpose of marrying her off to the Crown freaking Prince. She barely knew him!

She jumped up out of her chair, wrenching her hand free. "I'd like to leave."

Prince Eithan stood next to her, trying to retake her hand, but she stepped back. She was showing enough disrespect to warrant punishment, but she couldn't stop herself. She was going to be sick if she didn't get out of the room immediately.

The emperor hadn't moved from the hearth, but his voice was firm, "Sit. We still have much to discuss."

The prince held his hands out like she was a frightened animal he was trying to soothe, "Please, Veralie. I promise to answer any questions you have."

Gods, that name! Why did they keep repeating that name? Her chest started heaving in and out as her panic brushed the surface. She pushed her hands against her chest, trying to maintain her composure.

"Your Majesty—please—I need some fresh air—or I am going to vomit—all over this dress."

The emperor looked ready to deny her request, but to her shuddering relief, the prince stepped forward and, gently grasping her elbow, turned her toward the door.

"I'm sorry, I can only imagine how overwhelming this must be. I should have considered the fact I've grown up knowing all of this, and you've had it thrown at you all in one night."

He twisted at the waist, and he and his father stared at each other, communicating silently for a moment before the prince gave a small bow and led her back through the dining area toward the main doors.

Stepping through the doorway, Vera was shocked to see Trey still waiting, along with one other guard whom she recognized as one of the men who'd accompanied Prince Eithan to Midpath. Coleman, maybe?

Apparently, the prince didn't trust anyone but his own men to protect them. She supposed that made sense if he truly intended for her to marry him. She couldn't keep herself from wondering if Trey knew about all of it, and it only caused more bile to rise to her throat.

All she wanted to do was sprint out of the palace, but the prince was offering his arm and looking at her with concern. So, swallowing her anxiety, she wrapped her hand around his proffered arm and allowed him to walk her down the hallway. Trey and Maybe-Coleman followed, just far enough to give them privacy.

"Sul—my father can be abrupt and overbearing, but he has honorable intentions. He's not one to fall prey to conventional ways of thinking, but he has Aleron's best interest at heart. He has sought an alliance his entire reign, but our messengers to Bhasura have never returned." He sighed, pulling her closer.

"I know he may have expected your agreement tonight, but I do not. Although, I do hope you think about it, Veralie. It's about more than just us. It's about two lands and thousands of people. But I also, selfishly, don't want a wife who will resent me for the rest of our lives."

He spoke with such heart and conviction, she felt herself relaxing, just enough to quell the threatening nausea. The emperor had no qualms about ordering her into a marriage, and she had no doubt he would, but at least his son seemed to care about her opinion. So, she nodded as if she had a choice.

When they finally took a step outside, he released her arm. The instant lack of his warmth, along with the chill of the night, had her shivering. She welcomed it, allowing it to calm the remnants of panic still clinging to her chest.

"I must return, but Gibson will escort you back to your room." She was momentarily confused until she saw him motion for Trey. Some friend she was. She'd completely forgotten his surname.

She held up her hands, "No, that's all right, Your Highness. I know my way back. I'm sure Trey has more important matters to attend to for you." The guard in question rolled his eyes at her.

"There is nothing more important than ensuring your safety, Veralie. And please, call me Eithan." He smiled, taking her hand

and brushing a featherlight kiss to her knuckles.

She knew by the way Trey's eyes lit up, she had to be ten shades of red. Again. But she managed to return his smile with a shaky one of her own. "On one condition."

His lips quirked to the side, and he squeezed her fingers lightly before dropping her hand. "Name it."

"I will call you Eithan," she said, and his eyes flared, "if you go back to calling me Vera."

"But your birth name is beautiful."

"I prefer Vera, *Your Highness*." She batted her eyelashes, and he stepped back, laughing.

"Very well." Inclining his head toward Trey, he said, "You answer to her the same as you would me, Gibson. Her life over yours."

Trey saluted with a fist over his chest and bowed, but Eithan only had eyes for her before he and Maybe-Coleman slipped back into the palace.

"So...VERALIE, HUH?"

She glared daggers at those laughing brown eyes. "Don't even start."

The clear night air was working wonders to settle the whirlwind within her mind. She knew there was no chance of finding sleep tonight, but walking across the grounds, she at least felt a little less suffocated.

It only took a second for Trey's long strides to catch up to her, and sensing him on her left, she asked, "Since you've been ordered to serve and protect me and all that nonsense, are you also allowed to speak openly with me?"

He tilted his head back to look up at the sky, contemplating her question. "I'd think so."

"And?"

He huffed a quick breath out through his nose. "And Prince Eithan said that you're some long-lost highborn noble and instructed us to protect you as dutifully as we would protect him." He nudged her shoulder with his, "I won't lie, I find it real fucking weird."

She fought back an answering grin. "You're not alone. I find it real fucking weird too."

She wasn't sure if she felt relief or sadness that Trey still didn't know where she came from. She supposed if she went through with the whole marry-me-and-unite-our-lands idea, he'd figure it out sooner than later.

"Whether you're a boring ass armory ward or a fancy noble lady, I got your back." His laugh burst out as he dodged the elbow she shot his way.

"It's not boring! You'll thank me if you ever have to draw your blade, you twerp."

He stepped closer, and before she knew it, they were crossing the training grounds. She couldn't help but wonder how much longer she'd live here if the emperor was set on his plan. It was a crazy thing to even think about. It just seemed too surreal. Like it was all some grand joke they were pulling to punish her for all her recent transgressions. She was an orphaned ward, as invisible as she was replaceable. She was no princess.

Vera looked around, already planning on coercing Elric to train with her in the morning. Regardless of how sore she might still be, it would help ease the frustration and pressure she felt around her soul. She was running through her possible persuasive arguments when she saw it.

Movement.

It was the same subtle movement she saw in Midpath. Just a slight flutter of the shadows. She drew up, darting her gaze around and quickly realizing Trey hadn't seen it.

Finally noticing she'd stopped walking, he turned to her, putting his back to the shadows. It was only a second—just one breath of a moment—when she saw the darkness shift.

Faster than she'd ever moved before, she lunged for Trey. His eyes widened in shock as she slid her arm across his body and tore his sword from its sheath. Spinning out, she pointed it straight at the imposing male body suddenly standing a few feet before them.

Now in possession of both daggers, he was practically dripping lethal promises. With one in each hand, he glared at Trey, and she saw his muscles tense to attack. Primal anger surged up inside her at the thought of him attacking an unarmed man— a man who'd shown her a taste of friendship and had sworn to always have her back.

Using all the pent-up emotion the evening had bottled up inside her, she adjusted her body to completely block Trey and bared her teeth in a growl.

Jaren

HE'D BEEN LEANING BACK AGAINST THE ROUGH WALL OF what he'd confirmed was the armory, when he saw two figures appear at the opposite end of the empty training field. It was well into the night, and he was perfectly tucked into the shadows along the edge of the structure.

He didn't recognize her at first. Her shimmering gown stood out starkly in the moonlight. Her hair had been pulled up, exposing an elegant neck and warm skin. The snug bodice cut sharply down the front, exposing the full breasts he'd already known were there.

And as she came closer, he could make out the muscles of her arms straining against the sheer fabric. She truly was like a fucking star, all at once ethereal and fierce.

The man accompanying her was a simple guard. The masks always made it difficult to appraise them fully, but the way he held himself indicated his youth.

The poor fool kept glancing at the stunning creature beside him. Jaren scoffed. As if a simple man could ever be worthy of a *zhu* like her. But his distraction would undoubtedly work in Jaren's favor.

He watched her survey the training area, and her eyes seemed to be memorizing the sight as if she didn't expect to see it again. The idea only solidified his plan. He had to act before she disappeared. He unsheathed his twin blades, shuddering at the raw emotion he felt at possessing both.

161

Before giving the guard time to notice his presence, Jaren tapped into his speed and lunged. Pulling his arm back, he was going to slam his blade straight into the man's chest before holding his other to her throat to warn her from screaming. It'd be fluid and fast.

He'd barely darted forward when she moved first. He had to rear back sharply to avoid slamming into her. His senses had scarcely seen her move fast enough to stop his body from impaling itself on the blade she now held.

The guard stood just to her side—eyes comically large. Jaren couldn't risk giving the man the chance to gather his wits, he needed to remove the liability *now*.

The thought had only just entered his head when she seemed to sense it and shifted completely in front of him. Dropping into a stance, she practically glowed in the moonlight as she raised the sword, and a vicious sound tore from her throat.

He hesitated. He couldn't allow the guard to live, not after seeing him this close to the palace. But she was staking a claim. He'd have to get through her first, and that certainly wouldn't help convince her to leave with him.

Fuck, fuck, fuck.

"Take one more step, and I will drive this through your heart." Her voice lowered and vibrated with the strength of her anger.

He couldn't stop the smirk that crept across his face, earning him another growl. He knew better than to underestimate her. She meant every word, but he couldn't deny the thrill it sent under his skin. She was so gods damn beautiful.

"I'd love to see you try, little star." His smirk deepened when she bristled. She didn't appear to appreciate his endearment, which only ensured he'd continue using it.

"Don't move, Trey." The guard had been edging forward, attempting to step around her, but she elbowed him back.

He snapped his head her way. "Dammit, V—"

"I said *don't move*." The words lashed out like a whip, and it was obvious the guard hadn't been expecting her to take charge. He kept looking back and forth between her and Jaren, completely befuddled. Someone was apparently keeping secrets from her little friend.

Never taking her eyes off him, she tightened her grip, "I'm not arrogant enough to claim my skill exceeds your own, but I can assure you, I will not make it easy for you."

The words hadn't even finished leaving her mouth before she darted forward, swinging. He brought both daggers up, blocking her attack, but she only came for him again and again, relentlessly driving him back.

She was a force to be reckoned with, a violent storm that called to his raging soul and demanded he succumb. Her scent was all around him, her anger trying to consume him with the strength of her blows and the flash of her furious gray eyes.

She spun, and he braced himself for the impact of her next blow. But as she moved, her skirt tangled in her legs, just enough to disrupt her momentum. She stumbled forward, straight into Jaren's outstretched blade.

He saw it happening, almost in slow motion, and had only a second to pull back. It wasn't enough to miss her entirely, but it made his dagger graze her side rather than cut straight through.

She hissed, jumping back, and raising her sword again, but he'd already lowered his blades. He may have considered hurting her the first two times they met, but he had no such feelings now. Quite the opposite.

Her eyes flickered down to his daggers as if expecting him to attack her with them at any point. "You got what you came for...just leave." She was breathing heavily, and her side was bleeding, but she kept her defenses up like the warrior she was.

Fighting down the instinct to check her wound, he forced himself to act nonchalant. He held up the dagger that had pierced her skin, flipping it in his hand. "Are you sure about that?"

He needed to hurry. The longer they stood here out in the open, the higher the chance someone would see him and raise the alarm, which was most likely her exact plan. Jaren had to force her hand and make her leave so he could get them somewhere far from the city, and safe.

His voice came out steadier than he felt. "If you fail to beat me, little star, I will slit his throat." He pointed his dagger at her wound. "Are you willing to bet his life?"

She didn't lower her stance, but he saw the flicker of doubt in her eyes. It was there and gone in an instant, but it was enough.

"There's certainly a chance you could still win and kill me where I stand. A small one, but still a chance, nonetheless. However, if you lose, I will not kill you. I will kill *him*." He didn't miss the way she flinched at the threat.

"Or..." he continued, "you can willingly agree to come with me, and I swear I will not kill him. Your choice. But I suggest you choose quickly."

Chapter 15

Vera

"What do you want with me?"

"I'm afraid you'll have to accompany me to find out. But I swear to you upon my life, and our people, that you will come to no harm." He crossed his daggers in front of his chest and gave the barest dip of his head.

Vera shifted her weight and fought the urge to look at Trey to see his reaction. Part of her knew the male was dangerous, knew, without a shadow of a doubt, leaving with a stranger capable of overpowering her was *literally* the stupidest thing she could do.

But the other part of her, the part she'd been hiding for fifteen years, rose to the surface. What if he could answer all her questions? He was Magyki, after all. What if he was her only chance at finding out more about herself?

At her continued silence, he clenched his daggers tighter, as if the idea that she wasn't immediately agreeing irked him. She was tempted to roll her eyes. What did he expect was going to happen?

Lowering her sword an inch, she breathed through the pain radiating from her side. "You said you won't *kill* him if I agree to go, but I want you to swear not to *harm* him either."

She could almost see the tension leave his body at the implication of her words. He opened his mouth to respond, but Trey grabbed her arm, and he emitted a deep warning sound instead, his green eyes flashing.

"What are you thinking? Absolutely not. I swore an oath. Your life over mine. You're not a prize for some Magyki scum to collect."

"Trey—"

"Your life over mine." He tightened his hold on her arm, and with his other hand, tried to pry his sword from her fingers.

Vera maintained her grip and refused to let go. "You can't beat him, so he gets me either way. The only difference is whether or not you live. So shut the fuck up and back off."

"I'd heed her warning if I were you, *tha*." The Magyki grinned, exposing his sharp canines.

"Just because you have no interest in hurting me doesn't mean I feel the same about you, Green Eyes." She saw the barest hint of real humor enter his eyes before he shut it out.

"He already hurt you!" Trey was staring at her like she was completely insane, and maybe she was.

LILIAN T. JAMES

She finally lowered the sword completely and took a step away from her friend. Her side was throbbing in pain, and she didn't need the reminder.

"He didn't do this. This happened because the emperor demanded I play dress-up for him, and I am unaccustomed to fighting in layers," she snapped, gesturing to her gown.

Trey's eyes followed her hand before he turned to Green Eyes, contempt coating every word, "Just tell me what the fuck you want with her."

"That's not going to happen." He pointed one of his daggers in her direction, "I will tell *her* as soon as we leave the capital. But my patience is wearing thin, so I suggest you hurry up, little star."

He looked at her, and after concluding she didn't plan on attacking him again, sheathed his blades and took one long stride toward her.

Vera offered Trey his sword and then reached down and gripped his free hand. She truly believed the Magyki wouldn't intentionally hurt her since he'd already had more than enough opportunities. He needed her for something. But no matter what he promised, she didn't believe for one moment he'd leave her friend untouched, not when Trey could alert the rest of the guard within minutes of their departure.

"I have a condition."

Green Eyes responded with only the raise of a dark eyebrow.

"Trey comes with us." She watched as his lip curled and his hands twitched toward his weapons.

"*Pha.*"

"Yes. You said you'll tell me what you want as soon as we're

167

out of Matherin. I am choosing to temporarily trust you with my life, but that does not mean I trust you explicitly. We both know you have no intention of letting him walk away unharmed."

He didn't bother denying it.

"If you want me willing, you will allow Trey to escort me. Otherwise, I will scream like the delicate damsel this dress makes me appear to be and bring every guard in the vicinity rushing this way."

"Who's to say I won't kill him once we're out?"

"Is your word truly worth so little? Should I question my own safety with you then?" Vera stared him down. For the first time in days, she felt no fear. Just pure conviction.

She was growing tired of men telling her what to do. The emperor wanted to marry her off? Fine. She could understand his reason, no matter how much she detested the idea. But she refused to be pawned off until she knew the truth about Bhasura, and the Magyki was the perfect person to tell her. He thought he was using her, but she would use him right back.

He must have seen something in her eyes because he gave a terse nod and gestured for her to follow. A humorless laugh escaped her lips, causing both him and Trey to glance at her.

"What? You think I'm going to go in this contraption? Yeah, I don't think so. My side will likely stop bleeding the second I get this deathtrap off."

Those piercing eyes darted down to her exposed cleavage, and she nearly growled again. Choosing the high ground, she ignored him, holding her head high as she walked away.

"Will you just listen to me?" Trey was right on her heels,

putting his body between them.

"No. You swore to Eithan to answer to *me*, not the other way around. I'm going, and if you value your life, I suggest you listen and come with me."

Moving toward the back of the armory, she continued, "Elric is inside, so I'm going to sneak through my window to change."

Trey's eyes flickered to the armory, and already knowing what he was thinking, she whipped around and stood a hairsbreadth from his face. "If you even think about alerting Elric and endangering his life, I will stab you myself." He stopped in his tracks, staring at her in shock as she continued around the building.

Vera had just gripped the window ledge to push herself up when she felt hands wrap around her waist. She tried to spin, but the hands held her in place, carefully avoiding her wound. With one smooth motion, she was lifted and positioned to slide easily through the opening without pulling at her side.

As soon as she landed, she twisted to see Green Eyes staring at her from the other side.

"Hurry up." He shot a glare her way and turned, placing his back to the window to give her privacy.

Ignoring the phantom warmth that still spread where those hands had gripped her, Vera darted for the lamp at her bedside, banishing away the creeping shadows.

She could hear a repetitive banging noise coming from the other side of her door and knew Elric was working in the armory. Her heart ached at the thought of how worried he'd be when he discovered her gone. She considered leaving a note, but after recent events, she couldn't bring herself to trust that he wouldn't run to the emperor.

Fighting the burning sensation behind her eyes, she grabbed a pair of clean clothes from her chest and stood. It wasn't until she reached around her back and felt the knotted laces that she realized she had a problem.

"Gods dammit."

Within seconds, Green Eyes had launched himself in the room, making her nearly jump out of her skin. "What's wrong?"

He was looking at her side and his brow creased, probably at how much blood had seeped into the fabric. It wasn't enough to cause her detrimental harm, but it would make her lightheaded soon if she didn't get it wrapped.

"I—" She paused, "Wait, where's Trey?" She wasn't stupid enough to believe he'd leave the guard unattended outside.

"Unconscious."

"*What?!*" She whisper-screamed.

"He'll be fine. Now, tell me what's wrong?" She could see the impatience in his eyes. If she didn't start moving, he'd likely throw her over his shoulder and sprint out like a heathen.

She looked away, fidgeting with her skirts. "I don't wear dresses."

"I've seen you in two *dusing* just today."

"Yes, well, the other was the first one I've ever worn, and it had loose laces and made sense." She bit her lip and looked at him, humiliated. But he just continued staring at her like the aggravating male he was.

Vera glared back at him, hoping her scowl would cover the

blush crawling up her neck, "I can't get this stupid thing off."

His head tipped to the side, and she swore his eyes darkened before he scowled, like her comment had personally offended him. "Then how did you put it on?"

"I sneezed, and it just slipped right over me." She placed a hand on her side, squeezing her eyes shut and sighing when he stayed silent. "I was wrestled into it by a strong-handed lady."

"Hm."

"Gods dammit, Green Eyes, just get this dress off me."

His nostrils flared, and he clenched his jaw, causing the muscles to visibly tighten. Vera could only gape at him as the rest of her body caught up to what her mouth had said. She rolled her lips and spun around. She felt the heat of his stare and desperately tried to level her breathing.

Moving in that silent way of his, he was suddenly standing directly behind her. Vera fought back a shudder as he rested his fingertips at the base of her neck.

"You don't plan on wearing this again?" His breath tickled her ear, sending a trail of gooseflesh across her skin.

"No—"

Before she could say more, his fingers dipped down and gripped the top of her bodice. In one solid movement, he ripped it in half, all the way down to the skirts. The abrupt pull against her torso caused her to lose balance, and she fell backward into his chest, hissing as it jarred her side.

His hands wrapped around her shoulders, steadying her, and she swore she felt his thumbs graze her bare skin before he twisted her to face him. She had to hold the front of the dress to her chest to keep it from falling to the floor. His eyes flicked down to where her hands were curled above her breasts, clutching the fabric, and his expression hardened, an almost palpitating fury pulsing from him.

"How did you get that scar?"

She subconsciously raised a hand and glided it over the base of her throat. His piercing eyes missed nothing and were stripping her soul with the same intimacy he had the first day they met. His pupils dilated, making his gaze even darker, and a warm sensation began to coil inside her.

"It happened a long time ago." Thank gods her voice came out steady even while her pulse threatened to put her in an early grave.

His hands twitched, as if tempted to close the distance between them, but instead he took a large step back, his jaw clenched.

"You have two minutes before I change my mind about your guard." Without waiting for a reply, he turned and was out of the room in a matter of seconds.

As she let the ruined dress fall in a heap at her feet, she realized with crystal clear certainty, she had no idea what the fuck she was doing.

Jaren

DOUBLE-CHECKING THE GUARD WAS STILL SPRAWLED OUT where he'd left him, Jaren allowed his pent-up anger to rumble through his chest. He clenched and unclenched his fists, pacing in a futile attempt to cool his burning skin.

Gods dammit, Green Eyes, just get this dress off me.

Fuck, if her words hadn't zeroed in and gone straight to his cock. He wanted to blame his knee-jerk reaction on the fact he hadn't had a female beneath him in so long, but he couldn't keep lying to himself. That wasn't the reason, and he knew it.

It was just her. There was something about that frustrating *zhu* that called to him and heated his blood. Something beyond just beauty.

As soon as he'd seen the flush crawl up her neck, he'd been unable to resist touching her. Her skin a flawless brown against the pristine white of her gown.

And fuck, if her physical reaction hadn't brought him seconds from exploding, hardening him without her ever having lifted a finger. Even now, her star-fire scent consumed his senses.

Jaren honestly didn't trust what he might've done if he hadn't looked down and noticed the thin scar at the base of her throat. His focus zeroed in on the clear evidence that someone—other than him—had taken a blade to her throat, and he'd almost lost it.

He wanted to know how it happened, why it happened, and by fucking *who*. But she'd barely said anything. The damn female was a mystery. One he very much wanted to solve.

A light scraping sound caught his attention, and he turned to see her stumble through the window, grimacing and clutching her side. Guilt crept forward, but he shoved it back. It was due to her own stubbornness that she'd been injured.

Her face was pink from what had to be quite a violent scrubbing, and she was wearing an outfit almost identical to the one he'd first seen her wear in Midpath.

He crossed his arms as he looked down at her side, "Will you be able to travel a few hours?"

"Yes." She straightened her spine and was about to say something else before she caught sight of the useless guard. She rushed over to check his pulse, her expression carefully blank.

"You promised not to harm him."

"He's fine."

"He'd better wake up."

"He's a liability and will only slow us down."

"Yeah, that tends to happen when you knock someone unconscious." She brushed his hair back and hovered her hand over his mask, indecision written across her face before seeming to come to some silent conclusion.

Jaren didn't back down. "I cannot promise we'll find more than one horse."

"That sounds like poor planning on your part. I will not leave with you alone. Not quietly. Now help me get him up."

Pulling his hood up, he tapped into his strength, grabbed the lifeless man from where she knelt, and tossed him over his shoulder. "Your liability is going to draw attention if we're seen, so pray to the gods it's late enough that no one will be strolling about."

A smile that all but guaranteed she was plotting his demise spread across her face, and he stiffened. Somewhere along the lines, she'd stopped being afraid of him, and even though part of him was pleased, he had a distinct feeling it was going to turn her into an even larger pain in his ass.

THE GODS, INDEED, seemed to be watching over them. Not only were they able to sneak through the shadows virtually unseen, but as they approached the stables, the guard began to groan, shifting in Jaren's hold.

The second they made it safely under the structure, he tossed him unceremoniously to the ground. Angry gray eyes bore into him, and he shrugged.

"Full stable. Looks like your luck is holding out, little star. He needs to be ready by the time I bring them out, or he stays."

Giving them a false sense of privacy, he tapped into his hearing while he prepped two decent-looking mares. He needed to be sure they didn't try to hatch some absurd plan to stab him in the back. If he happened to hear anything else—like her name— even better.

"I'm so sorry, Trey."

"No, I'm sorry. Anything could have happened to you while I was out. Are you all right?"

"I'll be fine. Don't worry about me. How are you feeling?"

"Rejuvenated."

A small huff of laughter. "You're an idiot."

"I'm pretty sure out of the two of us, you fit that description a little more than me right now."

A heavy pause. "I have to do this, Trey. I did it to save your life, but also because I'm shamelessly selfish. I want answers."

"I get it. Your life over mine. I'm with you." A slight shuffle, as if he'd moved closer…

Fuck that.

"Let's move," Jaren threw their way as he led the two mares out into the open night air.

He glared at them as they approached, sneering his displeasure at the guard before handing him the reins to the smaller mare. Then he tipped his head back and curled his finger in her direction.

"You ride with me."

She shuffled closer to the guard. "No, thank you."

"I wasn't asking."

As she opened her mouth—no doubt to voice another pointless protest—he cut her off, "You. Ride. With. Me."

And gods dammit if a zap of adrenaline didn't spike through his stupid ass when she held her ground in a firm stare-off. Jaren's look might have turned a little unhinged because she seemed to conclude that he wasn't going to change his mind.

Grumbling in defeat, she conceded with an exaggerated roll of her eyes, and the sight had the predator in him purring at the thrill of exerting his dominance over her. Schooling his expression as she stomped toward him was a feat in itself.

On instinct, he reached out to help her mount, but the vixen slapped his hand and launched herself up onto the mare. She turned away from him, but that didn't prevent him from catching the flinch she tried to hide. She was still wounded, and it was annoying how much it bothered him.

Fixing a carefully blank gaze on him, she arched an eyebrow and asked, "So, what now?"

"Unless the love tap to my head warped my ability to gauge time, I'd estimate a shift change should be occurring within the hour, probably half." Jaren felt the loss of her stare as she turned her attention to Trey. He spoke reluctantly, understandably unhappy about providing Jaren with any form of intel.

"If the goal is to leave the capital, the eastern gate is the best choice since we station the grunts there at night."

Jaren swallowed down his irritation and nodded to indicate he heard. The information was useful, but that didn't mean he wanted to feel fucking grateful for it. The man would have a dagger in his chest and a beast chewing on his corpse if Jaren had his way.

"Slide forward, little star."

Her eyes narrowed, but she complied. With one quick push, he heaved himself up and over the back of the horse to straddle her body with his own. Pure, male satisfaction rumbled deep in his chest at how perfectly she fit.

Given he was almost a foot taller, her head didn't quite reach his chin. If she leaned back into him, he could hold her against his chest without impeding his ability to scout or ride at all.

She tried scooting forward to separate them, but the movement only succeeded in rubbing her ass against him in a way that nearly had him groaning. Catching Trey's scowl, Jaren couldn't stop himself from flashing an arrogant smile.

He reached around her and she stiffened, looking back, and snaring him with those gray eyes. It only lasted a moment before she faced front again, but it was enough to shoot fire through his veins.

Gripping the reins tighter than necessary, he guided their dark mare out onto the cobbled street. He needed to get his shit together before she felt more than just his legs against her. He was positive she'd stab him if she knew half the images he'd just conjured up in his head.

Instead, he ignored the warmth of her body and urged them to move faster toward the edge of the city, Trey keeping pace at their side.

"Emperor Matheris doesn't enforce strict tabs on the people who choose to leave. He cares more about who comes in." He aimed a pointed look Jaren's way. "If we approach during the shift change, I doubt we'll get more than a cursory glance. But we'll definitely be noticed when I bring you back, so you need to be prepared for that."

Her small body jolted back, and instinct had Jaren whipping an arm to hover over a dagger. But then he noticed what she was staring at. *Who* she was staring at.

"You took off your mask!"

Trey smiled at her, his teeth a vivid white against his skin. And to Jaren's irritation, a carefree laugh burst from her lips.

"I knew it. I knew you'd have an amazing smile. I'm honestly surprised they let you join the guard at all with a face like that."

"Why is that?" Jaren asked, succumbing to his desire to draw her attention back over. She looked up at him and her lips quirked.

"Didn't you know? Women aren't allowed to join the Matherin guard. Since a lack of capability and skill is obviously not the reason, I assumed it had to do with some inane requirement to look masculine."

Trey raised an eyebrow and scoffed, "Are you saying I look feminine?"

"You're definitely too pretty." She laughed, and dammit if the sound didn't make Jaren draw in a little closer. Thankfully, before Trey could resume flirting, the gate appeared in the distance. They all went on alert.

"You're still in uniform, Trey. And your pretty face won't distract anyone from your sword." Untying her cloak, she tossed it at him. "These guards won't recognize me, and I can blend in far better than you."

Murmuring his agreement, Trey threw the cloak over his form and weapon. It would've been too small if he'd been standing, but it worked well enough on horseback.

His attention still on the man next to him, Jaren didn't register her movement until her entire form had already leaned into him. As the back of her head tucked next to his neck, he inhaled sharply, and her scent slammed down his throat. He froze, grinding his jaw back and forth.

Fuck. Fuck. *Fuck.*

"What...are you doing?" He gritted out between clenched teeth.

She ignored him, reaching around his body to grab the edges of his cloak and pulling it around herself, hiding most of her body. She stayed just like that, cuddled into him, the side of her face resting against his neck the entire way to the gate. The wind shifted her loose curls, and the brush of them on his skin mixed with the warmth of her body set him ablaze.

He forced himself to focus on their surroundings, Trey doing the same. And he had to hand it to the annoying man—he'd been right. The guards stationed at the gate looked tired and eager for their replacements. They glanced at their group, but seeing nothing of interest, they just nodded before looking away, bored.

As they rode past the outskirts of the city, Jaren felt a weight release from his chest. He'd been waiting for Trey to attempt something as they passed the guards, but he must have known his chances were slim to none with her pressed so close to Jaren.

He barely kept the manic grin from taking over his face. He'd successfully stolen the *zhu* from Sulian, and that knowledge alone was almost heady.

Now he just needed a nice cliff for Trey to accidentally fall off of, and everything would be going to plan.

Chapter
16
Vera

She was content. Her stress had all but disappeared, and she was tempted to close her eyes and fall into an easy, blissful sleep.

The cocoon she'd formed around herself chased away the chill of the night, and she shifted to get more comfortable, causing her nose to graze against something warm. An earthy smell caressed her senses, and blurry memories assaulted the walls of her mind.

The scent settled her and reminded her of her childhood, of *before*. Of laughter and chases, late-night mischief, and innocent pleasures. Why was it so familiar? She pressed her nose more firmly against the warmth, allowing the smell to curl around her.

She all but melted when she felt the soft brush of fingers stroking her cheek, purring at the sensation. When they glided over to caress just behind her ear, Vera's eyes shot open, and she launched herself forward. A wave of dizziness crashed into her, and she tipped sideways. If not for the strong arms holding the reins on either side of her, she would have face-planted right off the horse.

"Relax, little star. *Phrino mbi thothori.*" You are safe.

He gripped her waist gently and pulled her back. She wanted to argue, to fight back, to do anything other than give in, but her body refused to obey. She felt short of breath, and her head dropped against him like a dead weight, lulling to the side.

"She's in no condition to keep going. We'll head to the forest line and stop just long enough for me to check the extent of her injury." The vibrations in his chest rumbled up her spine with each of his words.

Trey's voice came from the right, and if she possessed any function of her limbs, she might've jumped. Her mind was so fuzzy, she'd almost completely forgotten he was with them. "I'll take care of her."

The body wrapped around her stiffened. "Her life over yours, right?"

"Yes," came the clipped reply.

"Then I suggest you fall back and follow like a good guard dog, because out of the two of us, only I can help her heal, Matherin."

She couldn't help but appreciate his ability to make *Matherin* sound more like a vulgar insult than a name. She chuckled, drawing his attention.

"You're good at that," she mumbled into his neck.

"At what?" A shudder went through his body.

"Being an ass."

Vera wasn't sure if he replied, the black dots that had been trickling into her vision finally taking hold and pulling her under, but she swore she heard a soft laugh.

"CHOOSE YOUR NEXT move carefully. Deal or not, I will watch you bleed out at my feet if you do not back up."

"That's an empty threat, and we both know it. You want her cooperation, and for the moment, that requires my heart to stay beating. So again, remove your hands from her person, before I make you."

A dark chuckle, "I would truly love to see you try."

Vera felt awareness creep up and she reached for it, trying to latch on. But the lull of sleep still clutched at her, trying to entice her back down.

"I said, remove your hands from her clothing, Magyki."

Wait...what? Her clothing? Her confusion helped clear more of the fogginess around her mind until she became aware of hands gliding up the naked skin of her lower stomach. Her eyes flew open, and she sat up so fast the world tilted, and she barely had time to twist to the side before vomiting.

"What—" she said between heaves, "are you doing?" She clutched her side as it burned and screamed with each spasm of her body. Trey came around and crouched in front of her, concern pulsing from him in droves.

"Are you okay?"

"Yeah." She sat back, scooting away from the puddle of bile and inhaling slowly to settle her stomach. "Just a little woozy. Where are we?"

"Not far enough."

She turned to look at the piercing green eyes of the male kneeling at her other side. "You passed out. I need to check your wound if you have any hope of staying conscious."

Trey glowered at him, but he had a point. Traveling with an injury was irresponsible, and she definitely didn't want to lose consciousness again.

"Fine."

Ignoring the disagreeing grumble next to her, she scooted farther away before lowering herself to the ground and peeling her tunic up just enough to expose the cut. She bit her lip, fighting to stay still when he leaned over her and gently pressed around it.

Murmuring almost to himself, he said, "It's a clean cut." She didn't doubt that. She knew from experience how sharp his daggers were.

"I just needed to confirm since you wouldn't be strong enough to heal from anything more significant. Drink some water. If necessary, there's food in my pack to help replenish your energy before sealing the cut." He shifted back, ready to stand.

"Oh, is that all?" Vera couldn't refrain from rolling her eyes. "A little food and water, and suddenly the throbbing wound will no longer be of concern. How silly of me."

Eyes narrowing, he leaned in, invading her personal space. His gaze moved over her face, trying to find the answer to a question he hadn't asked. He suddenly grabbed her arms and hauled her up into a sitting position. Crossing his legs and sitting directly in front of her, he seemed more annoyed than anything.

"How much do you know about your heritage? Do you not even know what you're capable of?"

Vera bristled at his tone and nervously glanced at Trey, still crouched a few feet away from her.

"If he hasn't figured it out yet, he isn't worthy of being your guard. Now, answer my question."

She ignored him, looking up into Trey's brown eyes. She was so terrified of losing her only friend, she couldn't even form words. She feared his rejection more than she wanted to admit, but Trey gave her an encouraging smile as if her unvoiced question was painted on her forehead.

"I figured it out when you aggressively stole my sword."

"Was it the growl?"

"It was definitely the growl."

She laughed, tension leaving her body like a tidal wave. It jarred her side, and dizziness threatened to knock her out, but she shook her head and concentrated on the Magyki.

His frustrated expression had her sighing, tempted to roll her eyes again. "No, Green Eyes, I don't know anything. My mentor was not lax with my education, but for my safety, he did not allow me books about Bhasura. I was encouraged to push the limits of my strength and speed, but heritage-wise, that was it. The less I knew the better."

His expression turned thunderous. "Were those his words, or yours?"

"Both. Although, I no longer believe it."

He was quiet, contemplating what she'd admitted. "Jaren Barilias."

Her body snapped to attention. "What?" The only part of her that dared to move was her heart as it pounded rapidly in her chest.

"*A aprenza.*"

Something knocked at the walls of her mind. A memory, barely more than a fuzzy photograph in her mind's eye, attempted to surface. That name. She knew that name. She tried to dig it out, but the more she grappled with the memory, the faster it disappeared.

His head tilted to the side, brows raised, and she realized she'd spent several moments gawking at him. Mentally chastising herself for acting like a fool, she let the sense of familiarity fade to the back of her mind. She'd probably just heard a similar name once.

He seemed to be waiting for her to return the favor, and she fidgeted. Her thoughts raced over what the emperor had said about the rebellion and her family's deaths. She didn't know where Jaren stood, or who his loyalties were to. She needed to be careful.

"Varian Lesta."

"That's not your name."

She shrugged, "It's one of them."

He glanced away from her, and she swore she saw disappointment flicker over his face. "If you expect me to be honest, I would like the same from you."

"Let me ask you this, Jaren." His eyes snapped to hers, heat flaring in their depths. "I was told Bhasura suffered major casualties when a rebellion took arms and murdered Queen Vaneara and most of the noble families. Is that true?"

Eyes narrowed; he gave a short nod. "That is a crude summary of the events that occurred, but yes."

"Then I'm sorry, but I don't trust you enough to give you any other name. But if it means anything, I'm not lying. I almost always go by Varian outside the armory walls."

Jaren's eyes roved over her face and down her body at her answer, as if desperately trying to unravel her secrets. She knew her answer had given away a hint about who she might be, but he didn't push for more.

"No. Fucking. Way."

She almost jumped out of her skin. Both she and Jaren turned to Trey, her in confusion and he in irritation. He was staring at her with the biggest smile she'd ever seen before he burst out laughing.

"Varian," he said when he caught his breath, "*You're* Varian? You're the toothpick who knocked Prince Eithan on his ass?"

"He told you?"

Trey's smile didn't waver. If anything, it grew. "No. Jensen did. Said it was the best thing he'd ever seen."

"Jensen?" she asked, brows crinkling.

"Brex Jensen? You had to have seen him. He's been training under Lesta for years. Giant of a man with hands the size of your head."

She sat up straighter. "You mean Boulder Shoulders? I didn't even know he talked."

"I've known him my whole life. We practically grew up together. He definitely talks. And he wasn't the only one that night. Damn. You know, I think you just became my new best friend."

Vera's heart burst with his words, his acceptance almost too much to bear. Closing her eyes briefly against the sting of her unshed tears, she shook her head. The action made her sway, and Jaren reached forward and gripped her arm.

"*Thyip.*" Focus.

It seemed someone didn't appreciate it when she failed to give him her undivided attention. Vera honestly didn't really care, but she decided not to snap back and listened. They needed to move, and that meant she needed to heal.

"Fine. What did you mean about me being able to heal myself?"

"You have the blessing of the gods running through your blood, just as every Magyki does, but it is not fully unlocked yet."

More like stolen from the gods, but she didn't say that. "How can you tell I'm not...unlocked?"

"Your appearance. We are born possessing remnants of power through our bloodlines, but besides minor physical differences, we still resemble humans."

His eyes flickered to her ears. "Fully unlocked Magyki have traits like mine and can no longer easily pass for human, whereas, even if your ears hadn't been mutilated, you still could."

She nodded, storing the information away. It was unreal to

finally have the chance to learn about herself and her people.

Jaren continued, "For now, you should still be able to tap into a small portion of power."

"Is this so-called *power* the reason why I always seem to be able to see and smell you when no one else notices you?" The corner of his lips twitched, and she figured she probably could have kept the whole *smelling him* part to herself.

"Even locked, your natural senses are superior to humans," he couldn't have looked more smug if he tried. "And you can also self-heal small injuries. You won't be able to fully heal like I can yet, but you should be able to recover from your blood loss."

"How?"

"Meditation."

Vera tried, she really tried not to glare at him. "Lovely. So can you maybe explain *how* I meditate the blood back into my body?"

"Do you trust me?"

"No." Her response was instant, but instead of seeming angry, he almost looked like he was holding back a smile.

"I meant do you trust me in this instance?" he asked, and she noticed his hand was still gripping her arm from when he'd steadied her.

"In this instance, and only this instance, yes."

Jaren looked at Trey, his expression fierce. "Back up, Matherin."

When he didn't move, Vera gestured at him to listen. He sighed, taking several steps back before planting his feet, arms crossed.

"If you succeed, it will not hurt, but it won't exactly feel comfortable either. It will be similar to feeling uncharacteristically warm."

His green eyes locked on hers as the hand on her arm moved across her breast to rest over her heart. His palm was hot against her chest, and his lips tightened into a thin line.

"Close your eyes, steady your breathing, and focus on your heartbeats until you can feel each beat individually as they pump blood throughout your body."

She found it difficult to breathe with him touching her and looking at her like that, but she obeyed. She wasn't sure how long she sat there, tense and painfully aware of his presence, before she finally settled into a semi-sense of calm.

She had no idea what she was doing, but she heeded his advice and focused on her heart, imagining how it felt and moved. The more she relaxed into it, the more she started to sense something else there. It was almost like another substance flowing with her blood—an essence that pulsed with each pump of her heart. She pictured herself reaching in and touching it.

"*Dodz watsrang*, little star. Now, direct it through your body and show it what you want. Picture your body healing."

The hand resting on her chest pressed in, and she felt his other gently wrap around her throat, over her pulse. She shut it out, pushing everything away until it was all just background noise.

She focused on that humming power and reached toward it again, urging it to expand, to flow through her body and make her whole. It instantly reacted, flaring bright and hot inside her.

Her back arched and she gasped, trying to shove it back, but no longer able to control it. She felt Jaren's hands grasp her face, but the heat continued building until she was burning from the inside out, fire consuming her body and soul.

Throwing her head back, the power exploded through her like star fire, and she screamed.

Chapter 17

Eithan

Walking back inside was the hardest thing Eithan had ever done. He should be the one to escort her back to her room. Gods knew he wanted to. He wanted to send his guards off and bask in her tentative smiles and nervous mannerisms, maybe even steal a goodnight kiss.

He sighed, leaning his forehead against the wall. She needed her space. Like always, Sulian had pushed too hard. The poor woman had honestly looked seconds away from a full-fledged panic attack.

He'd go back for her tomorrow. He knew he could win her over, one night wouldn't change that. It's not like she'd choose to stay in the armory over the life he could give her in the palace. She just needed the space and time to calm down, and she'd understand.

So rather than rush outside like a man possessed, he dismissed an amused—and too observant for his own good—Coleman for the night and attempted to speak to *his father*. Only to be turned away, the men standing outside the emperor's door claiming he'd "retired for the night."

Bullshit. Eithan knew his earlier interference in helping Vera escape had angered the temperamental man. Sulian would likely spend the rest of the night contemplating the best way to make him regret it. Typical.

Brushing it off, he returned to his rooms. After a quick bath, he spent the next few hours immersing himself in Bhasurian texts. He'd had the scribes in the royal library locate them earlier. Halfway through the second one, he was so engulfed, the sound of frantic knocking had him almost throwing it.

Coleman entered, breathing heavily. "I'm sorry for disturbing you, Your Highness, but Lesta came barreling into the barracks asking for an audience with you."

Sliding his legs off the bed, he threw on a tunic and snatched his boots. "Did he say anything else?"

"Just that it was urgent. Something to do with Miss Vera."

No. No, no, no. He'd never raced across the grounds so fast in his life, all the while praying it wasn't what he feared. That she hadn't chosen to run. When Eithan approached the armory and saw Elric's haggard face, his stomach plummeted.

She hadn't run.

He now stood, unmoving, in her deserted room. From a glance, nothing was amiss. The bed was made and the floor clean.

Not a single thing seemed out of place. Nothing would have even warranted him to worry if it weren't for that damn dress.

He stared down at the garment clenched in his fists. It'd only been a handful of hours since he'd last seen the gown, admiring how the fabric clung and accentuated her beautiful figure.

Now, the sight of it made him sick. There was a cut in the side of the bodice, the blood below it partially dried. Whatever happened had to have occurred almost as soon as he'd left her.

But even that wasn't what had his blood boiling. It was the back of the dress, torn almost completely in half. His jaw popped, and his stomach roiled when he considered what horrors might have taken place in that room. And where the fuck was Gibson?

Lesta came to stand next to him. He had large circles under his eyes and looked every bit his age.

"Tell me what you're thinking, Lesta."

"I'm thinking we should assume it was the same Magyki male as before, Your Highness."

"It is certainly plausible, yes, but there are other possibilities. Tonight, the emperor informed Vera of his intention for us to wed. Oddly coincidental, is it not?"

Lesta made a choking sound but rushed to cover it with a shake of his head. He disagreed with that assessment, and regardless of what Eithan had just said, he did too. The state of her dress indicated a struggle. Not to mention the fact that Gibson was also missing.

"It still could've been any man who attacked her. Gibson escorted her, and I trust him with my life. My hope is that he followed whoever took her and will bring her back home safely."

The older man crossed his arms, frowning.

"Speak freely, Lesta. If you know something, it is in her best interest, and yours, that you state it."

He seemed to be having a silent battle with himself, and the nervous twitching of his face had Eithan widening his stance. If his Weapons' Master looked nervous, it couldn't be good.

"Your Highness, I must urge you to believe me when I say it was no Matherin who took her."

"Explain." Eithan's stomach clenched with unease when Lesta's face fell. He looked exhausted and resigned.

"I raised Vera the same way I would have raised a child of my own. I taught her to read and count, as well as how to safely care for and sharpen a blade. But that is not all I taught her." He sighed, rubbing his hand across his head.

"Do you remember the lad you sparred? You called him a toothpick."

The sudden change in conversation threw him, but Eithan nodded. Of course, he remembered. It'd been the best bout he'd had in months. "Varian was the lad, if I recall."

Lesta laughed, but it was hollow. "She only goes by Varian when she needs to protect herself. The individual you sparred was Vera."

Eithan stared at him for several long, tense moments. That was preposterous. He would've noticed if he'd fought a woman. "No woman could have sparred like that."

Lesta shook his head, eyes narrowed in distaste. "That's what your father has raised you to believe, but that doesn't make it true. Vera's skill is exceptional, and it is not because of her sex or heritage."

Eithan swore the floor swayed underneath him. "So, what you're saying is I got my ass handed to me...by the same woman I plan to marry?"

Lesta released a raspy chuckle. "What I'm telling you is she is capable of kicking almost any man's ass. But she barely survived her fight with the Magyki the first time around. She's remarkable, but his abilities make him fully capable of something like this." He gestured to the ruined dress.

Snapping his mouth closed, Eithan turned to him, narrowing his eyes. "You could be imprisoned for this. For teaching her to use a weapon and hiding it from your emperor. Why risk it?"

"With all due respect, Your Highness, I did exactly what His Majesty demanded of me." He didn't look the least bit ashamed. "When Vera was brought to me, I was given a single order—to protect her. I not only did that, but I taught her how to protect herself if I were ever unable to."

Eithan didn't respond. There was honestly nothing left to say. All that mattered was getting Vera back. He needed to speak to Sulian. Giving a parting nod, he spun on his heel and strode out of the chamber, still clutching the dress in his hands.

He would've been happy with the marital arrangement for the sole fact of what Vera was and what an alliance with her could give him. Their marriage could change everything. He needed to get her back, and when he did, he'd irrevocably tie her to him.

Jaren

HE FELT HER *LUZH* RESPOND THE MOMENT SHE REACHED OUT and touched it. Every Magyki's ability stemmed from the same base source. They didn't all have different pools to dip into, rather they all accessed and took from the same one.

Because of this, when nearby, Magyki could sense when another was tapping into it, although it was far easier to do through touch. Wanting to instruct and encourage her, Jaren placed his hand over her heart.

Of course, he could have just pressed his fingers against the pulse in her wrist, but why waste the opportunity? He'd never claimed to be a gentleman. He enjoyed toeing the edge of her boundaries, just to see what she would do.

He felt a small jolt of pride when Varian was able to fall deep into her meditation with no issue. It was impressive for someone as inexperienced as she was. As time passed and the further she reached, the more drawn he became to her. It felt like she wasn't just calling up her own reserves, but also his.

He couldn't fight against her pull, his body demanding he move closer. She might as well have dug her nails into his chest and yanked. He placed his other hand at her neck, almost hypnotized, trying to get a more accurate feel of what was happening. He felt the snap and reflexively grabbed at her face to shake her, grab her, throw her. Something, *anything*.

But it was too late.

In a vibrant, golden light, Varian's power exploded out of her, and he was thrown several feet away. He saw Trey tossed even farther behind him. Jaren tried to stand, but the scream that tore from her throat shot straight to his chest, dropping him to his knees, his limbs shaking from the weight of it.

It didn't make sense. She'd never been near the crystals, let alone touched them. She shouldn't have been able to access more than the barest layer she'd been born with. She screamed again, and his body flinched from the agony in it.

In his peripheral, he saw Trey trying to move toward her. "*Pha!* Don't touch her!"

Trey's head whipped in his direction, his hand grabbing for his sword. "What the fuck did you do to her?!"

Jaren pushed to his feet again, prepared to tackle the guard if he took another step when the world seemed to pause. Just a second of pure silence before all the power radiating from her suddenly reversed, snapping back into her body. Her eyes rolled back, and he lurched for her as she fell backward.

Reaching her, he barely kept himself from collapsing in shock when he saw her face. It was still her, but at the same time, it wasn't. Her cheekbones were higher, her jaw sharper, and when her eyes fluttered open, vibrant silver stared back at him.

"Did I do it?"

The words should have been raspy and broken from her screaming, but her voice came out strong. The circles that had been resting under her eyes all night were gone, and her skin was practically glowing.

He lifted her tunic just enough to glance at her side. Smooth, unblemished skin greeted him. Shit. She hadn't just healed her wound. She'd done far more than that.

Jaren looked back into her eyes, the liquid steel color leaving him momentarily speechless. She'd been breathtaking before, but now her beauty was nearly catastrophic.

"Did you do what? Somehow connect and draw directly from a power source you've never actually touched before? Yeah, yeah, I'd say you did."

She frowned. "Wait...what?"

She blinked several times before her eyes widened, and her tongue slid over one of the sharp canines now occupying her mouth. The act was sexy as fuck, and he hoped to gods she didn't notice his body's response as he helped her sit up.

Trey hovered behind them, radiating tension, but clearly unsure of what to do. He was like one of those annoying insects, constantly buzzing around your face no matter how many times you swatted it away.

"I'm guessing that wasn't what was supposed to happen." She paused, looking up at him with narrowed eyes. "You said it wouldn't hurt."

"It shouldn't have. Your access should've been similar to that of a child. Enough for mild healing and the most basic of abilities, but not what you just did. I don't even know what you just did."

"So, then what happened? I did exactly as you told me to and it just..." Her eyes unfocused as she tried to find the words. "It exploded. One second it was at my fingertips, and the next it wasn't. Gods, I couldn't control it." She shivered.

"I think you somehow unlocked your full reserve of power, and without access to the *laskas*. I've never heard of it happening before, so I can't explain it. But I also can't deny what I saw. Your entire appearance is pure Magyki now."

He watched her reach for her ears, disappointment flickering on her face when her fingers met the still round, scarred tops. She dropped her hands into her lap. "The crystals? Is that what the relic from the gods is?"

Shit. His head whipped to the side, and he glared at Trey, contemplating killing him all over again. There was no way Jaren could let the Matherin live after everything he'd witnessed and heard. Following his line of sight, Varian's eyes narrowed.

"He's my friend, Jaren." He turned his glare on her instead, and she added, "I suppose I shouldn't expect a misanthrope like you to understand."

Oh, he understood friendship just fine, he just didn't give a shit about anyone else's apart from his own. He wasn't one for mercy. He killed without remorse, without wondering or caring whose friend, sibling, or lover they might be.

But as she held his gaze, he knew he wouldn't kill the guard. Not yet. The damn *zhu* made him weak, and it pissed him off.

"We've been here too long. We'll lose the cover of night soon and need to put more distance behind us, especially considering anyone within miles would have heard you."

He didn't wait to see if she'd reply, not caring if his dismissal angered her. She could join the club. He headed for the horses that had thankfully been tied far enough away to avoid her power display. They were skittish though, and he took a few moments to calm both them and himself.

Even if he hadn't heard her approach, Jaren would have

sensed her presence. From the moment they met, he couldn't shake the connection his body seemed to have to hers, but it felt even stronger now. She didn't say a word as she mounted Darling and leaned forward to pet the mare's neck. Why she'd decided to name it, he had no fucking idea.

He looked over to see Trey mounting his as well, the guard's eyes trained on her face, taking in her physical changes. He looked frightened, and for once Jaren had to agree with him. What she'd just done was unheard of.

Pulling his attention back, he threw himself up behind her slight frame, eager to have her close no matter how frustrating she was. The second he pressed his chest to her back something sparked between them where they touched, like lightning. She yelped, flinching away.

"What in Aleron was that?" She twisted, looking over her shoulder at him, brows drawn as if he'd done it on purpose.

"Just excess energy. You're practically pulsing with the power you tapped into."

Her eyes narrowed, but she accepted his answer and faced forward, if not a little stiff. It hadn't been a lie, but it hadn't been the entire truth either. Jaren's power still pushed against him, seeking to get to her, the remnants of the spark echoing in his core.

He reached around her for the reins, and his chest grazed her back again, but instead of another jolt, something he'd buried deep inside seemed to shudder in relief. His power pushed toward her one last time before finally settling.

An instinctual part of him understood what the feeling

meant, but he denied it with every fiber of his being. He knew without a shadow of a doubt it wasn't possible. There had to be another explanation.

Jaren spurred Darling into a gallop, a sudden sense of urgency biting at his heels. The only thing he knew for sure was there was something about her. Something important he couldn't quite put his finger on, and fate kept whispering in his ear, urging him to get her home as soon as possible.

THEY TRAVELED NONSTOP through the rest of the dark hours and into the morning, only stopping when the horses could go no farther. They'd made decent ground, but Jaren's skin still prickled with the need to keep moving.

Confident she wouldn't leave without receiving whatever answers she so desperately sought, he left her with Trey to see to the beasts and consume a meager meal. He hadn't packed much food to begin with, and now with an extra mouth to feed, they wouldn't have enough to make it to Eastshore. They'd have to stop in either Kilmire or Midpath to stock up.

Gods, he hated that damn guard.

They'd left the main road heading east, choosing instead to take a longer route. It was a rough path that cut through the Lakewood Forest. It didn't appear to have been used in years, barely even visible through the overgrowth. But it would hopefully keep them from encountering other travelers.

They were a few hours outside of Kilmire, but Jaren still

scouted the entire area, making sure there was no indication of another soul around.

The distance from her helped clear his head, but that tug remained. If he were to fall asleep, he knew he'd wake up instantly knowing where she was. He fisted his hands, digging his nails into his palms. He shouldn't be feeling this way about some random *zhu*, no matter how beautiful and enticing she was.

It had to be because of his physical reaction to her. Maybe if he fucked her, he could rid himself of this constant awareness. He hated it. Even as he turned back toward their camp—toward her—he hated it.

It felt like a betrayal to his mate's memory. But even as his chest clenched at the thought of betraying her, he still let the connection *tug, tug, tug* at him, back to that burning star.

Chapter
18

Vera

She felt the daggers Trey stared into the back of her head while she tended to the horses. She didn't blame him. Although she hadn't seen herself yet, she'd moved her fingers along her face and felt the changes.

Strangely enough, the changes in her appearance didn't bother her as much as she would have expected. Even with the power Jaren claimed she'd accessed; she didn't *feel* any different. But she did feel self-conscious about how Trey might see her now, especially considering the new teeth that screamed *I'm not human.*

So, she stayed hunched over their travel pack as long as she could, pretending not to notice his stare. She only lasted about ten minutes with his silent scrutiny before she'd thrown the pack down in defeat.

"Just ask whatever it is you want to ask. I'm not an idiot, I know you have questions."

Twisting to look at him over her shoulder, she met his gaze as he ambled toward her. His posture was more relaxed now that Jaren wasn't close by, and her heart lurched with guilt at everything she was putting him through.

"I have dozens of questions, but only one of them is important." He plopped to the ground next to her, snatching the dried meat she'd pulled out for herself. She elbowed him playfully in the side before she dug back into the pack for a water flask.

When he didn't immediately continue, she looked up and caught a glimmer of mischief in his eyes.

"I guess what I really need to know is…what do I smell like?"

She elbowed him harder that time but found herself laughing, nonetheless. "That's your important question?" She shook her head, smiling. "There is no way I'm talking to you about your smell, Trey."

"Come on, you told Jaren you smelled him, so I know you've taken a nice little whiff of me too. I want to know what I smell like to your *superior* senses."

She tried to elbow him a third time, but he jumped up, narrowly avoiding her. She stood, as well, stalking him as he backed away, his face drawn into a mock-serious expression.

In a deadpan voice, she said, "You smell like sweat and desperation."

He feigned outrage; a hand clutched at his heart. "You wound me. Must you lie? We both know, if anything, I smell like sex and temptation."

She launched herself at him, but he'd been expecting it. He

dodged her first few blows before she finally landed a solid hit to his stomach, eliciting a satisfying grunt. She stepped back, fighting a grin, ready to knock him to the ground when the hair on the back of her neck rose, and the air tensed around them.

"Don't stop on my account, we all know I'd enjoy seeing him eat dirt."

She turned toward his voice. Jaren stood just behind them, arms crossed, the corner of his lips pulled up in a smirk. She was glad he didn't seem to have overheard their conversation. That is until Trey opened his big mouth.

"We were just discussing my enticing smell. It seems she can't admit her attraction to me without needing to get physical." He winked, and she felt her cheeks warm.

Her reaction only seemed to encourage him. His entire face lit up, and he wiggled his eyebrows. "Come on, *Varian*, tell Jaren how sexy I smell."

"Gods! How am I supposed to know what sex smells like? You just smell like a pig-headed man!"

It wasn't until she was met with silence, and she looked between the two wide-eyed stares, that she realized what she'd just admitted. Her cheeks went from warm to flaming, and she bit her bottom lip to keep from throwing curses at Trey's stupid face.

It was Jaren who finally spoke, "Have you never had sex before?"

She glared at him in response, appalled he would be so forward with such a personal question. As her extended silence answered for her, tension built between them. He tilted his head in that predatory way of his as he continued looking at her.

"I don't know why you're surprised," she snapped. "I basically spent the last fifteen years of my life alone."

Her hands fisted at her sides, embarrassment coating her like a second skin. More than anything, she hated that it bothered her. It wasn't her fault she hadn't been allowed the chance to meet someone. Just because she hadn't had sex didn't mean she'd never *wanted* to.

"Well, now you know." Trey stepped up next to her, "Because I promise you, that's exactly what I smell like."

He wasn't fast enough to avoid the answering punch she delivered to his gut.

"SINCE I HAVE an unwanted mouth to feed, we need more provisions to make it to Eastshore. We're only a few hours outside of Kilmire, but I have no intention of stopping in a town within easy reach of Sulian."

Jaren was back to his irritable self, and he seemed to be growing more and more restless by the minute.

"Eastshore? That's several days' worth of travel from here. You told her you would explain what it is you want as soon as she was safely outside the capital. We're plenty far."

Vera wasn't sure if Trey was reckless enough to attack Jaren, but his posture made her seriously wonder if he'd give it a try.

"From what I've gathered from the two of you, she is quite valuable to Sulian and his brat. By now they'll have discovered she's gone, so no, we are not plenty far. I am headed to Eastshore.

She may join for as long as she desires, but by all means, feel free to stay behind. Preferably six-feet underground."

Vera stepped forward before Trey could spit a reply that was sure to start a fight. "So is your plan to stop in Midpath then?"

"*Ÿe.*"

"There could easily be soldiers there, just as well as in Kilmire," she said.

"Word will travel to Kilmire far faster; whereas, no one in Midpath will be looking for you yet. As long as your guard dog behaves, we should be able to rest and replenish without any trouble." She caught his unvoiced question. He wanted to know how long she'd stay.

"I'm not some toy you can string along with only the promise of information, Jaren. I won't follow you forever. I have duties I'm neglecting, and someone who will be worried about me."

"Like who? The *chinbi srol*? What do you think the princeling's going to say when he sees you now? Your rounded ears won't hide what you are anymore. Every inch of you screams enemy."

She flinched. She'd been referring to Elric, but the truth of Jaren's words still stung. Technically, Eithan knew she wasn't human, but she'd at least looked like one. To have the truth visually shoved in his face every time he looked at her now? Would he want that? Elric loved her, but even he might be wary of her now.

"We need to put more miles behind us if we have any hope of making it to Midpath before dark tomorrow. You may ask questions on the way, but I have my own as well. A truth for a truth. Deal?"

She glanced at Trey, who was shaking his head. She knew she should listen and head back with him, back to safety and the life she knew. But she found with each mile they traveled, it became easier and easier to keep going.

Jaren knew all about where she came from and could tell her about her history, and maybe even her family. The emperor may have known Vera's surname, but regardless of what he claimed, he didn't know everything. If she returned, she had a feeling the emperor would never let her out of his sight again. She'd truly be locked away, knowing no more than she currently did.

"Deal."

She saw the brief look of hurt that crossed Trey's face, and tried to pretend it didn't cut her in half. She walked toward her friend and took his hand, begging him with her eyes to understand.

"Emperor Matheris wants to use me, Trey. That's always been his plan. Eithan may have been willing to give me time to come to terms with my future, but the emperor will never give me a choice. This is the first taste of freedom I've ever had, and when I return, it will be the *only* taste I'll ever have. So, forgive me if I'm not eager to slip on my chains."

He wasn't happy, but his face softened, and he pulled her into a hug. He was only a few inches taller, so when he chuckled, his breath brushed against her ear, making her shudder.

"You truly are the worst noble woman I've ever met, but you're still my favorite person."

Vera stepped out of his embrace, her eyes stinging, but her

smile fell when she saw Jaren. He was glaring at them with such heat, she wondered how many ways he was imagining their deaths, or more specifically, Trey's.

She looked to the sky, begging the gods for patience. "If your eyebrows drop any lower, you'll trip over them." He didn't react. He just watched her mount before following.

She shuddered as he slid behind her. Ever since her healing episode, every time Jaren's body came into contact with her own, it caused a flutter of energy to erupt. It wasn't as strong as the spark that had jumped between them before, but more like the very essence of her was purring, like her soul itself craved his closeness.

He settled in and directed them back toward the road, and she couldn't help but close her eyes and breathe him in. There was something about him that settled her.

At first, she thought maybe it was because she'd been deprived of physical touch for so long, but she didn't feel the same when she embraced Trey. Only Jaren.

Vera loved the way he towered over her when he stood too close, forcing her to crane her neck to make eye contact, the way his earthy smell surrounded her, and his thighs pressed against her own as they traveled.

She may have been inexperienced in the pleasures two willing people could partake in together, but she wasn't completely naïve of the pleasures of the flesh. She'd explored her own body enough to know what tightened her core and pushed her over the edge.

She found herself wondering what it would be like to have him touch her that way. Wondered how it might feel to have his weight press down on top of her, the corded muscles of his arms caging her in.

A jarring motion behind her broke the spell. She was overheated, a tingling sensation building inside her, and she had the urge to squeeze her legs together. Gods, what in Aleron had gotten into her? She dared a peek over her shoulder, only to be ensnared by vibrant chips of emerald.

Jaren was staring at her as if nothing, and no one else, existed but the two of them. His nostrils flared, and his eyes seemed to darken as a light rumble in his chest vibrated against her, turning the tingling sensation into a pounding throb. She spun forward again.

She felt pressure against her lower back, but it vanished just as quickly when Jaren shifted away from her. His posture was stiff, and Vera convinced herself he was probably just still irritated. She was just imagining things because there was no way he knew what she was thinking. Right?

Jaren

HE WAS PISSED. THERE WAS NO WAY OF DENYING IT.

By the time he'd thrown himself up behind her, his anger was palpable. Seeing how comfortable she was embracing Trey, along with the smile she gave him, had every inch of Jaren craving violence. No Matherin man would ever deserve her affection.

It didn't help that Jaren's possessive instinct to snatch her away and saw the guard's hands off only further increased his anger. She wasn't his to possess.

He was so caught up in his irrational thoughts, he was in no way prepared for the sudden flare of arousal that hit him. The shock of it almost knocked him clean over. He'd barely tightened his legs and gripped the reins fast enough to keep balance, and it took a moment for his head to catch up with his body.

Yinlanem dupye.

She was aroused. Gazing off into the distance, nestled between his legs, she was fantasizing vividly enough for her scent to be drenched in it. And gods, did he hope it had something to do with him.

He sat straighter, fighting the urge to take her right then and there. The desire was so strong, he swore he could see exactly how it would play out.

He'd wrap his hands around her waist, pulling her off the horse, and pinning her to his chest. He'd release her just enough for her body to deliberately slide down his own before ravaging her mouth, hands burrowed in her hair, freeing it to curl around her shoulders. He'd lay her out right there in the road, pressing his body down onto hers, grinding against her core until they lost their minds.

He'd tear her clothes from her body, unable to wait another moment before feeling her, skin to skin. He'd finally see the firm breasts he'd felt and pull a nipple into his mouth before biting down, making her groan and buck beneath him.

He'd fuck her with his tongue like it was his only purpose in life, forcing her to scream his name before he thrust into her. He'd make sure she never forgot it was *he* who'd had her first. He'd ruin her from ever daring to desire another.

Sensing his stare, or more likely his mind-blowing arousal, she glanced back at him. She looked shy, as if nervous he might know what was on her mind. That look alone was all it took for Jaren to confirm she'd indeed been thinking about him, and his cock strained painfully against his pants.

He couldn't restrain the responding rumble that crawled up his chest as he imagined sinking his teeth into the delicate neck before him, claiming her as he forced her to swear herself to him and only him. To cover her scent with his own and mark her as *his*. Because he couldn't deny it any longer, he wanted her. Every single inch.

Eyes wide, she turned back around, and Jaren found himself having to shift back. If he allowed her warm body to press against his throbbing length, he knew he wouldn't be able to resist touching her. And he sure wasn't going to do that with their current company.

Jaren glared daggers at the back of Trey's head, riding ahead of them. He'd never wanted to throw a dagger at someone as much as he wanted to do it to that damn guard.

But luckily for all of them, his violent thoughts were interrupted by his little star, her voice was hesitant and hoarse. "So, a truth for a truth?"

He shifted again, trying in vain to readjust himself and get more comfortable without rubbing his erection against her back. "*Ÿe.*"

She tilted her head, thinking. "How old are you? I know your—our—people age differently than I'm familiar with."

"Twenty-five. What's your real name?"

She shook her head, "Nice try. If I have to answer honestly, I suppose I can't answer at all. I'm not ready to tell you that."

"Fine. How much Thyabathi do you speak?"

"I was once fluent, or as fluent as a child can be, but I'm out of practice. Are you a type of soldier?"

"In a way, yes, I am a *shuthish*. What does Sulian want with you?"

Her hands clenched into fists on her thighs. Jaren knew if he could see her entire face, her delicate brows would be pinched, and she'd be biting that plush bottom lip he so desperately wanted to kiss.

"He wants me to marry Prince Eithan."

He jerked, accidentally yanking the reins and causing Darling to rear back before he recovered enough to calm her and continue moving. Of everything he'd imagined, that had not been the answer.

"Why the fuck would he want that?"

"He said a marriage between our people had the potential to open communication and be the first step toward an alliance. He desires trade and peace."

Jaren scoffed. He highly doubted that's what Sulian's true goal was, but his plan certainly wouldn't fail. If King Vesstan discovered Sulian had stolen and forced a *zhu* to marry his son, he'd open communication all right. It just wouldn't be peaceful.

"Sulian doesn't care about fostering peace between our people. He has other plans, I guarantee it."

"I already figured as much." Her voice was flat. Resigned.

"So, when's the big wedding?" Jaren couldn't control the sarcasm dripping from his voice. The thought of her marrying the Matherin prince had him grinding his teeth.

"I didn't agree to anything." Her voice came out with more strength than her last comment, but her shoulders were tensed in a clear indication she either didn't like talking about it, or didn't like the idea period.

"So—"

"You've asked three questions now. It's my turn." She twisted around to look at him, and he shrugged. He wanted to demand she tell him more, but he'd wait.

She was silent, roving her eyes over his face and pausing on his lips. "What did you mean when you called me untainted?"

Jaren considered her for a moment. He hadn't realized he'd uttered that out loud, but he'd been in such shock, it didn't exactly surprise him. He'd promised the truth, and this truth might be the best way to convince her to stay with him.

"Our island has slowly begun to die. The *laskas* that strengthens our people and our land are growing weak. The soil is less fertile, the water levels lower, and our people no longer have access to the same amount of power they used to have.

"They are falling ill, unable to completely heal, and they are dying younger than ever before. Everything is tainted with the *laskas'* sickness, but we have no idea how to fix it."

"But you don't believe that I carry this sickness?"

"All I know is you have not stepped foot on Bhasura since it began, so you were likely untouched by its taint. I am even more convinced now that I've seen the strength of what you can tap into.

However, there's also the chance that you've somehow connected to the *laskas*, so you could now be tainted as well. I don't know."

She didn't respond, lost in her thoughts. Jaren wanted to tell her she should return with him either way. Tell her she belonged on Bhasura with her people. With him. But he didn't.

Instead, he tapped her thigh, pulling her from her thoughts to look up at him. "My turn again. Do you want to marry? Become a Matherin princess?"

Jaren was needling her, but he couldn't move past it. Couldn't get over the idea of the pretty-faced princeling having her, touching her, using her for whatever game he and Sulian were playing.

With irritation, he saw in his peripheral that Trey had pulled back to be within earshot. He wasn't looking at them, but he was definitely listening. Apparently, Jaren wasn't the only one who was curious about her answer.

"Why do you care?"

"General curiosity, I suppose." He smiled wickedly at her, exposing the tips of his canines.

Her lips parted, and he watched, unable to look away, as her eyes went slightly unfocused. His pulse spiked, and he nudged himself forward to press firmly against her as he leaned down and whispered in her ear.

"You haven't answered my question." With utter delight, his eyes followed the gooseflesh trailing across her delicate skin.

"I'm not naïve enough to believe the emperor will give me a choice. Marrying his son was the only reason he saved me." Her voice sounded small, as if she'd already accepted a future she didn't want. The sound tore at him, demanding he bring her fire back to the surface.

"What do you mean, saved you?" He tried to peer around to see her face, but she turned her head, avoiding his eyes. A fiercely protective instinct began to knock at his chest.

"You don't seem like the type of female who wants to be *kept*. So, what is it that you want, little star?"

"It's my turn."

He narrowed his eyes. "*Pha*. Admit it. Just admit the truth. You don't want that future. Say it."

"I don't want to be a pawn! I don't want to be tucked away in a palace for the rest of my life, only useful for my name and womb." The words lashed out, like curses torn from her throat. She paused, and her body shook as she took a deep breath.

Jaren didn't think she'd say more, and he didn't push further. She'd said exactly what he'd been waiting for. Exactly what he needed to convince both himself and her to leave together. The corners of his lips had just begun to lift when a whisper of words, barely audible, hit his ears. They echoed straight into his soul.

"I'm tired of being invisible."

"You could never be invisible, little star. You burn too bright. Sulian may seek to hide you away, to steal your future and crush your spirit, but even he could not hope to smother the intensity of your fire. You are more than the pretty trophy he wants you to be."

He tapped the underside of her chin and let his fingers caress her jaw as he pulled away. "You know I speak truth. You can feel fate whispering in your ear as strongly as I can. I'll be here when you decide to follow it."

Chapter 19

Eithan

"I know I've disappointed you, Father."

"You cannot even begin to fathom the extent of how I feel."

"Father—"

"Disgusted is a more accurate description."

Eithan's hands curled into fists, but he forced his face to remain blank. This wasn't the first time Sulian had forced him to appear before him for punishment, and it wouldn't be the last. He wanted to get a rise out of him, but Eithan had learned long ago how to shut out his emotions.

After twenty-six years, he was quite skilled at hiding his true feelings. He stood still, his court mask in place, letting it all fester. No matter how violent or desperate the storm inside him brewed, he never allowed it past his walls. He refused. He'd hold off until later when he could control it in a more constructive outlet.

He bowed at the waist, "Forgive me, Father."

Silence.

The midnight blue carpet mocked him as the minutes ticked by, and he remained frozen in a deep bow, his spine screaming at maintaining the position. He took a slow, steady breath and held it for a count of five before releasing it, prepared for the long haul. It was just another power move, a chance for Sulian to revel in exerting his control.

Once, when Eithan was still a boy, he'd been caught trying to sneak out of the palace. His father had sent a servant to inform him of his mother and unborn sister's deaths, not even bothering to tell him, himself. Distraught and confused, Eithan had run.

He hadn't planned on any specific destination. He'd just needed to escape, needed the chance to understand and come to terms with his anguish while safely outside of the suffocating, stone walls.

As punishment for his display of weakness, he'd received two lashes before being forced to bow, hands behind his back, at the foot of the dais until his body gave out. He'd fallen, face first, unable to catch himself. The ugly carpet doing nothing to soften the impact.

He may have only watched one parent be buried, but both his parents died that night—if his father had ever existed in the first place. From that day forward, Eithan cemented his court mask to his face, perfecting his ability to smile for his father on the outside, while raging at Emperor Sulian on the inside.

He didn't expect anything less degrading today, especially given the allegations. So, he continued the cycle—inhale, hold, exhale—refusing to show weakness. He'd walked into the throne room prepared, anticipating a drawn-out punishment.

Vera was gone, and it was entirely Eithan's fault. Most of his anger wasn't even directed at Sulian, but himself. He'd had her in his hands, literally, and he'd let her slip away.

"You may rise."

He forced his body to rise steadily, not daring to express the relief he felt with the blood no longer rushing to his head. He looked up at Sulian, seated on his monstrous, stone throne, and willed his face to remain blank.

"Did you know, this morning after your complete and utter failure, a stable boy reported two horses missing? It appears they were taken during the night."

Eithan fought against his jolt of surprise. Two horses? Had she gone willingly after all? Or had there been more than one attacker? He clenched his jaw to avoid voicing a demand to speak to the boy.

Instead, he replied in an even voice, "Since they have not been caught, it would be safe to assume they escaped the capital." Internally, his mind was saying so much more. Where would she have been taken? And for what purpose?

"Escape. Interesting word choice." Sulian smiled down at him, and it was a cruel thing. "They did not escape. They simply walked right out from under your nose." He stood, smothering Eithan under his demeaning stare.

"Yes, Father."

Eithan watched him take a step down the dais stairs and stop. It was his favorite stance. He liked to make his subjects nervous, questioning whether he'd remain next to his throne or if he'd descend to their level.

It never ended well when he descended.

"I had all the guards on duty at each gate questioned, of course."

He struggled to maintain his composure, damning the arrogant bastard for dragging out the information.

"It appears, late last night, a group of three individuals left on horseback through the eastern gate. The guards claim one of them—a small woman—was asleep, tucked closely into the arms of a man."

For the first time in years, Eithan's mask slipped, his nostrils flaring as he ground his teeth together. His spine straightened, and the desire to run out of the room and start issuing orders to his men was strong.

It was no coincidence. That had to have been Vera. After seeing the state of her dress, if she'd appeared asleep, he had no doubt she'd been unconscious. The thought made his anger rise to a terrifying height.

"The guards have been dealt with," Sulian continued, either unaware or uncaring of the pressure rising in Eithan's chest. "Your guard, however..."

The unfinished sentence finally brought his attention away from his dangerous train of thought. "You're referring to Trey Gibson?"

"It all played out quite conveniently, did it not? Her *attacker* knew exactly when to act. Then, not an hour later, two men were seen leaving with a sleeping woman through a gate guarded by some of our newest recruits."

Eithan bristled. "If you are suggesting that Gibson had any part in Vera's abduction, I must respectfully disagree. I hand-pick my guards myself. They are loyal."

Sulian cocked his head with a condescending smile. "Yes, but your decisions lately don't exactly make you seem entirely reliable, now do they?" He descended the rest of the stairs, his large strides eating up the distance until he invaded Eithan's space. He locked his legs, refusing to cower before the man.

"If you had behaved like the Crown Prince should have and demanded she stay and accept her place, she never would have left the palace walls. She'd have been safely put away, waiting for you, and you'd be halfway to having a Magyki in your hand and in your bed."

Eithan didn't argue. He couldn't. The accusation was painfully true. He remembered the way she'd blushed every time he'd given her his undivided attention, the red hue gorgeous against her skin. She'd been isolated her entire life, sheltered, innocent, and untouched. It would have been easy to woo her.

Yet, at the same time, she was somehow still feisty and strong. He still couldn't believe such a shy creature had fought with the brutal skill she'd possessed. What he'd give to know what had gone through her head every time they'd interacted since that day.

She'd challenged him for the sole purpose of defending her mentor. She was loyal and protective when someone she respected was insulted, but she was somehow still a quiet and unsure woman outside of a fight.

It was alluring and addicting. He wanted her back more than anything he'd ever wanted in his life. Not because his bastard of a father wanted her, but because *he* did.

His thoughts flew through his head in a silent response to his father's sharp words before he controlled himself enough to speak with a steady voice. "With your permission, I will leave the city with my remaining guards and follow their trail. They cannot have gotten far."

Sulian stepped closer until he was only inches away. "Fifteen years, boy. I have waited fifteen years for her to grow into her usefulness. Fifteen years of making sure she stayed hidden and simple-minded, so she'd be ready to be swept off her feet." His voice grew louder with each word, spittle landing on Eithan's face. *"I could not have made it any easier for you!"*

They were the same size, but somehow Eithan still felt small. When it was all said and done, he was just a worthless means to an end for this man. The unwelcome feeling rotted his insides.

He'd hated Sulian for as long as he could remember, but at that moment, he wanted the man to *know*. Wanted him to see the truth of what he'd created in Eithan's eyes. But he pushed it back, his mask back in place.

"I understand, Father."

"No, I don't think you do." Sulian leaned back and proceeded to tell him something that changed nothing—yet changed *everything*.

He felt the blood drain from his face, his shock a tangible thing. "I will find her, Father, I swear it."

Staring at Eithan for another furious moment, he finally stepped back. He raked his eyes down his form, disgust apparent on every inch of his face.

"Let us hope your word holds a little more weight this time. For I will punish you and every one of your guards who dares come back empty-handed." Turning his back and effectively dismissing Eithan, he strode to the dais, where he'd most likely stew and scheme for the next hour.

Eithan didn't hesitate. He spun, aiming for the doors. Not even waiting for the guards to open them, he pushed through himself, heading straight to his men's barracks.

He would find her.

Vera

WHEN THE SUN FINALLY SET, JAREN RELUCTANTLY LED THEM deeper into the forest to rest for the night. He clearly didn't want to stop, but the horses needed a break, and even he could do with some rest.

She'd noticed dark circles beginning to linger under his eyes like he hadn't slept in several days. She assumed he could heal himself, but he hadn't bothered. He'd never admit it, but she wondered if maybe he just didn't have the energy.

They tied the horses in a clearing with easy access to a river, before Jaren took off to scout, leaving Vera and Trey to set up camp. Something told her he wouldn't approve of them starting a fire, but Trey didn't seem the least bit worried and did it anyway.

She relaxed into their comfortable friendship and easy banter as he attempted to teach her how to start a fire. Although he didn't waste a single opportunity to tease her, he was patient and she squealed with joy when flames finally grew.

When Jaren returned, he circled them, glancing down at the flames and frowning, but blessedly refrained from commenting. She almost heaved a sigh of relief. She didn't have nearly enough energy for a lecture.

Slouching on the ground across from them, he picked at the food Vera had set out for him, and she felt the corner of her mouth lift in a small smile. He acted so tough and merciless, but she was starting to think it was just a mask. The more worn out he became, the more it seemed to slip.

She took a long drink of water before removing her cloak and wadding it up. Curling up as close to the fire as she safely could, she propped the bundled cloak underneath her head and yawned. Even the hard ground was no match for her exhaustion.

"If you wanted to cuddle, all you had to do was ask. I know a few ways we can keep warm without the use of a fire."

She tilted her head to throw Trey a mock glare. She hadn't realized how close she'd gotten to him when she'd laid down. She should've known his ornery ass wouldn't keep quiet about it.

"But, of course," he continued, "if you'd rather work off the day's stress first, I certainly wouldn't say no." He winked, and it took every drop of self-control she had not to laugh. Instead, she forced herself to form a bored expression.

"Being left unfulfilled and disappointed doesn't sound like the most enticing way to fall asleep."

Trey looked genuinely offended, but after a slight pause, he let out a strangled laugh and settled down next to her. "Damn, woman, give a man a chance."

Mere seconds passed before she felt Jaren come around to lay on her other side as if she and Trey needed a chaperone. She wondered if all Magyki males were over-protective of females, or if it was just because he distrusted Trey.

As Vera laid there, in the middle of nowhere with two people she barely knew, she couldn't help but think about how surreal her life had become. In only a matter of days, everything she'd known had been completely turned upside down.

The Crown Prince had proposed to her—kind of—and now here she was, sleeping under the stars, miles away from home with a proclaimed enemy. Gods, *she* now looked like the enemy. She flicked her tongue over her teeth, wondering how long it'd take to get used to them.

What would Eithan think of her when Trey told him everything? It would happen eventually, and Vera had no idea what he'd do. He'd likely be disgusted and accuse her of sullying herself, and she wasn't sure she cared. She'd never be able to be herself around him, and that just wasn't a future she wanted.

It was his own father who'd forbade women from training and fighting. Not to mention, he'd only saved her because of what he hoped to gain through her, not because she mattered as a person.

She wanted to believe Eithan was different, but she refused to trust her future to a wild hope. There was a high chance the apple didn't fall far from the tree, and she was tired of being smothered by misogynistic men.

Jaren was right. There was a voice whispering in her head, telling her she had so much more to offer than what the Matheris men wanted. She was strong, she could fight, and she needed to stop being ashamed of it.

She rolled over, already knowing Jaren was looking at her. She'd felt the heat of his stare since the moment he'd laid down. They both needed sleep, but his mind was apparently just as busy as her own.

His eyes seemed to devour her as they stared at each other. Neither said a word. She was scared to tell him the truth about her family, scared to trust that he hadn't supported the rebellion and wouldn't betray her. But as she laid there, she realized she wanted to tell him. Something in her craved his trust and acceptance.

She inched her arm toward him, stopping to rest her fingertips a hairsbreadth from his own. He didn't move, his eyes darting to their hands and then back to her face.

"I'm not against the idea of an alliance, I think it'd be wonderful. But I don't want to marry Eithan. Not because of who he is, but because I selfishly don't want a marriage that has politics as its foundation," she admitted, part of her hoping Trey was already asleep and wouldn't hear. She knew he'd protect her, but she wasn't sure if that protection extended toward his prince.

"Then don't."

She almost told him right then that she wanted to go to Bhasura with him. She wanted to see her true home, meet people who had known her family, and learn more about the taint and the crystals. But something held her back, a lingering fear he'd change his mind, and she'd be abandoned all over again.

The rational side of her knew he wouldn't, knew he believed she should never have been on Aleron to begin with. But the other side, the side that had experienced loneliness her entire life, was terrified of his possible rejection.

So instead, Vera pulled her arm back, tucking it under her head, and closed her eyes. She wasn't sure how long she laid there before sleep finally took over, but the last thing she remembered thinking was no matter how much she'd miss Elric, she never wanted to go back to the armory.

Chapter 20

Vera

The following day went by uneventfully. Jaren woke them just before the sun, pacing like a caged animal eager to escape.

They ate a quick, meager breakfast and took turns washing at the river. Vera had no qualms admitting she smelled at that point—they all did—so she opted to strip and bathe completely.

Ignoring Jaren's order for her to hurry, she submerged herself, scrubbing vigorously at her scalp. Between the humid air of the forest and her hasty finger-combing, her hair was bound to look worse coming out than it had going in. She'd just surfaced, her back to the bank, attempting to wrangle her tangled hair into a plait, when she sensed his approach.

Her entire body responded. Her heart rate increased, heat

crawled up her neck, and tiny hairs across her skin rose to attention. She glanced over her shoulder, only to be accosted by the sight of Jaren's bare chest, and her throat closed. He wasn't the first male she'd seen half naked, she'd caught sight of plenty of topless guards throughout the years, but he was by far the most attractive she'd ever seen. While the majority of Matherin guards were wide and bulky, Jaren was lean and sinewy.

Dragging her gaze up his body, she jolted at the intensity of his glower. He wasn't staring at her face, but at her bared back, as if the sight of it infuriated him.

"I tell you to hurry, yet somehow you translated that to mean you could turn the river into your own personal *wushech*?"

His eyes lingered on her back, and she sensed something else swirling and mixing with his anger—something stronger. "I won't apologize for having good hygiene. Now leave so I can get out."

His eyes finally flickered up to hers, flaring slightly, before he spun and stomped off. Well, maybe not stomped. She didn't think Jaren was capable of stomping. Even his angry movements were graceful.

She had barely come within sight of their camp when he brushed past her to take his turn at the river. Moving toward the horses, she spoke quietly to them, desperately trying *not* to think about Jaren half naked and wet.

She choked on a breath when he returned, his face smooth and clean. Beneath the shadow of facial hair he'd grown, she'd almost forgotten how sharp his jawline was. Had he seriously shaved with nothing but the murky water to show his reflection? And why did she find the image of him bent over the water, gliding his blade across his skin, to be so incredibly attractive?

They swiftly took off once they'd all finished. After her quiet confession the night before, Jaren seemed more willing to talk.

"Why are you on Aleron?" she dared to ask.

Jaren was quiet for so long, she didn't think he would answer. "Duty."

She nodded, attempting to hide her disappointment at his curt, vague response. "Your duty as a soldier?"

"Yes, and no. I swore an oath to King Vesstan. I do whatever he requests of me."

She glanced up at him, "How long have you worked for the king?"

"Since I was ten." His hands tightened on the reins and his words were clipped, dissuading her from further questions. He'd likely shut down entirely if she pushed. So, pasting a smile on her face, she asked about Bhasura instead. She wanted to know everything about it.

She listened with rapt attention as he described the vast woods that surrounded Bhasura's main city, the unique animals inhabited there that couldn't be found on Aleron, and the soft beauty of their beaches. It was obvious he missed it.

Not once did he provide a single detail about the cities or people, unwilling to share in Trey's presence. He'd never trust a Matherin guard with that kind of information, especially one who was a personal guard of the prince. She couldn't blame him.

So, they kept to safer topics. He wanted to know every minute detail about her and how she'd grown up, and in return, he helped her refresh her understanding of their language. Having gone so long without speaking Thyabathi, her pronunciation was abysmal, but she remembered more than she thought she did. She could hold a conversation in it as long as Jaren spoke slowly.

She told him about Elric. How he taught her to care and handle blades, and how she'd badgered him until he'd agreed to train her. Jaren didn't say much, but he listened with rapt attention, and his noncommittal grunt was enough to tell her he had mild respect for Elric. And for some reason, it made her happy.

When she confirmed their meeting at Midpath had been the first time she'd ever been allowed to leave, she thought he might turn them back to Matherin, just so he could throw a dagger in the emperor's chest.

His body had transformed into a flesh-covered statue, and he was gripping the reins so tightly, she thought they'd break. He didn't ask any more questions after that, choosing instead to stew in angry silence.

After a half hour of him sitting tensed to snap, Vera finally turned to look at him. When he begrudgingly made eye contact, she didn't say a word, just gave him a small smile and patted his thigh. Although his eyes still looked angry, he'd relaxed under her touch, and they rode in companionable silence for the rest of the afternoon.

Trey never said much, but she knew he'd listened to everything she and Jaren said. He was always alert, and ever since they left, she'd noticed his fingers constantly moving against his saddle. The sight made her sick with guilt, knowing it was her fault he was stressed and his thoughts chaotic.

He pretended to be easygoing, but she'd learned he used humor to brush off his actual emotions. She knew he was upset and anxious about the predicament she'd landed them in, and she didn't know what to say to fix it.

He didn't finally start to ease up until Midpath came within sight. The promise of a fresh meal and warm beds instantly improving his mood. But Jaren had them stop a few miles outside the edge of the city.

He was on high alert, and she knew he was tempted to risk traveling without the added provisions just so they wouldn't have to take the risk. He locked his spine and crossed his arms as he stared down at Trey.

"I may have threatened her to get her out of Matherin, but from this point forward, she is accompanying me of her own free will. I am not forcing her to go any farther."

"I wouldn't let you."

Jaren smirked. "You're like a yappy *tha*, barking to seem bigger than you are, but you're no pushover, and I respect that. However, this is where we part ways. Make no mistake, I want to kill you."

He glanced at her but continued speaking to Trey. "I gave her my word, so I won't. But if she chooses to stay and you try to interfere, it will not end well for you."

They both looked at her, and Vera fidgeted under the pressure of their stares. She knew what she wanted. And for the first time in her life, she was actually being allowed to choose it.

Stepping toward Trey, she took his hand, "I know you feel like it's your duty to protect me, but I can protect myself." She

233

gripped his fingers, her eyes burning, "I'm going with him, Trey. Bhasura is my home, and I want to see it."

He inhaled sharply, and his face bounced from shock to hurt. He ripped his hand from her grasp, and her heart cracked straight down the middle. His lip curled, causing his nose to scrunch up, and he looked at her like he no longer knew who she was.

"Your home is back in Matherin with the people who love you."

"That's a lie and you know it. I only had Elric, and he lied to my face and kept me shut away for fifteen years, pretending it was only for my safety. He cared, but not enough."

"*I* care about you, Vera. Prince Eithan cares about you."

She shook her head. She needed him to understand, needed him to not hate her for her decision. "If he does, it's only because—"

She choked on her words when Trey went flying backward, his body sliding across the ground. Dust clouds billowed around him, and he groaned. She opened her mouth to yell, but it caught in her throat when Jaren suddenly stood before her, snatching at her face with both hands.

She flinched, instinctively trying to pull away, but his look of utter devastation had her freezing in place. He didn't appear to be breathing, and he stared at her as if she might vanish into thin air.

Vera's breathing turned erratic, and her heart started pounding when his piercing eyes locked onto her own. When she finally remembered how to pull in air, his earthy scent was all she knew. It was so thick she couldn't focus on anything else.

She wasn't experienced with sensing emotions in that way,

but she understood enough to know the sharp change in his scent coincided with the expression on his face. Something was wrong, but she had no idea what.

"*Rab žu mbi thoots pash?*" The words came out hoarse like he'd torn them straight from his chest.

She didn't answer. She couldn't. She could barely concentrate past the intensity pulsing from him and smothering her. She'd never seen him express anything more than anger and the occasional shock. Nothing like this, and it frightened her.

"What's wrong, Jaren?"

Tightening his hold on her face, he shook her head, desperation clinging to him, "*What did he call you?!*"

She grabbed at his wrists, holding herself steady from his jarring movements. She could see Trey in her peripheral, creeping closer. His hand hovered over his sword, ready to intervene if necessary.

She continued gazing into those green eyes, so bright and still so familiar, seeing something there that brought the truth to her lips.

"He called me Vera." Her eyes flickered down to his parted lips, and she could have sworn she felt tremors in the hands palming her cheeks.

"Veralie?"

She pulled back, feeling like he'd struck her, but his hands were still clutching her, holding her in place. Her eyes whipped up, wide, and her heart beat faster and faster. How did he know that?

She thought back over all their conversations. She'd never

said anything that could have hinted at who she was. There was no way he'd know Vera was only a nickname unless he knew her from…before.

She forced her lips to move, "How do you know that?"

He relaxed his grip, and she felt a nervous warmth spread through her as his fingers caressed her scarred ears, his eyes never once leaving hers. She didn't even think he'd blinked since grabbing her.

She tightened her grip on his wrists, "Jaren."

Hearing his name seemed to snap whatever spell he'd been under, and he shook his head. "It's not possible."

His gaze dropped to her throat, a hand moving down to swipe a thumb across where she knew he'd seen her scar. His eyes flared, darkening. "I watched you die."

Her world was spinning, her mind trying and failing to keep up with what was happening. "I don't know what you mean. I have no memory of Bhasura, Jaren. Just random images that come to me in dreams." She swallowed, "I don't understand."

Understatement of the century.

"They took you," his voice cracked. "I watched my own blade slice your throat right in front of me. I failed you so horrifically that night, Veralie." His voice was guttural and raw, "Apparently, I've never stopped failing you. How could I not know—"

Her heart lurched. His pain was visceral, coating her and seeping into her pores. She didn't know what he was talking about, not even a little, but the pain in his eyes was so acute she couldn't ignore it.

Releasing his wrists, she stepped closer until her chest

brushed against him and wrapped her arms around his waist. He didn't hesitate, his arms immediately snaking around her, one hand flat against her back while the other cradled her head under his chin.

"Okay, so...feel free to explain at any time."

Vera raised her head at the sound of Trey's voice. He stood awkwardly to the side and looked uncomfortable and confused. With a start, she realized they'd switched to Thyabathi, and she hadn't even noticed. Her emotions had simply taken over, and she'd slipped into it naturally.

Releasing Jaren, she took a small step back, switching to the common tongue. "Tell me everything."

Jaren

HER NERVOUS SMILE DESTROYED HIM. HIS FINGERS twitched, desperate to hold her again, to kiss her and bury his nose in her hair, to completely lose himself in her. "I'll tell you whatever you want to know, little star." His resolve almost shattered when she sent a half-hearted glare up at him.

Veralie.

His *aitanta*.

She was his fucking mate. It was like the veil covering his eyes had been ripped off. Everything suddenly made sense—every single fucking thing. What he felt? That tug? It was their soul bond.

Emotion choked him, and he felt lightheaded. It was weak

and buried behind years of loneliness, but the bond was real. It existed. *She* existed.

She'd only been five when he last saw her. A child. She looked so incredibly different; he wasn't sure if he ever would have seen it on his own. She was breathtaking and fierce, and *his*.

Mating bonds grew stronger over time, maturing as they aged into adulthood. How the bond felt to him as a child was different from how it felt now. Even weak, he could tell the difference.

As kids, he'd felt compelled to comfort and protect her, but now as he looked down her form, his compulsions were far more possessive.

He was so sure he'd watched her die that night. He'd watched her bleed out before being knocked unconscious. When he'd awoken, his fathers were hovering over him, and her body and attackers were gone. Nothing remained but the scent of her blood on the floor.

Jaren had buried his heart under so much anguish and self-hatred, he never would have believed what he now felt so clearly, stupidly believing it to be lust. And now that he knew, he couldn't think past his need for her. As his soul acknowledged who she was, it demanded he take her and complete their bond.

"I remember your eyes," she said, pulling him from his thoughts. "I mean, I didn't know it was *you*, but I sometimes dreamed of eyes just like yours."

She frowned, her gaze unfocused. "When I first saw you, I had this overwhelming feeling like I knew you. I thought it maybe had to do with you being Magyki."

Jaren cringed, thinking back to how close he'd come to ending her life in Midpath. Would he have known the second her heart stopped beating? Would he have been forced to stand there, helpless, watching her die all over again?

"Are we related? Is that why you're so familiar to me?"

His head reared back, a choking sound leaving his throat.

"Gods, no, we're not related."

His chest thrummed with satisfaction at her look of relief. "We were raised together under my fathers' roof, but not because we're family. We're more than that, Veralie. We're mates."

Her head tilted to the side, "What does that mean?"

Sadness swept through him. His little star had no real memory of him, no knowledge of her people, and no understanding of the profound connection they could form. As much as he wanted to rush with her, make up for the fifteen years they'd spent apart, he knew he'd have to go at her pace. She didn't see him the way he saw her. Not yet.

"It's something I can explain in depth later when we're settled for the evening." *And alone.* He looked over her shoulder at Trey, still hovering near them like a lost mutt.

Jaren couldn't help but smirk when Trey looked at him. "It means that I am yours, and you are mine. The pull you feel deep in your chest? The impulse to be near me? It's a soul bond. A connection between two Magyki that no one, and nothing, can replace."

She looked at her feet, biting her bottom lip and causing his body to heat. He wanted to pull that lip into his mouth and experience what it was like to sink his own teeth into the soft, plush flesh.

"Then why didn't you recognize it until now?"

He reached for a rogue curl, tucking it behind her ear. "I have no experience with a mature bond, Veralie. We were just kids, and then you..." He sighed, moving his hand to rub the back of his neck.

"The years apart have weakened our bond, but it's still there. Our bodies have known from the moment we touched. Our minds were simply in denial. I know you feel the same."

Desire shot through him when fire lit up her eyes, the silver color turning molten. "And what is it that I feel, Jaren?" She attempted to put space between them, but he reached out and yanked on her hand, pulling her flush against him.

"You want me just as badly as I want you, little star."

Her eyes narrowed, and she honestly looked ready to punch him, but her body told him otherwise. Her arousal went straight to his already semi-hard length, that star-fire scent teasing him with the thought of her taste.

He knew she could feel him pressed up against her stomach. She pushed away, her face flaming red, but didn't refute his claim. Raising her chin, she somehow found a way to stare up at him while simultaneously looking down her nose at him.

He was in awe of her. He knew she was inexperienced, knew—with no small amount of pleasure—that no other male had yet to touch her, but although easily embarrassed, she didn't feel shame for anything she felt. She didn't hide or deny her desires, and it was so fucking enticing.

"Gods, Vera, this is insane. You can't be serious. Mates? Like he has some animalistic claim on you? He's done nothing but manipulate you this entire time."

Jaren whipped his head toward Trey, a snarl bursting from his lips when the guard dared to reach for his star. He'd kill him. He'd fucking kill him right now if he laid so much as a finger on her.

Trey's eyes flicked to him, and sensing his impending death, he wisely lowered his outstretched arm.

Veralie stepped between them with one arm spread in both their directions. "Just stop! You hate him, and he hates you. We all get it. It doesn't matter whether he and I have this soul bond or whatever," she said, making him bristle. "I already told you I was going with him, Trey. And I meant it. I'm leaving."

He smiled at the guard, letting every malicious and cruel thought fuel his expression. Trey's anger was potent in the air, and the predator in him reveled in it. Jaren hoped the guard choked on the truth.

"No, Vera. I am your friend, and that means telling you when you're being insane, even if you don't want to hear it. You truly believe the male you just happened to run into while he was *stalking our Crown Prince* also happens to be your soul bonded...whatever?"

Jaren watched his mate lower her arms, brows pinched together in thought. She looked adorable, and he had the desire to smooth out the lines and kiss her forehead. The pull he felt to her was growing stronger by the minute, and he unconsciously took a step toward her.

She glanced his way when he moved, before looking back at Trey. "I don't know. But I do feel a connection to him. I can't explain it, but something is there. I don't need you to understand,

I just need you to trust me."

She stared at the ground, worrying her lip, and Jaren was ten seconds away from wrapping his arms around her when Trey opened his stupid ass mouth again.

"I can't let you, I'm sorry."

Chapter 21

Vera

Her face shot up, and she clenched her hands at her sides, "Let me? Are you serious right now?"

Standing his ground against the force of her anger, he said, "Yes. Your life over mine. I swore an oath. Don't make me break it."

She stepped closer, pointing a finger at his chest. "You swore an oath to protect me, but you made that oath when neither you nor Eithan understood that I don't need protection. I can protect myself." She forced herself to stay firm, communicating the truth in her words, "I won't go back, Trey. Not until if, and when, *I* decide to."

"Gods dammit, Vera. Prince Eithan isn't the enemy here. He's trying to build a relationship, not take advantage and scandalize you. Are you really going to walk away from that chance just so you can go gallivanting off with some stranger?"

"Eithan's even more of a stranger to me, so try again. Don't talk down to me. I'm not stupid."

"Then stop acting like it!" he spit. "I stayed with you and supported you running off because I understood your need for a taste of freedom. But this? Leaving? It's selfish."

She flinched back, stunned. Was she being selfish? Blinking back the burning in her eyes, she tried to breathe through the pain his verbal daggers were inflicting.

"I'm not against an alliance," she said. "We could still forge one. Did it ever occur to you that by going back I could be doing more for both Aleron and Bhasura?" She looked at him beseechingly, but he just continued glaring.

"My father was related to King Vesstan so maybe I could talk to him, convince him to open communication without having to sacrifice my future to achieve it."

Jaren stiffened, inhaling sharply through his nose. His head twitched in her direction, and he looked like he was about to say something before he glanced at Trey, quickly snapping his mouth shut. She knew he had a few choice words—or threats—he'd like to express, but he stayed silent, letting her fight her own battle.

"What am I supposed to tell Prince Eithan when I show up in Matherin without his betrothed? 'Sorry, Your Highness, but she decided to elope. Hope there are no hard feelings.' I'm sure that will go well."

She shoved him hard enough, he stumbled back, "You're being an ass."

"And you're being a coward."

Trey barely dodged in time to avoid her fist, but she wasn't nearly done. She followed through, twisting, and ramming her elbow back into his stomach. He grunted, his body curling forward before he leaped back, sidestepping her next strike.

"Putting myself first for once doesn't make me a coward," she said through clenched teeth. "I'm allowed to care about my future."

A single tear escaped, and she shot her arm out again, but there was no heat behind it, her anger turned to nothing but crushing disappointment. He blocked, catching her arm.

They stood in silence, staring at each other. Vera tried to keep her face from crumpling. If this was what it was like to care about people, she didn't know if she could survive ever doing it again. It hurt.

"I won't apologize for the choice I'm making, Trey. But I am sorry for involving you. I shouldn't have forced you to come. That wasn't fair of me," she said.

"Don't do this, Vera." His face was pale. "If you leave knowing what your emperor wishes, it will be considered treason. You might never be allowed back."

"He's not my emperor."

Wiping the wet streak off her cheek, she pulled her arm out of his grip and walked toward the horses, refusing to argue further. When she reached Darling, she paused.

"If you see Elric, tell him I forgive him." Pushing back her tears, she threw herself up, not once looking back at her friend.

Jaren's body silently encircled her, not hesitating to direct

Darling toward the road to Midpath. His presence alone eased the overpowering anxiety threatening to cripple her.

She didn't know if she believed what he'd said about them being mates, but she couldn't deny the connection that existed between them. Her attraction to him wasn't just physical. It felt deep, like her body recognized and needed his.

She'd already felt drawn to him, but it was like the longer they were together, the stronger it became. Just having him behind her, his scent wrapped around her, was enough to calm even her worst emotions.

Jaren was right, she wanted him. Even now, her body desperately wanted to lean back into him, craving more of his touch. Her mind just wasn't quite sure how to handle the revelation yet.

UPON ENTERING THE city, Jaren wasted no time in stabling a very deserving Darling and finding them an inn for the night. It wasn't anything like the one Vera had stayed in when she'd last been to Midpath. It was dirty and rundown, and she definitely wouldn't be offered a hot bath.

She wasn't sure if the promise of food and a bed made up for the fact that she'd probably contract food poisoning or a disease. But the room was cheap, the mystery stew flavorless but warm, and none of the other residents paid them any mind.

They traded small talk while they ate, and it wasn't as awkward as Vera had feared. She panicked when he casually removed his hood at the table, but his unruly hair curled around his ears in a way that covered their uniqueness. She was pretty sure an ink stain on a white sheet would blend in better than they did, but Jaren didn't seem the least bit worried.

"So," she cleared her throat, "we're mates."

His eyes flared, his attention narrowing on her with intense focus. "We are."

"How are you—I mean, how was that decided? You made it seem like this bond was different as children?"

Jaren leaned toward her, his voice lowered. "It *was* different. All I wanted was to be near you and protect you, but it was nothing like the strength of those instincts now."

"The blade you held to my throat begs to differ."

He smirked.

"How did you even know that's what we were?"

"I didn't. I was barely more than five when you were born. It was my father, Jaeros, who realized it. Apparently, I couldn't stay away from you. After you were born, he said I kept sneaking off and heading to some random house in the middle of the woods. Our people are well-versed in soul bonds, so as soon as he saw you, he knew."

"Are soul bonds common?"

He shifted back. "Yes, and no. They're not rare, but not everyone is blessed with one in their lifetime."

"Why are two people chosen? What decides it?"

"Depends on what you believe in. Fate? Destiny? Luck? What matters is our souls match, Veralie. The moment yours entered the world, mine went searching for it. The how and the why didn't matter. They still don't.

"I volunteered to travel here, to scout for King Vesstan. I felt an overpowering need to do it. I wrote it off as some need for penance but...I think my soul was just trying to bring me to you."

Vera swallowed the sudden lump in her throat and looked away. She wanted to ask more about their childhood, about her parents and why they apparently hadn't raised her, but she wasn't quite ready for those answers. Not yet. Her head was already spinning with information overload as it was. She'd have plenty of time to ask later.

Instead, she pushed him for details about the last stretch of their journey to the coast. His look told her the change of subject didn't fool him, but he humored her and told her about the small ship he'd hidden near Eastshore, and how long the voyage to Bhasura would take.

Now that they were down a mouth, he had enough coin for them to stock up on provisions, but they'd have to steal another horse. Vera knew she should feel guilty about that, but she felt nothing but excitement. She was about to *live*, and she didn't care if she had to steal fifty horses to make it happen.

They'd just finished their meal when he quirked an eyebrow at the eager expression she'd failed to hide. "Don't get too excited. It'll take at least a week to get there, and you won't enjoy most of it."

"Why not?"

"You'll likely spend the majority of the trip vomiting over the side. Seasickness is no joke."

Her smile fell, her excitement drying up. She'd vomit for

weeks? "Can't I just heal myself?"

He shifted forward, resting his arms on the table. Not for the first time, Vera noticed how beautiful his hands were. "It doesn't work like that. You'd have to heal yourself constantly every day, several times a day. Even with the strength of your ability, that would drain you."

"Do you get sick?"

"Not anymore. Although, I imagine watching you hurl over and over will be enough to make me want to." He pushed off the table and stood.

Vera made to glare up at him but halted, her mouth parting when she looked up to see him stretching his arms above his head, smiling mischievously down at her. Holy Aleron, he was gorgeous.

She'd always thought so, but the strange connection between them seemed to be changing, and now she *really* noticed. She watched his tongue glide over the tip of one of his canines, and heat pooled in her core.

She may have been inexperienced with intimacy, but her thoughts certainly weren't innocent. He wasn't the first person she'd ever fantasized about. She'd been physically attracted to a few of the guards—not to mention Eithan—but nothing measured up to what she felt for Jaren.

At that moment, all she could think about was sinking her fingers into his hair and running her own tongue across his teeth.

He went completely still, his arms frozen above his head. His gaze zeroed in on her, and her breathing quickened. Did he know what she was thinking? Was that something he could do through their bond? She suddenly regretted not asking more questions.

Shooting to her feet, she headed for the stairs, her face on fire. She didn't stop to see if he followed. She didn't need to. She could sense him directly behind her, his mere presence pressing in on her until she thought she'd explode.

Pausing at the door the innkeeper had directed them to, she awkwardly waited for Jaren to unlock it before rushing past him into the cramped room. She almost groaned with anticipation when she caught sight of the small, dingy tub in the corner, but then her eyes drifted to the other side of the room. To the single bed.

She chastised herself. They'd touched more on the horse than they'd have to touch sleeping on the bed. Not to mention, they'd already slept side by side on the ground. Doing so on a mattress wouldn't be any different.

Even if they were now alone.

In a private room.

And he'd claimed she was his.

She dared a peek at him. He was leaning against the closed door, his perfectly sculpted arms crossed over his chest as he watched her. She allowed her eyes to travel down his lean torso, admiring the muscles in his legs before moving back up.

How was she supposed to have any appropriate thoughts when he looked that good, just *standing* there?

His posture tensed, and for the second time that night, she wondered if he somehow knew what she was thinking. He'd said before that he wanted her, but she didn't know if he meant the same kind of want that she felt at that moment.

Vera's entire life had consisted of men making decisions for her, choosing what was best, and telling her what she needed. Every single one of them wanted to control her. Even Trey hadn't cared about what she wanted. Not truly.

And right now, she wanted Jaren. She wanted to touch him and feel the heat of his skin against hers. She wanted to experience a kiss and the kind of bliss she'd only heard about. She wanted to lose herself in pleasure and forget how chaotic and messy her life had become.

She wanted to *feel*, and she wanted it to be with him.

Gliding forward, Vera didn't hide her intentions from her eyes. After tonight, they would travel hard toward the coast, and then they'd be gone. Nothing would ever be the same again. Tonight, she just wanted to forget it all.

"You said we're bonded, that our souls are connected." She reached up, placing a hand on his chest, hoping it wasn't obvious how nervous she was. "I don't know what that means yet, and right now, I don't care. You were right, I want you."

The muscles along his jaw spasmed. He hesitated only a moment before dropping his arms to his sides. Butterflies erupted in her stomach, and she prepared herself for him to pull her close and kiss her.

She let her eyes flutter closed, feeling the heat that had begun to tease her spread through her body.

After a beat, when he still hadn't touched her and the silence began to grow heavy, she opened her eyes and looked up at him.

"I'm not going to fuck you, little star."

Chapter 22

Vera

She stepped back, wrenching her arm off his chest like he'd struck her. She felt her entire face go up in flames, the rejection stabbing her in the gut and twisting.

"I didn't mean—"

Jaren moved away from the door, but she took another step back, desperately trying to keep both her distance, and what little remained of her pride, intact.

"It's fine, don't worry about it. I just got the wrong idea. Not surprising since I've— You know what, never mind. We should probably get some sleep." Gods, she was rambling.

It was like her entire body was awake. The fire she'd felt building now felt like it was going to suffocate her. She needed fresh air and possibly a long soak in freezing water.

She tried to walk away, but she only made it an inch before

his hand whipped out, snatching her arm and spinning them until it was *her* back against the door. He caged her in with a hand on either side of her head, leaning so close his breath tickled against her flushed skin.

"You have no idea, do you?" His eyes had darkened, and she was unable to look away, a shudder coursing through her body.

She swallowed hard. "About what?"

Her voice came out throaty, and his expression turned positively devious. She got the barest glimpse of his canines. Gods, what she would give to feel them against her skin, her lips, her—

A dark rumble echoed from his chest, and his nostrils flared. Like an unwelcome epiphany, she had the sudden realization he could *smell* her arousal. That he'd been able to every damn time. If she thought she couldn't have been more embarrassed than she already was, she'd been painfully and irrevocably wrong.

She opened her mouth to say something else she'd probably regret, but his hand reached down and grabbed her own, pressing her palm to the hard length straining against his pants.

Her eyes felt like they might fall out of her head. Her breathing was erratic, her heart smashing against her chest. Instinctively, her fingers curled to cup him more fully, but faster than she could process, he'd snagged both her wrists and pressed them against the door, pinning them above her head.

He grazed his nose along her throat, inhaling deeply. "Did that feel like you got the wrong idea?"

She shook her head, unable to form coherent words.

"If you'd been taught how to focus your senses, you'd be able to tell by my scent alone." His body was flush against hers and she lifted her hips, desperate for the smallest amount of friction to ease the ache overwhelming her body—her fucking soul.

His grip on her wrists tightened, his pupils dilating. Pushing forward, he pinned her hips to the wall, stilling her. "I will not fuck you for two reasons, Veralie."

She felt a pang in her chest, the rejection hurting more the second time. But before she could spiral further into mortification, he brushed his lips against hers, so softly she might have imagined it.

"Reason number one being that we're in a small room that is severely lacking in both space and creativity. I would need a gods damn palace for everything I want to do to you and all the surfaces I want to do them on. And somehow, I doubt even that will be enough to sate this uncontrollable hunger I have for you."

Her entire body was shaking now, throbbing with need. Jaren was telling her why he wouldn't fuck her, but all it did was make her want him to even more.

"And two?" It came out as nothing more than a breathy whisper, and his eyes dropped to her mouth as she bit her bottom lip. Leaning forward, he licked the seam of her mouth, causing her to gasp and release it.

"And two, you don't understand enough about Magyki mates or soul bonds to understand the implications of it. It would not mean the same to you as it would to me."

She opened her mouth to deny it but closed it when she met his eyes. He was right, she didn't remember their history like he did. He'd told her they were mates, but it was just a word to her, it didn't hold meaning like it clearly did for him. And she wouldn't invalidate his feelings to argue it.

"Okay," she whispered, trying to push down her crushing disappointment.

She was still on fire, still burning for him, and it left her feeling both heavy and empty at the same time. She lowered her eyes and tried to pull her wrists out of his grip, but he only thrust his hips forward, grinding into her.

She gasped, looking up at him to discover his eyes devouring her. "Oh, my little star. I said I wouldn't fuck you. I never said I didn't plan on touching you."

And then his lips were crashing into hers. His earthy smell enveloped her, the firmness of his body touching the center of hers, and the press of his lips soft, yet unyielding, as he demanded every inch of her mouth.

She tried again to pull her arms down, but he tightened his hold, demanding she submit. A sharp pinch had her pulling in a breath as he sucked her bottom lip into his mouth, nipping it with his teeth. Her lips opened in surprise, a moan escaping her.

Jaren didn't miss a second. He thrust his tongue into her mouth like he wanted to taste the sound. His tongue danced with hers, and her mind emptied of everything except the feel of him.

He released her wrists, wrapping one hand around her plait and yanking, bringing her face sharply up as his other hand wrapped around her throat. His thumb pushed her chin up until she was completely at his mercy.

Reaching up, Vera combed her fingers through his dark hair, almost moaning again when she confirmed the strands to be just as soft as she'd imagined. As he continued to kiss and nip at her lips, she curled her fingers, digging her nails into his scalp.

It snapped the restraint he must have been clinging to. Moving the hand at her throat to her jaw, he squeezed, forcing her mouth to open even more for him, and snarling in satisfaction, he *consumed* her.

She ground against him, the buildup in her core growing. But just as she thought she might break apart, he pulled away, leaving her gasping for breath. She knew she had to look as desperate as she felt, but she couldn't rein in her emotions. They were too potent.

"Don't worry, little star, I won't leave you unfulfilled." He released her, only to grip her ass, lifting her as easily as if she weighed nothing. He held her pressed against him, wrapping her legs around his waist.

She'd thought he was only going to kiss her. He'd made it clear he wouldn't have sex with her, but maybe he'd changed his mind? Her confusion must have shown.

"If you think I'm going to stop at just the taste of your lips, you have severely underestimated my intentions."

Oh gods. She was going to explode into a thousand pieces.

He walked over to the bed and gently lowered them both until she was lying on her back, and he leaned over her shuddering form. His eyes traveled from her face down her body, stopping between her legs as if he could see the wetness now pooling there.

"The desire to bury myself inside of you is destroying me, Veralie. To feel your wet heat clench around me as I pound into you until you can't remember any name but mine. I want to ruin you, worship you, claim you and make you burn only for me."

He licked his lips as he began to ease her tunic up her torso. "But until that moment, I will settle for enjoying you another way."

He pushed the fabric up, halting right below her breasts, and she vocalized her disappointment when he didn't remove it completely. A smirk—one only an arrogant male could have—appeared on his face. "I don't plan on indulging in the entire meal during the first course."

She choked, the sound half laugh and half groan, "You're trying to kill me."

*Tsk*ing at her, he lowered his face to her stomach, trailing his tongue down the center and swirling it around her navel. "Trust me, my restraint is just as painful for me, if not more."

"Then why torture yourself?" she breathed. The words came out sounding whiny, but she didn't care. Her entire focus centered on his tongue now moving below her navel.

"I wouldn't call it torture. I'd call it...heightening the experience."

As his fingers twisted in the top of her trousers and began to pull, she tensed, suddenly self-conscious. He'd clearly done this before, and with who knew how many partners. While she had no idea what the fuck she was doing.

Jaren's movements froze, sensing the change in her body. He lifted his head, staring into her eyes. "Did I ever tell you that you smell like a burning star?"

"What?"

"Your scent, it's like a burning star. Like your soul itself was made from a swirling storm of fire and iron. It's intoxicating,

Veralie." He placed a kiss on her stomach, and her heart fluttered.

"There is nothing about you that does not draw me in. You never have to second guess with me. I know intimacy is new for you, and there is not a single part of me that is not aware of how fucking lucky I am to be the one to experience and show you."

He kissed her, and it was nothing like the clash and pull of their first kiss. This one was slow and deep, as if he wanted to pull her heart out of her chest and hold it to his own.

His fingers again began to pull the fabric down her legs, and he left her mouth to kiss along her throat, across the tunic still bunched below her breasts, and down her torso. Vera fisted the blanket on either side of her, still tense but thrumming with anticipation. What would those long, calloused fingers feel like against her? Inside her?

Finally removing the last of her clothing, he flung it across the room. A sound she could only describe as predatory burst from his chest as he sat back and stared down at the apex of her thighs. His nostrils flared, and she swore his eyes darkened even further, making them seem more black than green, before he gripped her hips with inhuman speed.

Sliding his hands around to cup her ass, he tilted her up to meet his mouth. Before her startled breath could leave her lips, he buried his face between her thighs. Inhaling deeply, he emitted a dark, pleased growl, and it vibrated against her core, drenching her even more.

Her back arched when his tongue began to move, and she reflexively reached up and dug her fingers in his hair, holding his head in place.

Her reaction seemed to encourage him as another sound rumbled through his body, and the licks and thrusts of his tongue became more enthusiastic and determined.

Never pausing his ministrations, he lowered her ass to the mattress, ran his hands down her thighs, and pushed them out. With her legs spread as wide as possible, he continued to devour her completely. She'd never felt more exposed, and the sensation was altogether exquisite and sinful.

"Gods, Jaren, I can't—"

He paused, lifting his head just enough to look at her. Her heart skipped a beat at the possessive gleam in his eyes. "I could bury my tongue deep inside you every day and still never be satisfied."

His voice was rough, and the grip on her thighs tightened, his nails biting into her flesh. "I will *never* not crave the taste of you, nor the intoxicating smell of your desire. You are *mine*, little star. Every inch of you was created for only me."

His claim should have terrified her, but it didn't. He didn't want to own or control her. He just wanted *her*. The knowledge was freeing, and she couldn't fight the flare of arousal, nor the incoherent words that burst from her lips.

Any resolve he had, shattered, and he attacked her with fervor, licking and sucking on the bundle of nerves at the same time he slid a finger inside her. Not anticipating the invasion, she gasped as her back arched higher. She'd touched herself before, but not like this.

Her fists were gripping his hair so tight, it had to hurt, but he didn't seem to care as he started moving that damn finger faster.

His thrusts were firm and demanding, but he was careful not to hurt her. Her entire body tensed like a bowstring; the pressure so strong she wasn't sure she'd survive it.

"Fuck yes, Veralie, come for me. Let go."

"Oh my gods."

He growled into her, and the hand on her thigh, squeezed. "You don't belong to the gods, you belong to me. The only name I want to hear you call out is mine."

He sucked hard exactly where she needed him to right as he curled that damn finger against her inner wall, and she screamed his name as release tore through her.

His finger continued moving, working her through her orgasm, while his tongue lapped at her desperately, determined to taste every last drop of her release. When her body finally sagged in his arms, she looked up through heavy-lidded eyes to see him smiling at her, his lips glistening with her arousal.

He removed his finger and sat back on his heels, and she could see the rock-hard erection still pushing at his pants. With trembling arms, she pushed herself up and reached toward him before pausing, unsure.

"I don't—I mean, I'd like—" she stumbled over her words, her brain still mush from her mind-blowing orgasm. She licked her lips, "I don't want to leave you unfulfilled either."

Groaning, he shook his head. "As delicious as that sounds, my restraint is not strong enough to be able to feel your lips around my cock and not fuck you after. Because when you make me come, it will be while I'm buried deep inside you, not in your mouth."

Trying her best to appear confident, she continued reaching

for him, gripping him through the fabric. "What if I just touch you then?" She rubbed her palm down to his tip and back up, hoping she wasn't making a fool of herself. She smiled when he twitched in her hand.

"Fuck, Veralie, I—"

She rubbed him again, harder this time, and watched his defenses crumble to ash. He rushed forward, grasping her face and kissing her deeply.

When they finally broke away, she again reached for him, "Will you show me what you like?"

"Yes, but know that I'd like anything you did, little star. You can't do it wrong." She shifted closer until their knees were touching, watching his long fingers work to undo his trousers.

When he sprang free, her mouth dropped open. *That* was supposed to fit *inside* her? And he'd mentioned her mouth…gods. "How is that…" she trailed off, a furious blush filling her cheeks.

He grabbed her hand, pulling her down until her fingers wrapped around him. "Do not finish that question. My restraint is only so strong, Veralie, and if you put that thought in my head, it won't be your hand that is working me."

Her mouth dried, her pulse pounding in her ears. She gave an experimental squeeze and he lurched, eyes flaring as he cursed through clenched teeth. "*Yinlanem dupye!*" It was all the encouragement she needed. Seeing him lose control by her touch alone was invigorating. It made her feel powerful.

She kept her grip firm as she began to move up and down his shaft, reveling in the words of praise he rained on her like she was his own personal goddess.

He groaned out her name, tipping his head back, and digging his nails into his thighs. When his body stiffened and his breathing became irregular, she had a feeling he was close. She increased her effort, determined to make him feel as good as she had.

One second, she was working her hand up to his tip, and the next, she was flying backward. Her back had barely touched the bed when he leaned over her, gripping her hip, and covering her torso in hot spurts as he came completely undone. Her eyes widened. She'd known what happened when a male orgasmed, but she hadn't known it could be so *fucking hot*.

She leaned up onto her elbows, desperately wanting to kiss him, but he placed a single hand on her chest, pressing her back down. "Jaren?"

He snarled, flashing his canines and flinging her thighs open. "We're not done." And with that, he descended, feasting on her again like he had no other purpose in life.

After he had her screaming his name a second time, he pushed off the bed, standing in one fluid movement. He ran his tongue over his lips and hummed in approval.

"Can't say I'm not disappointed your guard wasn't here to see me between your legs. I want him and his princeling to know that you are mine." His look was nothing short of wicked, and even in her exhausted state, it sent a thrill through her.

"I'm going to map out our morning route. I'll tell the innkeeper to have water sent up. Bathe and rest, little star."

She nodded. Her eyes already felt heavy, but she'd rather dine alone with the emperor than refuse a bath. She watched him throw on his cloak and walk out of the room, and she'd never felt so content in her life.

Chapter 23

Eithan

They'd kept a hard pace along Eastmore Road for two days, and he still had no idea where she was. After Sulian's barely veiled threat, he'd left with his remaining guards as soon as possible. But with every hour that went by with no sign of her, he came closer and closer to snapping.

There wasn't even a guarantee she'd been taken this way. For all he knew, they'd taken the eastern gate as a diversion before redirecting west. But he had no choice, *east* was the only lead he had to go on.

Eithan questioned every traveler they encountered, but no one had seen anyone fitting Vera or Gibson's descriptions. He wasn't stupid, he knew whoever had her would have wanted them off the main road and out of sight. They likely never even touched

Eastmore, choosing instead to follow one of the old, unused paths through the Lakewood Forest.

Eithan's group was too large to attempt any of the smaller paths through the trees. He'd considered separating into several small groups before shutting down the idea. If it was a Magyki, he'd need his entire guard to take him down. Eithan had no idea how powerful a trained Magyki male could be, and he couldn't risk it.

So they kept to the main road and pushed their mounts to the limit, desperate to move as fast as the beasts could handle. By the time they'd come within a few hours of Midpath, he still had no leads, and he was seconds from ripping his hair out.

When a single traveler on horseback appeared in the distance, Eithan didn't even deign to give him more than a cursory glance, confident the traveler would be as useless as every other. But as they steadily came closer, the traveler kicked his horse into a gallop, aiming straight for them with purpose.

His men surrounded him, their weapons at the ready. If he gave the signal, Hayes could have an arrow in the man's chest before he even knew what was happening. But Eithan waited.

When the man finally got close enough for Eithan to make out his mask and uniform, he almost leaped off his horse. Pushing past the barricade, he ordered his men to stand down.

Where was she? Where was she?

"Gibson!"

"Your Highness." Eyes wide, he dismounted, lowering himself into a bow. "I was on my way to Matherin to report to you. I did not expect to see you outside—"

Eithan silenced him with no more than an impatient flick of his wrist. He was in no mood for guilty rambling, his father's words trickling into his ears, mocking him.

By nature, Eithan wasn't a trusting person. His life among nobles and vipers had made sure of that. But he'd been meticulous with who he'd chosen to guard his back. He'd permitted himself to trust those men with his life and his friendship. The possibility that his choice may have been made in ignorance was a hard concept to swallow, like a jagged stone caught in his throat.

"I am only interested in Vera. Report. Where is she?"

Gibson rose, eyes flickering to the men as he stood at attention. "In Midpath, Your Highness, with a Magyki who goes by Jaren." His lip curled over the name.

Eithan gritted his teeth until his jaw felt like it'd pop. After his conversation with Elric, he'd been sure it was a Magyki who took her, but hearing it confirmed still infuriated him. His mind went to the blood on her dress. "Is she hurt?"

"No." Gibson paused, stuttering over his words like he wasn't confident about his answer. "At least, she wasn't when we separated. She's confused, Your Highness, but I don't believe she's in danger." He lowered his eyes to the ground.

Eithan glared down at the worn-looking man, fighting the urge to punch him in the face. To do more than that. "I trusted you to keep her safe, yet here you are, having abandoned your duty."

Gibson kept his head down as if his pathetic act of subservience would help him. "She demanded I leave, Your Highness. I fought to return her home, but she is adept with a blade. Even if she couldn't have bested me, the Magyki would have killed me if I stayed. I would've laid down my life for her with no hesitation. But I feared no one knew where she'd been taken, and if I did not return, she'd never be found."

Eithan's anger ebbed—barely. "You said she's in no danger, but I find that hard to believe. He won't hurt her?" The question was pointless. He knew she'd already been injured. But Gibson shook his head, finally glancing up.

"Vera could stand on her own if he tried, but I don't believe he will. He seems to care about her well-being, but everything he's told her has been cryptic. He's hiding something, but she's blinded by his fantastical stories of Bhasura. All I know is he's desperate to get her off Aleron."

Eithan nodded. That sounded like something one of those pointy-eared barbarians would do, especially if he knew who she truly was. What he wasn't sure was whether or not *Vera* knew. The idea that she was willingly leaving rankled him.

"I spoke with the Weapons' Master. I know she was trained, and I know it was she, whom I sparred. But even her skills are no match against a skilled Magyki. Now that she's alone, she has no choice but to follow him." He glared at his guard.

"She's…changed, Your Highness."

Three seconds. That's all it took for Eithan to dismount, his long strides eating the distance between them. He tried to calm his racing heart, but the adrenaline pumping through his veins told him he was failing.

"Changed how?" His voice came out harsher than he'd intended.

Gibson's eyes widened. "After she was accidentally injured, Jaren tried to teach her about whatever abilities they possess. But something happened." He grimaced, "She doesn't look human anymore."

Eithan stood, spine locked and fists balled, as he told him about Vera's surge of power and how it'd altered her appearance. That it had shocked even the Magyki native.

Gibson fidgeted in shame. "I have failed you, Your Highness. May your blade run true where my actions have not," he said, quoting part of the oath all Matherin guards were sworn to.

He had failed, willingly and knowingly, and Eithan would be expected to take his life as punishment. That festering anger *wanted* to take his life. But he pushed it down. Not yet. Not until Vera was returned safely home to him.

"You have been a loyal guard for several years, Gibson. For that reason alone, I will not decide punishment until we are back within the capital walls. Be thankful I am giving you that much."

Eithan motioned for the rest of his party to prepare to move. "Get back on your mount and tell me everything. Leave nothing out. We make haste for Midpath."

Jaren

HE TOOK A LONG PULL FROM THE MUG OF ALE HE'D ORDERED downstairs, swishing it around his mouth before swallowing. The sleazy innkeeper had charged him double what it was worth, which was definitely more than he should've spent given their impending necessities, but he was desperate. He flung back the rest, half drowning himself in the process.

He needed to get her taste out of his mouth. Needed to forget how her inner muscles had clenched around his finger, and how the smell of her sex overtook every other gods damn thought in his head.

He'd never recover. She was everything he could ever want and so much more. He'd never be able to take another female to bed, nor would he ever want to. He'd fantasized for days about ruining her, but her innocent, inexperienced ass ruined him instead.

He was in so much fucking trouble.

Jaren ran his hands through his hair. He needed to leave. He told her he would plan out the next steps of their trip, and he hadn't been lying. He needed to do it, and the quicker he did, the quicker he could get back upstairs to wash and sleep. The thought of holding her body close to his and falling asleep with his nose buried in her hair already had him semi-hard.

He could just say fuck it and go back upstairs now and pull her to him. She was probably soaking in the tub now, with her long legs and perky breasts peeking out of the water. The pathetic excuse for a tub was too small to join her, but after she finished, he could take her glistening, naked form and sprawl her across the bed.

Before he knew it, he was hard and had taken two steps toward the stairs before stopping. The war between his head and his cock was painful. He was drawing attention from some of the straggling, late-night patrons as he continued to stand there, drowning in desire, staring at the stairs like they were his greatest nemesis.

Get yourself together, Barilias.

He couldn't take that next step with her, no matter how badly their bond demanded it. How badly his body demanded it. It was just as true now as it was earlier when he'd told her. She didn't understand what would happen if she allowed him to claim her in that way. How their bond would change.

He wanted it to change, he craved the completion of it. He wanted Veralie to be tied to him in every possible way, to share everything between them. But he also wanted her to choose it, knowing and understanding exactly what she was choosing.

For over a decade, fate had kept them apart. He, having mourned her with every dark corner of his heart, and she, having been trapped in a life she didn't want or deserve. Now that they'd finally found each other again, he refused to risk ruining it. He wouldn't take advantage of her ignorance.

Then there was what she'd told Trey about her father. Gods, she didn't know anything. He needed to tell her that too. She'd be pissed that he hadn't immediately told her, but he was too selfish and scared of what she'd decide to do with the knowledge. There were so many things they needed to discuss and figure out, but he'd help her through it all, even the dark parts.

He continued staring at the stairs for another moment longer, imagining his *aitanta*, sated and washed, curled up in bed, waiting for him. He swore right then and there he would tell her everything as soon as he had her safely on his vessel.

Pulling his shit together, Jaren forced himself to leave the inn and headed out into the night.

IT HAD TAKEN him longer than he'd hoped to get back, and he was exhausted. He couldn't even remember the last time he'd slept well. If he fell on the bed now, he could still get several blissful hours. But he also knew if he found his mate awake, sleep was not what would happen.

Turning the key slowly, he eased the door open and stepped over the threshold. The room was filled with Veralie's star-fire scent mixed with the dull aroma of cheap lavender soap. The tub was still full of water—albeit cold now, but it was the scene on the other side of the room that stole his breath.

Veralie was curled on her side in bed, her damp curls strewn about the pillow as if they were stretching out, enjoying the rare freedom from the plait she normally forced them into. Her mouth was parted, and one hand rested just under her chin.

The blanket was pulled up just under her chest with one long leg pushed out, seeking the cool air. She'd apparently chosen to scrub her clothing and had instead donned one of Jaren's newly purchased tunics while hers laid out to dry across the floor.

She was fucking beautiful. It took every ounce of self-control he had to head toward the tub instead of her. He wanted to climb in beside her, but even he knew he smelled. Sucking in a breath against the temperature, he washed up the best he could with the used soap and water and scrubbed his clothes before finally climbing behind her in just his undershorts.

His star twitched but didn't wake when the mattress dipped beneath his weight. He wanted nothing more than to wrap his arms around her and pull her flush against him, but he hesitated.

She'd initiated their intimacy earlier, but that didn't automatically mean she'd be okay with him touching her again. She'd acknowledged *he* thought they were mates, but she hadn't verbally accepted it herself yet.

Cursing himself for even considering it, he rolled onto his back. He closed his eyes, desperately trying to ignore the body lying mere inches away.

SOMETHING ROUSED HIM to consciousness, and he was tempted to fight it. He couldn't remember the last time he'd slept so deeply. He usually had a habit of lurching awake to every noise, and if he dreamed, it wasn't pleasant. But lying there, he'd never felt so completely content.

A subtle movement caught his attention right before a voice broke the silence. "Jaren."

Cracking his eyes open, he glanced down, spotting the female prostrate beneath him. She was lying on her stomach with her face smashed into her pillow, causing his name to come out muffled. He'd gravitated to her sometime during the night and wrapped his limbs around her. He hummed in approval.

Sprawled across her like he was, he could feel the contour of her ass beneath his hips and couldn't fight the thrill that raced through him. He remembered the toned, naked leg he'd seen peeking out last night and reveled in the fact that only their underclothes separated them.

"Jaren."

"Hm?"

She struggled to lift her head, trying to uncover more of her mouth. "I know we agreed not to kill each other, but if you don't stop trying to suffocate me, I'll launch your ass across the room."

He sighed, shifting farther on top of her. "I'm actually quite comfortable. You make a good—"

She raised her arms, pressing her palms flat against the mattress, and giving him just enough of a warning. As she shoved off the mattress, Jaren wrapped his arms around her waist. True to her word, she launched him straight off the bed. He just made sure to take her along with him.

Taking the brunt of the fall, Jaren landed with a loud *thunk*, the still-damp clothes on the floor rumpled and cold under his bare back. Neither of them moved for a moment—him recovering from the landing, and her likely trying to convince herself not to throttle him.

"I know we agreed not to kill each other, little star, but if you don't stop trying to suffocate me..."

She stiffened, exactly how he knew she would, and he smirked. Point one for him. "You know, you're heavier than you look."

She slammed her elbow into his stomach, causing him to relax his hold enough for her to roll off. She jumped to her feet, glaring down at him as he tried, and failed, to rein in a painful chuckle.

Clutching his stomach, he stood, finally able to look at her head-on. Veralie's eyes were narrowed, and her frizzy hair billowed around her like its own entity. It was honestly impressive in its size. He let his eyes roam about her face, watching the subtle changes as her irritation rose.

"Stop ogling me."

"I'm not. Your hair was just telling me good morning."

She crossed her arms, a blush creeping up her neck as she furiously patted her curls down. "Well, something of you is telling me good morning, but it's not your hair."

Jaren glanced down at the erection tenting his undershorts, and then with exaggerated slowness, raised his eyes up her bare legs. He shrugged, unconcerned, even though the sight of her wearing his clothes made him anything but calm. "I don't blame it."

Dropping her arms, Vera took a single step toward him, her face beet red with both frustration and something else. Jaren didn't feel the least bit guilty. He couldn't remember the last time he'd felt playful, not since he was a kid he supposed.

Not since he'd last had *her*.

Chapter 24

Vera

She was going to kill him. Or at least rip the smirk off his face and shove it right up his—No. She couldn't. She needed him to get her to Bhasura. Not to mention, he was kind of, sort of, her mate. Or something. But still, she was tempted to whack him upside his stupid head.

She knew she was seven shades of scarlet at the turn of the conversation, and she had only herself to blame. She hadn't meant to point out his erection, but she'd been trying so hard not to look at it, that it'd been front and center in her mind, when her mouth decided to spew its lovely word vomit.

Now, all she could think about was the way he'd worshipped her body the night before. The images taking over her mind, filling up space and leaving none left for any amount of intelligence.

Jaren didn't move, apparently content to just watch her. Finally remembering how to work her tongue, she shifted from one foot to the other, "I assumed we'd be in a rush this morning?"

"We are."

"Then, do you mind? It'll only take me a few minutes to get ready."

He tilted his head to the side, raising a brow. "By all means. I'm not stopping you."

She huffed, throwing her arms up only to instantly regret it when his eyes shot to the hem she'd inadvertently raised up her thighs. "Privacy, Jaren. I'm waiting for privacy."

"I know that tunic is clean since it's mine, so I'm assuming the only thing you need to do is pull on the trousers that are currently at our feet. I've seen and tasted most of you already; there's nothing to be embarrassed about."

"This is different." She rubbed her hands over her face, pressing her palms into her eyes.

"*Tri?*"

Because changing her clothes and freshening up next to him felt intimate, something that lovers did. Was that what they were now? Childhood friends, mates, soul-bonded, and now lovers? It was all too much.

"I spent my entire life…well, almost my entire life, alone. It's just a little overwhelming to have everything suddenly be so different." She looked up, meeting his eyes. "I don't know how to act like your mate, or what I'm supposed to do."

She swore she saw a flicker of hurt, and maybe even

disappointment, cross his face, but it was gone before she could be certain. He stepped closer until only a foot separated them.

"I don't expect anything from you, Veralie." She flinched, but he continued. "I don't want you to *act* like my mate. I want you to act like *you*. I'll support your feelings, no matter what they may be."

"Half the time, I want to stab you."

Pleasure shot through her when he tipped his head back and laughed, his smile showing off the canines that had so deliciously nipped at her. It changed his entire appearance. He looked younger, less violent and bitter.

She almost changed her mind and closed the distance between them when he leaned down, grabbing his clothes from the floor.

"Careful, little star. I might like that." The corner of his mouth lifted, and he walked to the far side of the room, giving her his back while he changed. She considered walking after him, but shook the thought out of her head. They shouldn't linger.

Taking advantage of the semblance of privacy, she put on the rest of her clothes and wrestled her mane back into something a little less scary.

EVERYTHING SEEMED TO be going according to plan until they approached the stable. Vera already knew it would be difficult for them to sneak off with a horse in broad daylight, but now it was impossible.

Three Matherin soldiers were standing near the stable, looking very much like they were guarding it. She remembered from her last trip that there was a battalion of soldiers near Midpath, but it didn't make sense for them to be guarding a stable.

"They know we're here." Jaren's voice cut through the air, slicing through her thoughts.

She shook her head. "That doesn't make any sense."

"Doesn't it, though?" He speared her with his eyes, frustration and anger bleeding through. "Not even a full day since we left your guard dog, and suddenly soldiers are guarding not just any stable, but the eastern stable? It makes perfect sense." He shook his head sharply, "*Te thori ma trush zhumo dzind.*"

"Sparing a man's life who was only doing his job doesn't make you a fool. Disregarding a life because it makes your own more convenient would have made you a fool," she flung back at him.

He stared at her for a moment, and his eyes softened. "We'll have to walk. As long as we push hard and are careful about food, we should be fine. But I can almost guarantee these are not the only soldiers here. We need to be careful."

She shook her head again. "How would Trey have had the authority to send soldiers here? He may be one of Eithan's guards, but he's still just that—a guard."

He seemed to consider that as he tucked them farther out of sight. "Does the *chinbi srol* know who you are?"

"What? Of course, he does. I already told you what Eithan wants from me."

He gripped her biceps, looking down at her. "Let me rephrase. Who does he think you are? You've yet to give me a surname."

Vera blinked; shame weighing heavy on her shoulders. She still hadn't told him. She'd all but asked him to fuck her, but hadn't even given him her full name. Gods, she was an ass. "Palacia. The emperor told me my father was a cousin of King Vesstan, although I don't know how close they were."

Jaren released her, exhaling heavily, and her brows furrowed. Why did he look like that? What had he expected her to say?

He intertwined their fingers and leaned in close, his breath tickling her skin. "We can't slink in the shadows and try to sneak out of the city. That's exactly what they'll be expecting. We'll have better luck trying to blend into a crowd." He paused, a grin teasing the corners of his mouth. "Think you can convince the masses that there's a cock under those clothes, Varian?"

Her answering grin was nothing short of wicked. She released his hands and raised her arms to tuck her plait into her tunic, but he stopped her. Grabbing her wrists, he held them at the nape of her neck and ran his nose along her jaw. He pulled back, peering down into her eyes, and she melted under the heat of his stare.

"I want to kiss you, little star."

"You couldn't wait just a second?" Her voice was breathy, even to her own ears. Damn this male and how easily he could fluster her.

"Varian is who Aleron forced you to become. I don't want to kiss Varian. I want to kiss *you*."

She blinked back the burn in her eyes. Isn't that what she'd always wanted? To be able to be herself and not be punished or judged for it? Wasn't that why she'd wanted him last night? Not just because of how her body reacted to him physically, but because he saw her.

Sure, he pissed her off and she'd lost count of how many times she'd wanted to punch him, but Vera was beginning to think that was the whole point. Jaren drew passion out of her—pulled and demanded it—and he didn't shy away, no matter how she responded. He liked her fire.

And she wanted to give it to him. She wasn't going to let him kiss her. She was going to take it for herself. Closing the last inches separating them, she captured his mouth with her own. She bit his bottom lip hard enough to taste blood, demanding he open for her, and he obliged.

He brought her arms down, pinning them behind her back with one hand, while his other wrapped around her throat in a claiming gesture.

She could probably break out of even his strongest hold if she knew how to consciously tap into her strength. But even if she could, she didn't want to. He was the one exerting dominance, but it made *her* feel powerful because it was *her* who made him lose control. She fucking loved it.

They stayed like that, devouring one another, both taking and giving in equal measure. It could have been minutes or hours, and she wouldn't have noticed. When she did finally break away, he leaned his forehead against hers, his pants matching her own.

She kept her eyes closed, enjoying the feel of his fingers along her throat before he released her and stepped back. "We need to move."

"You're the one who distracted me," she quipped. He only

shrugged, smacking her on the rear.

THEY'D MADE IT to the edge of the city successfully avoiding attracting attention. Vera felt relieved, but Jaren had never been more tense. It was clear he didn't trust the ease with which they'd made it so far.

"Maybe we were wrong, and those soldiers had nothing to do with us. You did steal a horse the last time you were here. Maybe someone saw you sneaking around last night."

"*Pha.*"

She pursed her lips but didn't argue. His pessimism may be infuriating, but his instincts were far better than her own. He grabbed her arm, practically dragging her in his haste to leave the city limits. They'd traveled no more than a mile or two when they froze to the distant sound of hooves.

Vera whipped around, her breath catching in her throat when she saw the group heading toward them. There were thirteen of them, the one in the center dressed in finery and wearing no mask.

"What in Aleron is Eithan doing here?"

Jaren shot her a look, telling her without words that she was an idiot if she didn't know the answer. He tried to push her behind him, but she pushed back, refusing to hide.

"He can't force me to do anything, Jaren."

He laughed humorlessly. "Are you willing to kill all of them to make sure of that?" When she didn't answer, he scoffed and shook his head, "That's what I thought."

Eithan's group was almost to them now, and she caught sight of Trey riding just behind him. "Let me talk to him, Jaren, please. Let me explain, and maybe we can leave without all the sneaking and hiding."

"I trusted your judgment about your *friend* and look how that turned out," he snapped. Her anger rose in response, but she held back her retort. He was right. "If you attack the Crown Prince, there will be all-out war."

"I don't care about a fucking alliance."

She was about to bite back, but Eithan's voice beat her to it. They'd finally reached them.

"Step away, Magyki." His voice carried with an air of authority, and Jaren responded by tightening his hold on her arm.

"Jaren," she muttered so only he would hear. "Let go. It looks like you're restraining me." His grip turned painful for a split second before letting go, but she didn't step away.

"Are you all right, Vera?" Eithan's question forced her eyes back to him. Gone was his stern expression, and in its place was concern. It caused her chest to squeeze in shame.

"I'm fine, Eithan."

He smiled, whether from her answer or her casually using his name versus his title, she wasn't sure.

"How can we help you?" She cringed. *How can we help you?* Seriously? Gods damn word vomit.

He flung a leg over and dismounted in one smooth movement. She'd forgotten how large and muscular he was, but as he stood there, mere feet away, she couldn't help but acknowledge how magnificent the prince truly was.

"It's okay, Vera. I know you only left that night because he threatened Gibson's life. I also know what tales he's been feeding you to keep you from changing your mind."

Her eyes flicked from him to Trey. Eithan didn't seem mad. If anything, he seemed like he pitied her. Like she was an ignorant child, led astray by a pied piper.

"I don't blame you, Vera. I understand, I do. But that male—Jaren, I believe—is lying to you."

And just like that, she was pissed. They were all the same, assuming Jaren to be the enemy simply because of where he came from.

"Why?" She spit, stepping forward. "Because Trey said he was, or because he happens to be Magyki?" She saw a few of his guards shift in their saddles, clearly uncomfortable with the way she was addressing their prince. In hindsight, it probably wasn't her best idea. But Eithan didn't react at all.

She wanted to hold firm and tell him to shove his opinion right up his ass, but instead, she mashed her lips into a thin line, reminding herself that he'd only ever been kind to her.

"Did he tell you what caused the rebellion?"

She cocked her head, brows pinched. She had asked Jaren about the civil fighting, but his answer had been vague. She glanced up at him, but his face revealed nothing, his focus trained on Eithan. "No, but—"

"You."

"Pardon?" She'd clearly misheard him. "You think that *I* caused the rebellion?"

"From what I've recently learned, your mere existence did. It seems your family hid you for years, never telling anyone about you. When the truth was discovered, many Magyki rebelled trying to find you."

"What do you mean? Why?"

He pointed at Jaren, "Ask him. I can almost guarantee he knows who you are."

She crossed her arms, scowling. "You apparently know as well. So, everyone knows something I don't. Big surprise." She shrugged, "I've grown used to it."

But even as she said it, she felt something prick at her skin, unease at the thought Jaren might have lied to her.

"The difference, Vera, is I didn't know until after you left when my father decided to inform me. *Jaren*, on the other hand, has apparently just chosen not to tell you."

She crossed her arms. "And who am I exactly?"

"Veralie Arenaris. King Vesstan's daughter, and heir to Bhasura's throne."

Her arms dropped to her sides, the blood rushing from her face. "What?"

She looked at Jaren, waiting for him to deny it, but he said nothing—not one word. Her heart stopped, his silence all the confirmation she needed.

Why would he keep that from her? He'd just asked her earlier who Eithan thought she was, and when she'd told him, he hadn't corrected her. He'd looked relieved at her answer. Why would he lie?

Eithan came several steps closer, ignoring the growl of warning emanating from the male beside her. He stared at him, a challenge in his eyes. "Go ahead, Magyki. Tell her why she was hidden."

"How do you know any of this, Eithan?" she snapped.

"My father already told you. The loyalists bartered information to save your life. Part of that included your identity and the knowledge that the rebels were a danger to you. They claimed not to know the reason, but my father never did believe them. All we know is there is something about you. Something important enough, your mother was murdered for trying to hide you."

Jaren threw their pack of supplies to the ground and unsheathed his daggers, snarling, "That is not knowledge Sulian should possess."

The guards responded instantly, dismounting and surrounding Eithan, blades raised. Ryn Hayes, the guard Trey had once warned her about, nocked an arrow.

"What is he talking about?" she asked.

The pieces began clicking together. She remembered Jaren saying they grew up together. She'd been given to her mate's family...to *hide*. She felt like her life was about to crumble underneath her feet, and she took several steps away from Jaren so she could look at him head-on.

His eyes were angry, but his voice softened as he spoke in their native tongue, for her ears alone. "He's wrong. They were looking for you, but they would never have intentionally killed the queen. She was too important.

"The crystals connected to her bloodline differently. It was rumored that her death, and thus the end of her bloodline, was what caused the taint. But no one knows for sure. I didn't tell you because I did not wish to upset you."

"But her death couldn't have been the cause if I'm her daughter. Her bloodline never ended."

"You were locked, Veralie. You had yet to connect to the crystals."

She was quiet for a moment, processing what he'd said. She'd been the cause of her mother's death. Hundreds of innocents had died in the rebellion because of *her*. Her stomach roiled, and she swallowed down the bile threatening to come up.

"You think I might be connected now, right? Does that mean the taint might be gone?" She couldn't hide the thread of hope in her voice.

Eithan's cough interrupted Jaren's reply. He was frowning and shaking his head. "Whatever he's telling you, Vera, you can't trust him. The night you left, I was researching your culture, hoping to learn more about you before we courted."

A loud snarl ripped from Jaren's throat, causing Eithan to stumble back. He caught himself, glaring at Jaren before linking his hands behind his back and continuing.

"I read something interesting about the previous queens. As you know, the average lifespan of your people is around two-hundred years. But the female rulers? Not one of them even made it to half of that. Each queen living a shorter life than the one before.

"I didn't think much on it until my father admitted to who you are. There's a reason your people went to war over you, Vera. It's not safe there."

His words were a slap in the face, and she felt a sharp pain in her chest, like a dagger piercing her heart. "No," she whispered in denial. "No, it's not true. Jaren wouldn't—"

"Wouldn't what?" Eithan interrupted. "Wouldn't endanger your life for his entire people? You don't know him; you don't know what he's willing to do."

In her peripheral, she saw Trey looking her way. He hadn't told Eithan about her being Jaren's mate. Even after their fight, even though he was sworn to his prince, he had her back. Her eyes filled with tears, and she wished she could hug him and tell him how sorry she was.

"Come home, Vera. Elric is beside himself with worry. You will be safe with me, I promise."

Jaren was gripping his daggers so tightly; his knuckles had gone white. "Touch her, and you're fucking dead."

Vera's body felt numb. She couldn't have raised her arms or moved her legs if she tried. Her head was spinning, trying to connect the dots and see the truth behind everything. Was Eithan right? Would Jaren be willing to take her back even if it wasn't safe for her?

No. No, it wasn't true. It couldn't be. Not after what they'd shared. He wouldn't take her back unless he knew he could guarantee her safety.

"*Te wi yadz tsas mbi*, little star," he whispered. She believed him; believed he'd never hurt her. Their bond was real. She could feel it—feel him.

"I appreciate your concern, Eithan. Truly, I do. But I have a feeling it's too late anyway." If every queen had died young, and what Jaren said about her bloodline was true, she assumed their deaths had something to do with the connection. And without even meaning to, she might've already connected to the crystals.

"If what you say is true, then that means I'll have more sway as a princess on Bhasura than I would as a princess here. I can talk to King Vesstan, tell him about my life, and try to encourage him to open communication. It could work."

His gaze darkened, a dangerous look entering his eyes before he blinked it away. "You're not thinking clearly, Vera. I'm sorry, but I'm doing this for your own good."

He raised two fingers on his right hand, and she watched in horror as Hayes drew his arrow back and released it.

Chapter 25

Vera

Jaren's reflexes were quick enough to avoid a hit to the heart, but not quick enough to deflect it completely. It struck his shoulder, making him stagger. Vera cried out, her hands flying to her mouth at the sight of the arrow's tip shooting from his back.

Her sudden movement hurt, a strange pain radiating through her shoulder and down her arm. "Eithan, stop! Please!" He didn't reply to her plea. He didn't even look at her.

Regaining his footing, Jaren sheathed his daggers just long enough to grasp the arrow and snap it, snarling viciously. He then reached around his body and slowly pulled the remaining piece out, tossing it to the ground. "You want to take me down...you'll have to do better than that."

Hayes nocked another arrow, but Jaren didn't so much as flinch. He stood firm, but Vera could see the strain in his eyes, the way his chest heaved, and his hands shook just slightly.

She didn't know how affected he was by the taint. Didn't know if he would have the energy to enhance his reactions and also heal the wound. He met her eyes, and in that moment, she knew he'd choose to defend her over healing himself.

Her eyes flicked to Eithan to see his fingers rise a second time, and her world stopped. There was no dipping into her power this time. No reaching out or coaxing. It came rushing to her without conscious thought, responding to her terror. Before Hayes's arrow even left his bow, she was moving. Her body screamed, unaccustomed to the maelstrom pulsing through her as she focused it on her legs and lunged.

One second she was standing several feet away, and the next, she was shoving into Jaren, fast as a shooting star. She felt the sting of his dagger sinking into her side as she barreled into it, sending him flying. But it was the arrow piercing her chest that ripped an agonized scream from her lips. It had narrowly missed her heart.

The sound of her knees hitting the ground echoed in her ears, but she forced herself to ignore the shaft protruding from her body to find Jaren. He was crawling across the ground toward her, clutching his chest, his eyes filled with pain.

He'd finally found the strength to push up off the ground when a booted foot shoved him back down, a sword pointed at his throat. Hayes stood over him, apparently having tired of his arrows not finding their mark. He glanced back at Eithan, a smirk on his pock-marked face, seeking the go-ahead to end Jaren's life.

Vera tried to get up, tried to get to him, when her vision suddenly went black. She blinked, swiveling her head around, terrified and bewildered.

She wasn't on Aleron anymore.

She was in a dark corridor, kneeling on a stone floor. The cold penetrated through her clothes, and she could smell the metallic scent of blood in the air. Looking up, she watched in horror as an enormous male held a boy at sword point.

Her shout lodged in her throat. It was Jaren. He was little more than a child, but it was him. She looked into those familiar eyes, widened in fear, and held her hand out toward him like a lifeline between their souls. All she knew was he needed her.

And she needed him.

The vision faded away as quickly as it had come, but it remained seared into her mind like a parasite. Something tensed and hummed in her chest, and then it was burning and flaring as she lurched to her feet.

Staring straight at Hayes, she wrapped her fingers around the arrow and wrenched it from her chest, her roar of agony echoing out as blood soaked her tunic. His head whipped around, his eyes widening in fear as he met her gaze.

Because at that moment, Vera was gone. Something dark had twisted inside of her, and nothing but fury and violence remained, demanding she make him hurt. Make them all hurt. She swore to the gods, she would fucking kill him if he moved. "*Sphe zhimb praÿ bra, ÿu te a tsha dupye tseb, te adez̈ mbi zab.*"

He didn't need to understand her to know her intent. It was

radiating off her in waves. His mistake was glancing at his prince for orders. The second his eyes flickered, she was on him, savoring the feeling of cartilage breaking as her fist made contact with his face.

She could hear clashing start up behind her, but she didn't dare look away from Hayes. He wiped the back of his hand under his nose, smearing blood across his cheek, and she smiled, her expression manic.

Fuming, he rushed her, but she dodged his swing, throwing him off balance. He cursed, coming for her again and again, but she darted past his pathetic advances, landing blow after blow, delighting in his grunts of pain as she tried to see how many ribs she could crack.

She circled him, the new angle allowing her to spot Jaren fending off three of the guards who'd targeted him while she'd been distracted. Although most of the guards, including Coleman and Trey, stayed back around Eithan, a few more had begun to creep forward.

She saw red, and the sound that escaped her was anything but human. They wanted to play games? Fine. She'd play. She ducked Hayes's next lunge, pivoting and striking him directly in the chest. He flew backward, his head cracking against the ground, and he didn't get back up.

Swiping his sword where he'd dropped it, she then snatched the closest rock from the ground, and aiming at a particularly ugly guard, she focused her strength and launched it. It met its mark with a gratifying *thunk*. She watched his eyes roll back, blood running between them as he crumpled to the ground.

Glancing at Jaren, she saw he'd taken down two of the three who'd attacked him. He was breathing heavily, but with relief, she saw that he appeared fine. She raised her stolen blade, edging closer to the third man while his attention was still trained on Jaren.

One of the other guards called out a warning, and her prey twisted toward her, but it was too late. Like a woman possessed, she leaped on him. In his surprise, he dropped his sword, and she wasted no time straddling him and pressing her blade to his throat.

"If anyone moves, he dies." She looked up at Jaren, who was standing next to her, sweat glistening across his skin. She fought back her shuddering relief that he'd chosen to heal himself. In fact, she no longer felt pain either. She'd healed herself without even realizing it.

"I'd listen to my *aitanta* if I were you, princeling."

Vera pulled her gaze away to lock on Eithan, barely visible behind his wall of guards, all of them looking equal measures of shocked and horrified. All except for Trey, who stood behind him, arms crossed, his sword still in its sheath.

Eithan raised his hands, placatingly, "You don't want to hurt him, Vera."

"Actually, I do." She bared her teeth and put just enough pressure on the guard's neck to draw a line of blood, snarling in satisfaction at the hint of fear she could scent on him.

"I'm guessing with all the bonding you and Elric did, he failed to mention I have a bit of a temper. You see, I don't like people touching my things, and he," she said, tilting her head toward

Jaren, "is *mine*."

She felt a small pulse of warmth in her chest, like a flutter of pure joy, and it was so at odds with how she currently felt that it distracted her, pulling her out of her rage. She frowned, confused at what she felt, and glanced back to see Jaren smiling wickedly.

Feeling calmer and more like herself, she asked him, "Are you okay?"

A rumble in his chest was his only reply.

Sighing, she didn't even bother looking down at the man beneath her before ramming the hilt of the sword into his temple, knocking him unconscious. She tossed the weapon out of reach and stood, swaying slightly. She felt suddenly dizzy.

"I don't want to continue fighting, Eithan. But I will. All of this could have been avoided if you'd just listened. I will not go back." She looked at him, feeling more drained and exhausted by the second. "But I swear, even after all of this, I will still talk to King Vesstan. I will not refuse to help with an alliance out of spite when it could benefit all involved."

Jaren sheathed a dagger to intertwine their hands. Side-eyeing the group, he led her to one of the horses that had run several yards away in all the excitement, grabbing their pack along the way. She tensed, expecting Eithan to try to stop them, but none of them made a move.

"This isn't how things were supposed to turn out." Anger coated Eithan's words, clashing with the controlled mask on his face.

"I know. And believe it or not, I don't hate you." She looked behind him and made eye contact with Trey, her next words meant more for her friend, "I understand that you had to follow orders."

Trey looked heartbroken, like he didn't expect to ever see her again. She placed a hand over her heart, ignoring the sticky tear in her tunic, praying he'd hear what she couldn't say. The corner of his mouth lifted, and he dipped his head.

Feeling Jaren's hands slide across her waist, she finally turned, for once accepting his help to mount. His body had scarcely curled around hers when he reached around for the reins and spurred the horse into a gallop.

Jaren

THEY'D BEEN TRAVELING IN SILENCE FOR CLOSE TO TWO hours before he finally broke under the tension. He knew Veralie's mind was awhirl with everything that had occurred. Fuck, he could *feel* how anxious and angry she was, like part of her soul had nestled in beside his own. Their bond was so close to being complete that he thought he'd go insane with anticipation.

"I should have told you about your family."

"Yes, you should have." Her words were clipped, and she remained facing forward.

"My motives were selfish. I knew how you felt about becoming a Matherin princess, and I feared you would feel the same about being Bhasura's *Nlem Snadzend* and change your mind." Her posture loosened a smidge, but she still didn't turn.

"You let me believe I had no living family, Jaren. Yes, I'm

upset about my mother, but I'd already known she'd died during the rebellion. Finding out I'm partially to blame is painful, but the joy I feel knowing my father is alive?" She shook her head, "I suppose I don't need to explain it. I think—I think maybe you can feel it."

He hesitated. "I can."

"I think I felt you earlier. It was strange, like I was suddenly feeling two different emotions at once. Is the bond complete?"

Gods, did he wish that. "No, but it's as close as it can be without taking the last step."

She tilted her head, "What made it change? What step is there left to take?"

"A soul bond is fated and exists whether or not two Magyki wish for it, although it can be…rejected if one or both refuses to recognize it. Even if acknowledged, it does not solidify unless it is also accepted. When I told you we were bonded, your body instantly acknowledged its existence, strengthening the pull between us, but you did not accept what it meant."

"So today…"

Jaren pulled her hands out of her lap and laced their fingers, unable to resist the need to hold her. She sighed, relaxing into him. "Your soul fully accepted my own."

Tipping her head back to look up at him, Veralie's silver eyes roved over his face, bright with understanding. "I claimed you."

A thrill shot through him. "You did, little star." He brushed his nose along hers, savoring her scent. "Our bond will be complete when I claim you."

An emotion that was not his own flickered through him. It

was there and gone in a flash, but he'd felt it—confusion and...hurt.

She tried to face forward, but he grabbed her jaw, forcing her to meet his eyes. "You misunderstand me. I've wanted to claim you from the moment your star-fire scent invaded my senses and my life. But I want every piece of you before I do."

He leaned down, watching her eyes flutter shut as he kissed her forehead. "I want your thoughts," he dropped his lips to her eyelids. "I want your body," he brushed a featherlight kiss to the corner of her mouth. "I want your soul," he let his breath ghost across her ear. "But mostly, I want your heart." He placed an open-mouthed kiss on the column of her neck, watching her skin erupt in gooseflesh when his canines scraped against her.

"I want to claim *all* of you, preferably while I'm buried deep inside of you."

She tilted her head, baring more of her neck to him, and he almost lost his mind. Wrapping his hand around her throat, he slid his other between her thighs. Veralie's body began to shake as he deftly undid her trousers and, ever so slowly, eased his fingertips inside. He bit back the desire to thrust his hand all the way, instead caressing her skin in teasing strokes, working his way down.

He clenched his jaw, biting back a curse when his fingers finally met their goal; his cock hardening almost painfully from how ready she was. Her scent alone could send him to an early grave.

"You're so wet for me, *aitanta*."

He adjusted his posture to keep them steady before focusing

his attention on her clit, pressing down and causing her to moan and buck against him.

He rotated his fingers in tight circles, his motions hard and demanding. Her head fell back, and the whimper she released was fucking ecstasy. He kept up a steady rhythm, kissing and licking along her neck and ear as he did.

She gripped his thighs, her nails biting through the fabric as her breathing grew ragged. Shifting, she desperately tried to grind against his fingers, only to let out a frustrating mewl when their current situation prevented it. He chuckled and picked up his pace, eyeing the unblemished skin of her neck and shoulder.

In-tune with every subtle change in her, he sensed when she was about to break. Unable to control the urge, he struck, sinking his teeth into the flesh of her shoulder. The sound of his name on her lips turned into a scream as her orgasm slammed into her, and he fought not to shoot his load.

As it ended, her muscles went lax, but he tightened his hold, refusing to move neither his hand nor his mouth until the last tremor left her body.

Wrapping a fist around her plait, he twisted her face to meet his, capturing her mouth with his own and drinking in her pleasure like he was a male dying of thirst.

"Don't heal."

Veralie looked up at him, fighting to regain her breathing, "What?"

"My mark. Don't heal it."

She raised a hand to the small puncture wounds on her shoulder, "Your mark?"

"When we get home, I don't want anyone, *pizlath* or *zhu*, to question that you are spoken for." He didn't miss the flare of excitement in her eyes when he said the word home, but she quickly covered it, narrowing them.

"That's quite presumptuous."

He released her, moving his hands back to the reins. "I presume nothing. You're spoken for."

Her eyes sparked. "Well, maybe I'll change my mind once I have the opportunity to meet a few more, *less arrogant*, options."

He raised a brow, "Less arrogant?"

"And less violent, for sure."

"Violent. Hm. Tell me, little star, did I, or did I not, see you crack a man's head open with a rock?"

She flushed, facing forward. He laughed, then laughed harder when the color intensified. Ignoring him, she adjusted her posture and inadvertently rubbed against him. He hissed out a breath, and she froze. He was still hard as fuck, and the fresh mark visible on her neck was not helping in the least.

"Jaren—"

"Just rest, little star. We have several long days of travel still before we reach Eastshore."

Her scent deepened, and gods if he didn't love the way she responded to him. "What if I want to touch you?"

Groaning, he tightened his grip. "*Pha.* I am one touch away from ruining a perfectly good pair of trousers."

She shuddered, her arousal flaring once more. "Rest, Veralie. We have all the time in the world."

Her body stiffened, and a sudden sense of uncertainty pulsed in his chest. "Do we?"

She might as well have dumped a pail of cold water on him. That fucking *chinbi srol*. He should've ripped his tongue out for making her fear her future.

"Do not let the rash words of a jealous man put fear in your heart. We do not know the truth about the queens."

"You promise?"

Shame slithered through him. "Yes."

"I think it's true. It's too coincidental to be anything else. I think it's all connected, their bloodline—my bloodline—and the taint. Either they caused it, or they were the ones preventing it. I think it's what killed them."

Fuck, how had their intimate moment suddenly turned so dark? Jaren felt like he might be sick. He'd already feared the same, but hearing her voice it was terrifying. He couldn't lose her, not now, not in ten years, not even in a hundred.

She sighed, looking out across the open expanse and tucking a few wind-blown curls back behind her scarred ears. "It's ironic, isn't it?"

"*Rab?*"

"You thought I could help Bhasura because I was the only untainted Magyki left, but that didn't turn out to be true at all. I'm probably more tainted than them all."

"We'll figure it out together, little star." And they would. The princeling was wrong. Jaren would sacrifice the entire island rather than let anyone or any*thing* harm her. She was his to protect. He'd fight the gods themselves if he had to.

Epilogue

Eithan

It had been a week since he'd failed to obtain Vera, and he was still in a rage. That piece of shit Magyki had taken her and turned her mind into such a mess, she had no idea what she was saying or doing. She'd been saved and kept for *him*, not some pointy-eared bastard who decided he wanted her. Eithan clenched his fists and breathed heavily through his nose, fighting the urge to punch the wall.

If things had worked out the way they were *supposed* to, he would have dragged the Magyki back to the palace dungeons, letting Hayes give him a proper welcome.

Eithan would've held his betrothed and swore the male died quickly and painlessly, but he would have lied. He'd have hung his body from the ceiling and taken his time, peeling his skin off in strips, enjoying his agonized screams.

Then, Eithan would've been able to take his time with Vera, wooing her and gaining her trust. He'd have claimed both her hand and her body, making her scream, too, but from a very different set of skills. It would have been fucking perfect.

Now, he'd have to work twice as hard and play dirty to force her hand. She'd grown powerful. Her display near Midpath had certainly proven that, even if her appearance hadn't already. He wasn't arrogant enough to believe he could physically force her into anything anymore. She had to return of her own free will, and luckily for him, he had the perfect leverage.

He took another deep breath as he strolled down the corridor to the back cells, relishing in the sounds of pain and misery. Eithan loved it down here. Up there, he had to be the perfect prince. He had to obey his bastard of a father and smother every emotion and desire. He had to be a friend to his men, smile for his people, and say all the right things. He had to be patient and wait for Vera when all he wanted to do was take, take, *take*.

Down here was his sanctuary, the only place his real self could run wild and free. The only place that allowed him to let the darkness out, that welcomed the roiling, poisonous malevolence festering inside him. Being down here was almost better than sex.

As he approached the last cell, he heard the scuffle of chains dragging across the stones and shuddered in anticipation. He stepped up to the bars and looked in at the two men inside. They were filthy, and neither appeared to be sleeping well, but they otherwise appeared perfectly fine.

"Good day, gentlemen. I assume, by now, I've given you

plenty of time to swap stories." He smiled, watching them shift uneasily, but neither man said anything.

Tapping his fingers against the bars, Eithan let his smile fall. "You have both been charged with treason against His Majesty. However, I've convinced Sulian to delay your sentences. For now, at least."

Both men glanced at each other, but it was the Weapons' Master who finally croaked out a response, "Your mock leniency is wasted on me. I already admitted to my guilt. I take pride in both Vera and her skill. Execute me. I will not help you drag her back."

"You see, Lesta, that's the beauty of it. You *will* help me whether you wish it or not. Tell me, how do you think Vera will react when she finds out where you are? How will she react when she finds out where *he* is?"

Lesta's face fell, and his stoic expression morphing into horror was all the confirmation Eithan needed. Vera would do anything to keep them safe. She'd already proven that when she stood up for her mentor that day in the training yard.

He turned his attention to the second man, continuing his mindless tapping and enjoying the way it made Gibson's eyes twitch. He pursed his lips. Two eyes too many.

"Not to worry, Lesta, you will be released on the promise that you will continue training our men until a replacement can be found." He flicked his gaze to the young guard, the man he had laughed with and trusted. "You, however, do not deserve my leniency. You not only broke your oath to protect Vera, but you lied to me."

"I did not—"

"*Do not insult me further by denying it!*" Eithan slammed his fists into the bars of the cell, breaking the skin of his knuckles. "Vera's disgusting display over the Magyki was evidence enough that you left out some vital information that would've changed the entire outcome."

Gibson swallowed hard, his nerves giving him away, and Eithan smiled. It wasn't the perfect, princely one he had to give above, but one that showcased the darkness inside.

"I won't kill you yet. I have a far better use for you while we wait for our messenger to return." He opened the bars and laughed when Lesta thrashed against his chains, cursing, realization dawning on his worn features.

He took his time walking the few steps across the cell, soaking up the power their fear gave him. Once upon a time, he trusted these men, but now he wanted nothing more than to see them crumble at his feet.

Snatching Gibson's chains, he unlocked them from the wall and all but dragged him from the cell. He'd work off his anger and find out why Vera was so willing to abandon her life for a male she'd just met.

She may not accept it yet, but she belonged with him. He'd bind her to him, and then he'd rip Matherin's pathetic excuse for an emperor off the throne he so desperately clung to. Just the thought had adrenaline racing through his veins.

Then Gibson's screams began. The day was looking better already.

Glossary

A aprenza – My name
Aitanta – Soul bonded mate
B'u mod – Little star
Chinbi srol – Baby king/princeling
Dodz watsrang – Good job
Dunduwaw – Lovers
Dupye - Gods
Dusing – Dresses
Duwabi – Thief
Ga - Fuck
Kúltha – Hello
Laskas – Crystal
Luzh – Power
Nlem Snadzend – Daughter to the Throne
Pha – No
Pizlath – Male
Rab - What
Shuthish – Soldier
Tha – Dog/mutt
Thyip – Focus
Tsiw – Pathetic
Wushech – Bathhouse
Ÿe – Yes
Yinlanem dupye – Holy fucking gods
Zhu – Magyki female
Zhumo dzind – Stupid fool

Acknowledgements

My first, and most heartfelt, thanks goes to my mother. Not only is she my best friend, but she is, by far, the most amazing woman I have ever met. No matter how many times I've messed up in my life or made a wrong turn, she has pushed me back on my feet and pointed me toward the light again. I would not be who I am today if it weren't for her.

We have always shared our love of reading. Even now, at thirty years old, I call her at least weekly to talk about books. We gossip about plot theories, fawn over spicy scenes and fictional boyfriends, and mourn character deaths like they were real people. I am truly blessed to have her in my life.

Second, I want to thank every person who helped me make my vision a reality. I want to thank my beta readers who gave me amazing, honest feedback, and my editor, Paige Lawson, who took my manuscript and helped me perfect it.

Next, I want to thank the talented Murphy Rae for my amazing cover design, artist Kudriaken for her gorgeous character art, musician Whitnie Means for creating breathtaking music for this story, and my dear friend, Angie, for being my own personal cheerleader and always listening to me vent, whether about publishing or just mom life. This wouldn't be nearly as incredible and fantastical without each of them!

Finally, I have my nerdy, sexy, hardworking husband to

thank. That man loves me better than any book boyfriend could. He is constantly aware of me and knows every single one of my tells. He knows when I need a break, when I'm tapped out, when my head is secretly killing me, or when I desperately need a massage.

He is also the single most supportive person in my life. When I told him I wanted to publish a book, he could have laughed. He could have pointed out that I had three children at home, two of which were homeschooled and the third barely two years old. He could have told me it was a fool's dream. But he didn't.

When imposter syndrome punched me in the face, he was there to tell me I'm amazing. When the stress of planning out pre-orders and newsletters made me feel like I was drowning, he was there to tell me that those things didn't make my book any less successful. Even if no one read it, it was still amazing. Even if I never published it, I was still amazing.

Not a day goes by that I do not realize how absolutely lucky I am to have that man at my side. I could never have written this book if he didn't work so hard every day to put a roof over our heads so that I can stay home with my children and write.

The love stories we read about? I have it.

About the Author

Lilian T. James was born and raised in a small town in Kansas until she finished high school. Enrolling at a University on the east coast, she moved there with her son and obtained degrees in Criminal Justice, Social Work, Psychology, and Sociology. After graduating, she met her husband and moved to the west coast for a few years before they finally settled back in Kansas. She has three kids, one miniature dachshund, and has been an avid fantasy and romance reader her entire life. Lilian was finally able to publish her first novel, Untainted, in 2021 and has no plans of stopping.

Next in the Series

Vera had always hoped to one day leave Matherin. To travel the world and escape a life that was never meant for her.

Bhasura would have everything she could ever want. Freedom, respect, family, and her mate. Her *aitanta*.

But behind the island's beautiful cities and smiling citizens, she can hear the lies poisoning their stories.

She wants to believe it's all in her head, but a dark anger starts to grow inside her, and she can't ignore the feeling that something is wrong.

Something besides the vivid dreams that plague her sleep the moment she sets foot on the island.